Ker... Career
Ach... as been
nominated in the Best Contemporary Paranormal category of the *Romantic Times* Reviewers' Choice Awards.
S... dessert and function cook by trade, and lives with
h... aughter in Melbourne, Australia.

Vi... her website at www.keriarthur.com

Bound to Shadows

KERI ARTHUR

piatkus

PIATKUS

First published in the US in 2009 by Bantam Dell
A division of Random House Inc., New York
First published in Great Britain as a paperback original in 2009 by Piatkus

A CIP catalogue record for this book
is available from the British Library.

ISBN 978-0-7499-4222-9

Printed in the UK by CPI Mackays, Chatham ME5 8TD

Papers used by Piatkus are natural, renewable and
recyclable products sourced from well-managed forests and certified
in accordance with the rules of the Forest Stewardship Council.

Mixed Sources
Product group from well-managed
forests and other controlled sources
www.fsc.org Cert no. SGS-COC-004081
© 1996 Forest Stewardship Council

Piatkus
An imprint of
Little, Brown Book Group
100 Victoria Embankment
London EC4Y 0DY

An Hachette UK Company
www.hachette.co.uk

www.piatkus.co.uk

Acknowledgments

I'd like to thank:

Everyone at Bantam who helped shine

this book—most especially my editor, Anne; her

assistant, David; all the line and copy editors

who make sense of my Aussie English;

and cover designer Juliana Kolesova.

I'd also like to thank my agent, Miriam, as well as

my buddies and crit partners—Robyn, Mel, Chris,

Carolyn, and Freya. You all rock, ladies.

Chapter 1

I've come to accept the fact that I'm a guardian. I'll even admit that I enjoy hunting down those rogue supernatural elements who prey on humans and non-humans alike.

But that doesn't mean there still aren't times when I absolutely hate my job.

Getting a call-out at three A.M. on a bitterly cold winter night was definitely one of those times. Especially when the call sent me to an area rapidly gaining a reputation as the "it" spot for blood whores—which was the common term for humans hooked on the pleasures of a vampire's bite.

Normally I didn't have a problem with people getting their kicks any damn way they pleased, but for humans—and it only seemed to afflict humans, not the rest of us—becoming addicted to a vampire's bite was definitely one of the quicker ways to court death. They simply didn't have the strength, the speed, or even the willpower to battle a vampire if things went wrong. Hell, many supernaturals didn't, either.

And while most vampires were generally law-abiding and took only enough to give the addicted his or her hit, there were always some abusers who pushed for longer, stronger rushes, and there were always vampires willing to oblige.

And sometimes that meant death.

It had become such a problem in recent months that the government had set up a think tank to find ways of curtailing the growing numbers flocking to the vampire bars. There were even calls to outlaw the practice—though how the hell anyone was going to police *that,* I had no idea. It wasn't like ordinary cops had much hope of tracking down and arresting vamps, and there simply weren't enough of us guardians. Not if they wanted us to do our real job.

Personally, I think they had about as much hope of stopping this craze as they did stopping all the designer drugs that were constantly hitting the streets. If a junkie wanted his fix, then he'd find it no matter how difficult or how illegal the government made it. And at least all the whores were of legal age—the vampire "pushers" were careful about that. They had to be, because otherwise they had to deal with the Directorate. Regular drug dealers just got jail time, at worst.

Of course, there was no proof that the murder I'd been called to tonight was yet another pleasure seeker who'd pushed too far. Jack had simply told me to get my butt over there pronto, and the edge in his voice had me scrambling for clothes and not taking the time for questions. But the murder had happened in the older section of Fitzroy, in a parking lot behind Dante's—and that club was a prime location for blood whores and their vampire johns.

I slowed the car as I passed through the Smith Street intersection, then turned left onto Budd Street. Several of the streetlights were out, and darkness closed in around the car. The buildings here were mainly old factories and warehouses, their brick walls grimy and covered with graffiti. The few houses squeezed in between the larger buildings were dark—and with the graffiti on their walls and the filth littering their front fences, it was hard to tell whether they were occupied or not. But I was a dhampire—part werewolf, part vampire—and had inherited many gifts from both parts of my heritage. The vampire part of my soul could see the blood heat within those buildings—although unlike my twin brother, I couldn't hear the siren call of their heartbeats.

And I was damn glad of that, because it meant I'd also missed out on the vampire's hunger for blood. Rhoan hadn't, but he *had* missed the fangs, and his blood hunger rose in tandem only with the full moon.

The crime scene came into view and I pulled up behind a Directorate van. The wind's icy fingers slapped across the back of my neck as I climbed out, and I hastily zipped up my jacket then pulled up the collar. It didn't help much. I might be a werewolf, and therefore supposedly immune to the winter, but the cold and I had never been on friendly terms.

I shoved my hands into my pockets and walked toward the parking lot. The rotating blue lights of the squad cars washed the night and the few bystanders in a ghostly glow, but as far as I could see or feel, there were no actual ghosts in the area. And if this *was* just a feeding taken too far, then there probably wouldn't be. As far as I knew, the souls that hung around tended to be the ones who'd met a violent end or who had something they needed to finish before they moved on. And blood whores didn't fit either of those categories, because they'd gone to their deaths knowing the dangers and not caring one bit.

And that's probably what annoyed me most. These people were knowingly flirting with death, yet when he answered, everyone got righteously moral and wanted the vamp responsible caught and killed. And the guardians were obliged to obey, because that was the law. But killing a blood whore wasn't a simple act of murder. It was consensual, and that raised a whole different set of issues. And although I *did* believe the vamp involved needed to be punished, killing him seemed a step too far. Most of the vampire community agreed.

Meaning that the worst part of the whole situation was the fact that our pursuit of these vamps was raising a lot of bad feeling in the supernatural community. And having the city's vampires angry at us could only ever end badly. There were a whole lot more of them than us, and as well trained as we guardians were, we didn't have a hope if the vamps decided we were too much of a problem.

Of course, the two vampires who dominated my life—Quinn, my lover, and Jack, my boss—thought I was making too much of the situation. Jack even kept trying to reassure me with the fact that the vampire council had a handle on it. I didn't believe it—or them. They weren't out on the street dealing with the ill feeling day in and day out. They simply didn't understand how bad it was getting.

I did, and I didn't mind admitting that it scared me.

The parking lot had several cars in it. The mobile light towers weren't trained on any of them, but rather on the corner of the lot, where it intersected with Dante's back wall. There were several overall-clad men there, and relief slithered through me as I caught the glint of silver hair. Cole might be our top guy when it came to crime scene forensics, but he also hated these early-morning call-outs as much as I did. That meant he'd be doing his best to find the clues and get the hell home as quickly as possible.

As I ducked under the blue and white police tape lining the parking lot, one of the cops keeping an eye on the small crowd huddled in the middle of the road took a step in my direction. I grabbed my badge and flashed it his way, shivering a little as the wind hit my fingers and chilled them in an instant.

The cop gave me a nod and turned back. I stepped over the gnarled roots of a small tree struggling to survive in a little corner of bare ground then flared my nostrils, drawing in the flavors of the night.

Blood was the strongest scent, and that surprised me. Most vampires hated wasting their food, so maybe this murder *wasn't* as straightforward as I'd been presuming.

Cole looked up as I approached, his lined face weary and dark shadows under his normally bright blue eyes. "You took your time."

"And you look like shit." I stopped beside him and stared down at the victim.

He was male, probably in his mid to late forties if his worn features and gray-flecked hair were anything to go by. There were no obvious wounds on his body, and very little in the way of blood on the front of his clothes. His arms had been crossed over his chest, almost as if he were asleep rather than dead. But someone had separated his head from his neck, and even a vampire couldn't survive that.

The blood that was missing from his clothes formed a lake around the area where his head should have been.

"Have you bothered looking in the mirror lately?" Cole snapped off his bloody gloves and tossed them into a nearby contamination bin.

"I'm trying to avoid them. Between working day shifts and getting call-outs at night, the bags under my eyes feel large enough to pack a lunch in. Who's our victim?"

"Grant Haven, a local vampire who owned a café up on Smith Street." Cole handed me a pair of slip-on shoe protectors. "Apparently he finished locking up at one and was heading to Dante's for a little top-up feeding."

"There were no witnesses?" I slipped on the shoe protectors then stepped forward, avoiding the thickening pool of blood as I studied the severed flesh. It wasn't a clean wound. In fact, the edges were all ragged, as if the killer had used some sort of serrated blade.

"No witnesses have come forward," Cole said. "But there's a whole club of people just waiting to be interviewed."

"You're fucking kidding me." I glanced at him. His blue eyes were filled with amusement and a smile twitched at the corners of his lips. My long night had just stretched into an interminable morning. "You're a bastard."

"Those were Jack's orders, not mine."

Then Jack was a bastard. God, he knew I hated interviewing these idiots. "We'll never get anything sensible out of them. They'll all be high."

Although, truth be told, the high from a vamp bite didn't last all that long—just like the pleasure received from sex, really. And like sex, most humans could stand only several hits before it weakened them to the point of sleep.

I guess we were lucky nonhumans didn't get addicted, because I very much doubted there'd be enough vampires in Melbourne to cater to a werewolf's hunger.

"If it helps any, there aren't many customers. Tuesday is apparently their slow night."

Well, thank God for small mercies. I nodded down at the victim. "Who called it in?"

He motioned toward Dante's. "The caller was

anonymous, but we traced the line and location. The cellphone belonged to a Mandy Jones, and the call came from inside Dante's."

Meaning she was likely still there. "She obviously doesn't know a lot about Directorate practices if she thought she could remain anonymous."

Cole smiled. "I don't think the Directorate actually advertises the fact they trace every single call coming in or out."

That was true. I'd only discovered it because I'd been horribly nosy during my time as Jack's assistant, and I'd often gone trawling through the computer system to see what I could find. "Do we know who owns Dante's?"

"Unsurprisingly enough, a vamp named Dante Starke."

"What do we know about him?"

Cole shrugged. "He has a rep for preferring to handle his own problems. Other than that, you'll have to check the system."

"Preferring to handle his own problems" probably meant he hated cops. And guardians. Great. "What was used on the victim's neck?"

"Rough-tooth saw. Dusty found it discarded in one of the bins behind the club. But it's been wiped clean of anything useful."

I glanced around and saw the shifter in question hunkering down over what looked like an oil stain. Cole's other assistant, Dobbs, was nowhere in sight— but given the three of them usually traveled together, I knew he'd be around somewhere. "Was it a new or old saw?"

"Brand-new. It still had the Bunnings price tag on it."

"Any chance of tracking down which store it was purchased at?"

"Maybe. But even if we found the right hardware store, I don't think they'd be much help. They probably sell hundreds of the things each week."

"Still, it's worth a shot." I frowned down at the vamp's unmarked body. "He doesn't appear to have put up a fight of any kind."

"None at all, which leads me to suspect that he's probably been drugged. We'll run the full toxicology when we get him back to the lab."

"So there's no indication so far of who our murderer might be?"

"Well, sawing through a person's neck takes strength, so we're probably looking for either a large male or a nonhuman."

"Gee, that really narrows down the field."

"Best I've got for the moment," Cole said, snapping on a new set of gloves. "Now, if that's all you've got, I've really got to get back to work. I have a bed and a lover waiting."

I raised my eyebrows. For as long as I'd known him he'd been relationship free, so the woman who'd finally caught his interest had to be someone pretty special.

"She has to be new, because anyone familiar with our line of work wouldn't bother waiting." Hell, Quinn hadn't. He'd mumbled something about bundling up against the cold and had promptly gone back to sleep. Anyone would think I'd worn the old vampire out. "So, is it anyone I know?"

"No." His smile bloomed bright. Man, he had the love bug *bad*. "And no, I will not share details. Now go do some work."

"You do realize that I am now officially intrigued?"

He groaned. "Please don't go investigating. I don't want to scare her away."

I grinned as I stripped off the shoe protectors and tossed them in the hazard bin.

"Riley, don't." He almost sounded worried.

"Don't what?" I raised my eyebrows, pretending an innocence that probably wasn't believable given the grin I couldn't quite control.

"Don't try and play innocent. You're as far from that as anyone could get."

He had a point there. "I just want to protect your interests. I'd do the same for any friend."

"Then please consider me an enemy."

I patted his shoulder as I passed. "Sorry, I've got suspects to interview. We'll continue this discussion later. Over coffee."

"You are such a bitch," he muttered, but the twinkle in his eyes took the bite out of his words. "And you'd do anything to get a free coffee, wouldn't you?"

"Totally," I said, and left him to it.

There were two uniforms stationed at the entrance to Dante's, along with a dark-eyed man who looked in serious need of a good feed. He was standing to one side of the doorway, under a blue light, and it gave his sallow features an even sicker glow. His dark gaze was never still, flickering from the cops to me, then onto the surrounding streets.

I showed the cops my badge and met the other man's gaze. "Who are you?"

"Valentine Smith. I'm the bouncer here."

He didn't look as if he could bounce a kitten out the door let alone anyone larger. But then, if he was a vampire—and given the rather pungent scent he was emitting, he couldn't be anything else—his looks would have been misleading. Even the scrawniest of vampires had more strength than the average nonhuman. And far more than any human.

"How long have you been on duty here?"

"I just came on shift. The boss asked me to help out these officers, in case some of the customers got antsy about being detained."

I glanced at the cops. The older of the two nodded in confirmation. I returned my gaze to Valentine. He wasn't looking at me. He was studying the street, as if he expected something to happen. Though I guess having a dead vamp on your back doorstep and cops on your front would be enough to make anyone jumpy. "How many people are inside at the moment?"

He shrugged. "Maybe twenty customers, and half that again of vampires."

Interesting that the vampires weren't considered customers. "And who's in charge tonight?"

"Dante Starke."

"The boss himself?"

The bouncer's gaze flicked briefly to mine then moved on again. "He lives here."

That surprised me. The old warehouse was as grimy and as run-down as the rest of the buildings in this area. Surely a wealthy businessman would prefer a more . . . well, if not opulent, then less dangerous area to reside in? But maybe the key word was "wealthy." He might be a vampire, he might own a nightclub, but that didn't necessarily mean he was rich.

"Could you please tell Mr. Starke that I'll need to speak to him?"

He looked at me again, then nodded. His gaze became slightly unfocused, and a buzz of energy caressed the air. He had to be a newer vampire. Any vampire with more than a few years behind him had learned not to let anyone know when they were using telepathy.

I stepped past the cops and pushed the nightclub's door open. The smell hit me immediately. It was a miasma of hunger and lust, of humanity and vampire, all entwined with the aroma of sweat, booze, and blood. I wrinkled my nose in distaste. Normally I loved the scent of lust when it rode on the air, but this was different. This had an almost desperate edge to it.

Which made sense, since the club was catering to those addicted to vampire bites.

I stepped into the darkness. The door shut behind me, closing out the light and making the shadowed confines of the room appear even more unfriendly.

That feeling was coming from the vampires in the room, not the humans. The majority of the humans were either busy boozing or getting their fix.

I scanned the room, taking note of the black walls and carpets—and wondering if they chose that color because it made the blood less noticeable. Booths lined three of the walls, some with curtains, some without. A good fifteen of these were currently occupied, and it was from them that the lusty scent was the strongest. A small dance floor filled the front half of the room, but hardly anyone was on it. There were quite a few vamps sitting at the tables in front of the bar that lined the fourth wall. None of them seemed to be drinking, but all of them were brooding.

I could feel it—feel the heat of it rumbling along the edges of my thoughts. They weren't trying to get into my head, just sharing their unhappy vibe.

It made me glad that Cole and his team were right next door in the parking lot.

I walked across to the bar. The bartender strolled over, idly drying a glass and chewing gum. "What can I do for you?"

I showed him my badge. "I believe your boss has been informed that I need to speak to him?"

There was a slight pause, and though I didn't feel the caress of energy, I knew he was communicating with said boss. After a moment, he nodded and said, "He'll be down in a minute. Do you need a drink?"

"Not yet." Though I definitely might by the time I finished this gig.

I turned around and let my gaze sweep the room again. The humans who were engaged in drinking rather than being drunk from were all clustered around the far end of the bar. Most of them were women, and all of them looked as unhappy as the vamps.

Though I heard no footsteps, awareness tingled across my skin. I shifted my gaze and saw a golden-haired man walking toward me—although "drifting" would have been a more accurate term, because his feet didn't appear to touch the carpet. Then again, he knew exactly what had been spilled on it.

"Dante Starke," he said, coming to an effortless halt several feet away.

His scent swirled around me, and though I'd been expecting him to smell as bad as his club, he didn't. He was orange blossom and dark spices, a combination as elegant as the man—and one that stirred the embers of desire deep in the pit of my stomach. Even Quinn didn't smell *this* good.

I shoved the thought away and concentrated on the vamp rather than his delicious scent. If Starke was a pauper, then his suit certainly didn't advertise it. I'd seen enough suits on Quinn to recognize the cut and quality of a Zegna, and they certainly weren't anything the average Joe would be buying off the rack in any old department store. But as classy as the gray pinstripe was, it was the man wearing the cloth that drew the eye. He was power, passion, and beauty all rolled into a six-foot-four-inch golden frame, and he seemed totally out of place in this run-down dump.

I ignored his offered hand, not wanting to touch his flesh when my inner wolf was taking so much notice, and showed him my badge. "We're investigating the murder in the parking lot behind your club."

"So I've been informed." He crossed his arms, his expression bored. And yet his golden eyes were alert and hungry, reminding me of a hawk with its prey in its sights.

A tremor went through me, though I wasn't entirely sure whether it was fear or something else. Damn it, I was a werewolf who'd found her soul mate, so technically I shouldn't feel *anything* for *anyone* other than the man I was destined to spend the rest of my life with. But of course, things were never that simple for me. Not only did I have Quinn as my lover, but I didn't *want* Kye—my said soul mate—anywhere near me.

And now it seemed I was attracted to this man. Or vamp. Or whatever the hell he was.

Sometimes I wished fate would just stick to the rules when it came to my life. It would have made things a whole lot easier.

"How can I help the Directorate, Ms. Jenson?"

His voice was like buttered honey, smooth and rich. I licked my lips and tried to shake the lust from my thoughts. "I'd like to ask you a few questions, then I'd like somewhere a little more private to interview each of your guests."

One golden eyebrow arched upward, and part of me ached to lean forward and kiss it. Damn, this was weird.

"You don't actually need my permission to do either of those things."

"No, but given the current climate, I've discovered it makes things easier to be polite."

A smile tugged at his lips. "I suppose you could be

right." He waved an elegant hand toward the door just behind the bar. "My office is through there. Would that be suitable?"

"Perfectly. Thank you."

"Good." His fingers touched my spine, lightly guiding me toward the door. It was a heat I felt all the way down to my toes. "Boris, a bottle of champagne for the two of us, please?"

"Not for me. I'm working." I opened the door and stepped away from his touch.

"Surely even the Directorate would not begrudge their guardians a sip or two?"

"My boss is rather old-fashioned when it comes to mixing alcohol and work."

The office was sparsely furnished, with a filing cabinet, an old desk neatly stacked with books and paperwork, a leather office chair that had seen better days, and a coat stand. The only luxurious items were the two plush, burgundy velvet armchairs. I walked over and sat in the one closest to the door.

It didn't make me feel any less trapped.

God, what was it about this man that was getting to me? Hell, I'd faced a god of death. One golden vampire shouldn't have worried me in the least.

And yet he did.

"Ah, but this isn't mere alcohol," he said softly, seductively, "but rather the finest ambrosia ever made."

I shrugged. "He'd still class it as off-limits."

"Tragic." He sat down and crossed his legs, the action elegance itself. One shiny shoe briefly touched my calf, and delight shimmered up my leg.

I shifted fractionally. Amusement twitched at his lips.

"What is it you wish to know, Ms. Jenson?"

"What do you know of a vamp called Grant Haven?"

Starke didn't answer immediately, waiting as the bartender came into the room and deposited a bottle of Bollinger champagne and two glasses on the table. Once he was gone, Starke picked up the bottle, popped the cork with ridiculous ease, and began pouring it.

"Please, none for me."

"Ms. Jenson, it is totally uncivilized to be sitting here without partaking of one of life's great pleasures." He held out the glass of liquid gold, his gaze meeting and holding mine. The hunger was stronger in those watchful depths, and suddenly I wasn't so sure he was talking about the champers. "And I refuse to answer questions until you at least take a sip."

"I could just haul your ass down to the Directorate for questioning."

"You could," he admitted calmly, "but that would cause a rise in the ill feeling you're so desperate to avoid."

He had me there. So I accepted the glass, careful not to touch his fingers in the process. The delicate lemon and grapefruit notes teased my nostrils, making my mouth water. I'd become something of a champagne freak since I'd begun hanging around with Quinn, and Bollinger, with its fresh flavor and teasing under-notes of fruit and coffee, was one of my favorites. I took a sip.

"There," I said. "I've upheld my end. Now answer the question."

He smiled again, and my stomach knotted in response. "Haven is one of the regulars here. He services my guests."

"So the vamps here are under your employ?"

"Not all of them, no. Haven wasn't, but this place was close to his café and handy for a nightly top-up." He took a sip of champagne, then sighed. It was a sound of sheer pleasure, and it curled around me as lovingly as a caress. "There is no sweeter taste than the nectar of the gods."

"Oh, I could think of one or two things that are better," I said, trying to keep it light. Trying to ignore the net of hunger that he seemed to be spinning around me. "Hazelnut coffee, for instance. I'd die without my daily dose of *that*."

"Good coffee is a must, although I'm not sure hazelnut could be classified as good." His heavy-lidded gaze met mine again, and something hot unfurled inside me. "Though I do agree that there are things in this life whose sweetness equals that of champagne. The juices of a woman in the throws of ecstasy, for example."

The words were barely out his mouth and I was imagining him between my legs, licking and teasing and savoring. I blinked and the image shattered, leaving me aching and hungry.

"Will you stop that?" I said sharply.

"Stop what?" he asked, the innocence in his voice at odds with the wicked smile teasing his lips and the dangerous glint in his eyes.

"Spinning the seduction web. I'm here to find a killer. Nothing more, nothing less."

"I weave no web. I merely enhance what is already there."

"You can't enhance it because it *isn't* there, so start concentrating on answers." My voice was sharp. "Otherwise I *will* arrest your ass and drag it down to the Directorate."

He merely shrugged. Which probably meant he'd tone it down but not give up. "What else do you wish to know?"

I crossed my legs and took another sip of champagne. The cool liquid didn't do a whole lot to ease the fires burning within.

"Why do you employ some vamps and not others? Don't you get enough vampires in here to cater to the needs of your human customers?"

"This club is not one of the more popular ones, but we still get plenty of humans in on the weekends." A small smile teased his lips, briefly drawing my gaze. "The vampires I don't employ are the ones I know I can trust *not* to go too far. There are fewer problems that way. The others help act as additional security should the need arise."

"So Haven has never acted as one of your bouncers?"

"No."

"Then did he ever serve someone and perhaps go a little too far?"

The small smile became full-blown, and my toes curled in response. Damn, that was one *hot* smile.

"Despite the way my establishment looks, we run an orderly club. There are very few problems here."

I took another sip of champagne and decided Quinn really needed to get a case of this stuff. "That didn't answer my question."

"No, he has never caused any problems. He's actually been on vacation for the last couple of weeks. Tonight was supposed to be his first night back." He paused to take a drink. "I never knew they had pretty guardians. I find it quite refreshing."

"Considering most guardians are vampires who don't actually wash a lot, that's not really the compliment you think it is."

His expression became contrite, but I didn't believe it for a second. "It's very remiss of me to make such a remark, then. I shall endeavor to make it up to you."

"Don't bother. Do you know if Haven had any problems in his personal life?"

Starke raised his eyebrows. "Why would you think I'd know—or even care—about the intimate details of my friends' private lives?"

"Because you seem the type of vampire who likes to know these sorts of things."

"You could be right." He flashed me a smile that was as playful as it was sensual. "I could tell you two truths right now, in fact."

"Well, I'm not here to hear lies, Starke."

He put the glass down on the table then leaned forward, so that his long golden body was only inches from mine. Tension ran through me, yet I honestly couldn't say it was totally due to the readiness to fight.

Part of it—a tiny, dark, and altogether *stupid* part—was sexual.

"I know, for instance," he continued, his voice as smooth as silk, "that if I took you in my arms and kissed you right now, you'd fight. Eventually. Yet there would be several moments beforehand when you would melt into that kiss and enjoy the passion of it."

I didn't bother refuting it. I couldn't when my heart was beating like crazy at the mere thought of that kiss.

"And the second truth?"

It came out somewhat breathless, and he reached forward, taking my free hand in his, turning it over and gently caressing my wrist. His skin was smooth against mine, his fingertips warm. And the caress . . .

The tremor that ran through me was all heated desire.

"The second truth," he said softly, raising my wrist to his lips and placing the gentlest of kisses on it, "is that this is not the first beheading to happen in this area."

Chapter 2

$\mathscr{I}$ jerked my hand away, but his kiss seemed to have seared itself into my skin. My wrist burned.

"What do you mean, this is not the first beheading?" I surreptitiously glanced down at my wrist, but there was no mark on it, despite how it felt.

He leaned back in his chair and picked up his glass. "Just that."

I frowned. "We've had no reports of other incidents."

"No, because the sun was rising by the time he was discovered. His body was consumed by fire."

"Meaning he was a very young vampire."

"One would presume so. We older souls can take at least a few hours of sunshine."

If he could take a few hours, then he was at least eight hundred years old. "When did this happen?"

"Two days ago."

"Do you happen to know the victim's name?"

If we had another murder, Jack would want me to check it out, even if we didn't have the body.

Starke shook his head and shifted his foot again. He must have surreptitiously moved his chair, because though I had my legs pointed away from him, he managed to run his toe up and down my calf. He might be wearing shiny leather shoes, but somehow it felt like skin on skin.

And that dark part of me wished it was.

"As I mentioned," he said softly, amusement playing around the corners of his delicious mouth again, "he was ashes by the time I got there."

That raised my eyebrows. "You went to the crime scene?"

"The man who reported it was a little on the inebriated side. I thought perhaps a customer had merely fallen down."

"So why not send one of your lackeys to investigate?"

"Employees," he corrected gently. "And we were full that night. I could not afford to take anyone away for even a few minutes."

"So you don't personally service the blood whores?"

"No." He was still caressing my calf, and the movement, though gentle, was extremely erotic. "I prefer to take what I need the old-fashioned way."

And he'd be damn good at it, too, I thought, then pushed the thought away as his gaze met mine. He gave me a wicked smile.

Though he wasn't reading my thoughts—I would have known if he tried—I had a feeling he knew exactly what I was thinking.

Thank God the full moon wasn't near. I probably would have been all over him otherwise. My self-control was barely hanging on as it was.

"Do you know the name of the man who found the body?"

"His name was Henry Gateway. He's something of a regular here."

"Human?"

"Vampire. He's not in my employ, but I do have his address."

At least that was someplace to start. But that didn't explain Starke's "inebriated" comment. "Vampires can't get drunk."

"If they consume enough, any vampire can get intoxicated. Trust me on that. And Gateway doesn't normally imbibe, but he lost a close friend recently." His shrug was elegant.

I frowned. "Wouldn't it be dangerous having a drunk vampire serving the customers?"

"He is extremely popular with our customers." Starke waved his hand airily, the movement oddly sensual. "Something to with his dark good looks and French accent, I suppose. We keep a close eye on him if he's drinking."

"And you have his address because . . . ?"

"Because, as I said, he's good for business. It pays for me to keep him in once piece." He drained his glass then rose. "My presence is required outside. Are there any further questions, Ms. Jenson?"

He was standing right in front of me, which meant I was staring straight at his family jewels. And they were impressive, if that bulge was anything to go by. I forced my gaze upward and saw the laughter there. "No, but I'd appreciate it if you could start sending people in. The sooner I interview them, the sooner they can go home."

"Most will not be in a hurry," he said, then bowed slightly. "It's been a pleasure, Ms. Jenson. If you come and see me before you leave, I'll have that address for you."

"If you just give it to the barman, that'll be fine."

"What, and rob myself of a final glimpse of your beauty? Never."

I rolled my eyes. "You know, sweet talk isn't going to get you anywhere."

"Ah, but you hunger, and that's a start."

"I'm a werewolf. Hunger comes with the territory. But believe me, we know the fine art of self-control."

Even if mine seemed to be hanging on by threads.

"It's still fun to try."

"And I think it's fun to haul people back to the Directorate and interrogate their asses. But I'm willing to give up my pleasure if you'll give up yours."

He laughed—a warm sound that trembled up my spine. "If there were more guardians like you, Ms. Jenson, I believe there would not be as much disquiet in the community."

He walked out without waiting for a comment, and

I sighed in relief. At least I could now concentrate on the business of finding our witness.

*M*y long night did indeed turn into an interminable morning. Over the course of the next six hours, I consumed two glasses of Starke's fine Bollinger then moved on to coffee. Several cups later, I still felt like shit.

There might have been only thirty people plus Starke's bar staff to interview, but they were all reluctant to talk.

I leaned back in the chair and rolled my neck, trying to ease the cramp in my muscles, but it didn't help the tension any more than the coffee helped boost my energy.

I took another gulp of coffee anyway as a tall brunette sauntered into the room. Her clothes looked expensive and there was a lot of gold around her neck and wrist, which set her apart from the others I'd interviewed. But just like them, she plopped down with a decided lack of elegance, shoved her long legs out in front of her, and crossed her arms.

"It's taken you long enough," she said, voice tart and not in the least bit slurred. She had to be the only non-drinker in the place. "None of us had anything to do with that beheading, so this is all just a waste of time."

"I apologize for the delay," I said, picking up my vid phone and setting it to record again. "Once you answer a few questions, you're free to go."

She grunted, but it wasn't a happy sound.

"For recording purposes, can you please tell me your name and address?"

"Is it legal for you to record without asking me first?"

"Yes."

She sniffed. "My name is Mandy Jones, and I live at 14 Lytton Street, Elwood."

Meaning I'd finally found our anonymous caller—and it had only taken me half the damn morning. "How long have you been here at the club, Mandy?"

She shrugged and tucked a stray strand of hair behind her ear, revealing a wrist littered with bite marks. "I finished work and came straight here, so most of the night."

"And you haven't left at all?"

She shook her head. "I was about to leave when your lot locked us in."

I picked up my coffee and took a drink. It was vanilla and cinnamon rather than hazelnut, but it was still better than regular coffee. I wondered if Starke had raided his personal stash, because I couldn't imagine them serving it in the bar. It was too upmarket for this sort of establishment.

Mandy didn't seem to notice the drawn-out silence. She didn't fidget, either, just continued to glare at me.

Either she was a very good actress, or she actually had nothing to hide.

"Then how did you know there was a beheaded body out in the parking lot if you never left the club?"

"Because he paid me to call."

Meaning this case wasn't as straightforward as it

seemed. Why was I not surprised? "Who paid you to call?"

She shrugged again. "He was tall, blond, and green eyed. The eyes were contacts, though."

I raised my eyebrows. "How can you be so sure?"

She waved a dismissive hand. "I'm an optometrist. I know these things."

Maybe she did. But why would this guy—whether he was the killer or someone else—have paid someone else to make the call? And if it *had* been the killer, why call at all? That made no sense.

"He gave me five hundred dollars to make that call," she continued. "I wasn't arguing."

Five hundred dollars seemed like overkill to me, and I wondered if it was deliberately done to attract interest. Although why would a killer want to bring attention to his crime? Unless, of course, he was one of those freaks who liked notoriety. "And did you get the cash?"

"Sure." She reached into her pocket and pulled out a wad of bills. "I made him pay me first."

"Did it cross your mind that you might have been taking money from a killer?"

She frowned. "Of course he wasn't the killer. There was no blood on him."

I didn't bother pointing out the obvious flaws in *that* logic. I mean, it wouldn't have been hard to change clothes before he came into the club. I reached out telepathically and scanned her memories. Images flitted— insubstantial wisps of faces and fangs mixed in with resonance of pleasure. She'd talked to several men over the night and had taken enjoyment from many more. I withdrew, then asked, "Was there anything else about him that stood out? Anything odd?"

She was shaking her head even before I'd finished. "He was average. It was his eyes that made me remember him."

"Do you think you'd remember enough about him to work up an image?" Given what I'd seen in her mind, I doubted she'd remember more than what she'd already said, but it was worth a shot.

"Maybe." She wrinkled her nose. "I'm not much of an artist, though."

I smiled. "We'll send someone over to you. All you have to do is describe what you remember."

"That I can manage," she said, nodding.

"Do you know a man named Grant Haven?" I couldn't help adding.

She shook her head. "Why? Is he the one who lost his head?"

"I'm afraid so. He apparently used to work here."

"He might have done. I don't ask their names, you know?"

If it was me, I'd want to know the name of the man I was trusting to provide fulfillment in the form of a bite. But then, regular junkies often didn't know the names of their suppliers. All that mattered was the hit.

"That's it for now, then. We'll be in contact with you to get the image."

She nodded and sprang to her feet. "So I can go?"

"You certainly can." I waited until she'd opened the door before adding, "Oh, there is one more thing."

She paused and raised an eyebrow as she glanced around at me. "Yes?"

"Why this place? You obviously can afford to go to one of the better establishments."

Surprise flitted across her features, then she smiled ruefully. "If I go to the other places, I might run into people I know." She shrugged, and there were shadows of unhappiness in her eyes. "I can't seem to give this craving up. I want to, but I can't. So I come here, where no one I know would ever come."

"Thanks, Mandy."

She nodded and traipsed out, though I fully expected her to get one more pleasure hit before she left the club. She had that hungry look in her eyes, despite the sadness I'd glimpsed.

The remaining two patrons couldn't tell me anything more. Neither of them recognized the victim's name, and they didn't even seem to care that someone had been murdered close by. The only thing they cared about was the inconvenience we were causing them.

I let them go, then switched off the recorder and shoved the phone back into my pocket. It was time to go home and catch up on some sleep.

I pushed to my feet and headed out the door. The interior of the club was still dark, despite the fact it was close to eleven. Obviously all the windows had been blacked out.

I walked over to the bar and motioned to the bartender. Business had to be slow, because he was still chewing gum and polishing glasses.

"Your boss was going to leave me the address of a Henry Gateway."

He raised an eyebrow and, after a heartbeat, said, "The boss is on his way down again."

Damn. I did *not* need another confrontation with that vampire when my energy reserves were so low, but Starke was already gliding toward me, his body long and strong and beautiful, his skin glowing as if it was fired by the sun itself.

I blinked, and the image shattered. But not the desire.

I suddenly wondered if he was an emo vampire. Emos lived off emotion rather than blood, and they had the ability to augment the stronger emotions for their own feeding pleasure. A nightclub servicing the hungers of others would certainly be a perfect feeding ground for an emo vamp—and it would also explain my unusual reaction. I made a mental note to check his background when I got back to the Directorate.

He offered me a piece of paper. On it was Gateway's address. He lived close, meaning I might as well go see if he was home before I went that way myself. I folded the paper and shoved it into the back pocket of my jeans. "I don't suppose you have security cameras here, do you?"

"Regretfully, no. My patrons prefer not to have their exploits captured." He paused, mouth curving seductively. "What about you, Ms. Jenson? Do you like having your conquests recorded for future pleasure?"

"I prefer my pleasures to be of the moment," I said. Then, as the spark of desire burned deeper in his eyes,

I added hastily, "Thank you for your assistance, Mr. Starke."

"Anytime, sweet lady. Anytime."

I snorted and got the hell out of there. The brightness of the sun had my eyes watering after the gloom of the club, and I blinked several tears away and took a deep breath, clearing my lungs of the last vestiges of blood, desperation, and luscious vampire. Then I spun on my heel and headed for the parking lot.

Cole and his team had already left, and although the blue police tape still lined the lot, there were no cops guarding the perimeter. Obviously, Cole had gotten everything he needed and someone had simply forgotten to take down the tape.

I climbed into my car and typed Gateway's address into the onboard computer. He lived only a few streets away, so it didn't take me long to get there.

Gateway's house, like so many others in this area, had a run-down, grungy facade. But the little strip of grass between the footpath and the roadside was neatly trimmed, and there were geraniums lining the front fence. He obviously had a little more pride in his surroundings than was usual for this area.

I slammed the car door closed and made my way to the house. There was no bell so I knocked instead, my knuckles shaking loose several layers of dust as the sound echoed. I waited several minutes, then knocked again. The only response was the barking of a dog from the far end of the house. I wrapped my fingers around the knob and tried to turn it. The door was locked and I had no real reason to break into the house—although that had never stopped me before. But breaking in would mean more paperwork, and I really didn't have the energy for that right now. I'd have to come back later—or go back to the club to catch him there. Which wasn't something I wanted to do, despite the excited response from my pulse.

As I started walking back to the car, the dog's barking became more frantic. It wasn't the "get away from here, this is my place" bark that canines all over the world used when strangers came to the door. It was more the "something's wrong, I need help" type of bark.

Curiosity stirred. I stepped across the little garden bed and peered into the front window. The room beyond was a bedroom, but one that hadn't been slept in often if the dust coating the stacked pillows was anything to go by. The bedroom door was open, but I couldn't see much more than the shadows of a hallway.

There was a small metal gate to the right of the house, so I pushed that open and walked down the side. Several windows lined this section of the building, but the curtains were all securely closed. No surprise, given the owner was a vampire. The barking got louder as I neared the end of the old house. As I rounded a corner, a little white and brown terrier made a dash for my feet, nipped at my shoelaces, then raced back to the door. He might not be able to talk, but he was doing his best to tell me something was seriously wrong inside.

I peered through a window, but I couldn't see anything more than a washing machine that had walked halfway across the tiles and, beyond that, a basket half-filled with clothes. I flared my nostrils, drawing in the air, sorting through all the different aromas. Again, nothing seemed out of the ordinary.

And yet the little dog was frantic.

I scooped him up and held him one-handed, then opened the screen door and tested the door handle. Like the front door, it was locked. A punch in the sweet spot just above the lock soon fixed that, but as the door swung open, the smell hit.

Something was dead inside.

Or someone, given the terrier's reaction. He had relaxed a bit now that I was holding him, but I could still feel the tension in his little body.

I walked around the wayward washing machine. A clock ticked softly in the silence and the air was warm—a fact that wouldn't have helped preserve whoever was dead.

The small hallway beyond was shadowed. There was a toilet to the left and an open doorway to the right. The source of the smell also seemed to be coming from that way.

The terrier started wriggling as I walked into the large kitchen-dining area. I gripped him a little tighter, not wanting him to shake himself loose and disturb whatever evidence there was to be found.

Sunlight streamed in from the window above the sink, lifting the gloom. A small table had been set for breakfast—which for this vampire was a packet of synth blood that now smelled off and a cup of coffee that had long gone cold. The fridge held milk and more synth blood. Obviously, Gateway wasn't servicing enough customers at Dante's to keep himself fed.

I closed the fridge door then followed my nose, and found Gateway's body sprawled stomach down in the hallway. He was barefoot and wearing a towel around his middle, suggesting he'd just come out of the shower. His skin was pale and his body lean, his ribs and spine clearly evident. My gaze rose further and my stomach sank. Someone had separated his head from his neck, and the blood had pooled around his head like a dark, dried-out halo.

Which meant there'd be no ghost hanging about to help.

I swore softly and spun around, walking back to the kitchen and closing the door behind me before releasing the little terrier and dragging out my phone. As the little dog whined and scratched at the door, I called my boss.

"Riley," Jack said. "How goes the investigation?"

"No one saw anything, no one heard anything, and no one knows anything. And unfortunately, we have another beheaded vampire on our hands."

He swore softly. "Where?"

"In a house a few streets away from Starke's club. The victim's name is Henry Gateway, and he's been dead for a couple of days, if the dried blood is anything to go by."

Jack paused. "I don't know him."

Something in the way he said that prickled my instincts. Jack might not know him personally, but he knew him. So why wouldn't he say that?

"He serviced blood whores at Dante's."

Jack snorted. "Now, if there's one vampire I wouldn't mind seeing dead, it's that bastard."

"You know Starke?" It surprised me, although I'm not entirely sure why. Maybe it was just the fact that Starke didn't seem like the sort of vampire that would normally come under Directorate scrutiny. But I didn't know a whole lot about vampire society or how they socialized, so they very easily could have known each other on another level.

"He has a long history of seducing women and running less-than-stellar establishments," Jack said, distaste evident in his gravelly tones. "I'm actually surprised someone hasn't taken *his* head. It'd make more sense than focusing on those who work for him."

"So he really is a blood vampire?"

"Yes." Jack paused. "Why?"

"Because he has some mighty powerful vamp mojo happening. Enough that I wondered if he was another emo vamp."

Jack snorted. "He's not an emo, but he's gifted with what we call a sexual glamor. Combine it with his looks, and he could seduce a brick wall if he put his mind to it." He paused. "He didn't succeed with you, did he?"

"No, but someone could have had the decency to warn me."

"Sorry. It didn't even cross my mind that you'd have problems."

"Jack, I'm a werewolf. Sex is like food to us." And he was just lucky that Quinn was keeping me well fed.

"Anyway, according to Starke, Gateway claimed to have stumbled upon a beheaded vamp two days ago, but the sun destroyed any possible evidence before anyone could get there to confirm it."

"He should have notified us."

I didn't bother replying. What should have happened and what did happen were often two very different things. Especially when dealing with vampires.

"Three beheadings in as many days," Jack continued. "This is not good."

"No." We had trouble enough with the vampire population. We didn't need them getting antsy about some crackpot running around lopping heads off. "You don't think we've got a new anti-vampire gang on the loose, do you?"

"It's entirely possible," Jack said, voice weary. "But there's been no rumor of such a gang in action."

"There soon will be if they keep up at this rate."

"If they keep up at this rate, we'll have more than a gang to worry about."

Yeah, like vampires forming vigilante gangs of their own. It had happened once before—thankfully well before my time at the Directorate—but I'd heard the whispers about it and had seen the photographs of the resulting riots. It had damn near erupted into a race war, and from what I'd heard, it was only luck—and a whole lot of tough talking from Director Hunter—that had stopped a bloodbath.

"Has Cole gotten back to headquarters?"

"No. He's still en route. I'll redirect him."

"You want me to wait?"

He hesitated. "No. Finish your investigation, then go catch some sleep. I want the report on my desk by five, though."

Meaning I'd better do it before I went to sleep, because unless there was another death, I fully intended to sleep well past five. "Do you think someone is trying to get back at Starke through his employees?"

"I certainly hope so, because the other option is not one I want to contemplate."

Especially given the unrest already out there in the vampire community. "Then Cole's fast-tracking his report on this one?"

"Yes. It'll be ready by eight tonight."

So much for Cole heading back to his warm bed and his waiting lover. "I'll be in at eight, then."

I hung up, then scooped up the still-whining terrier and stepped back into the hallway. My nose wrinkled as the scent of rotting flesh wrapped around me, but I didn't bother trying to breathe through my mouth. I needed to explore the scents in this place. Besides, past experience told me it wouldn't help anyway. I stepped past his body and investigated the other rooms. Other than the dust that littered the basin and shelf, there were dirty clothes on the bathroom floor and a dog-eared toothbrush sitting on the sink, complete with a shiny strip of blue toothpaste. He'd obviously been about to brush his teeth when he'd been interrupted. I sucked in the flavorsome air, sorting through the undercurrents, finding the dankness of mold and something else. Something that was too nebulous to define, and yet oddly seemed out of place.

Frowning, I spun around and headed for the room opposite. It was a living room, and though sparsely furnished, it was obviously where Gateway spent most of his time. There were newspapers stacked beside the sofa and remotes neatly lined up on the stained coffee table. The rest of the room was surprisingly tidy. There wasn't even dust on the top of the TV, which isn't something I could claim in my own apartment. I swept aside the curtains to check the window locks, but again they were intact.

Which left me with the bedrooms.

I was walking toward the front rooms when the little dog suddenly began barking. I jumped slightly and glanced at the door as a shadow loomed. But as I reached for the door handle, I felt it.

A familiar—and altogether unwelcome—tingling that ran across every sense, every fiber, setting them alight. Setting my soul afire.

There was only one man who had that effect on me.

My soul mate.

Kye.

Chapter 3

My hand froze against the doorknob.

I didn't want to confront him. I didn't even want to see him.

I hadn't set eyes on him since he'd walked away six months ago, and if I never had to see him again, that would have been all right by me.

I might have spent most of my life longing for my soul mate, but the reality wasn't what I'd hoped for.

Kye was a killer for hire—a man who didn't care who employed him or who he had to kill. All that mattered to him was the money, the thrill of the chase, and the satisfaction of getting a job done as quickly and as efficiently as possible. He wasn't a man who wanted a wife or a family or entanglements of any kind. He was everything I *didn't* want in a soul mate.

But I couldn't deny that he was, or change the fact of it—no matter how much I might wish otherwise.

"Are you going to open the door or not, Riley?"

His voice was like a good red wine—rich and smooth—and it touched places deep inside that no one, not even Quinn, could reach. I closed my eyes, took a deep breath, then complied.

He stood in a halo of sunshine, his golden skin glowing with warmth and the dark red of his hair running with brighter highlights. He was a golden man with chilling amber eyes set in a face that was handsome and yet uncaring.

But not unfeeling.

Because I could feel his hunger. I felt it rip through my body before it settled down low. It was a fierce and unwanted ache that had nothing to do with my heart's desire and everything to do with my werewolf soul. But while she had wanted this feeling, she didn't want this man. That made it a little easier to ignore the hunger.

And if I kept telling myself that, I might eventually believe it.

"What are you doing here, Kye?" My white-knuckled grip on the edge of the door belied the calmness of my voice.

"I might ask you the same question." He glanced from me to the squirming, barking dog in my arm. "Found yourself a pet, have you?"

"He belongs to the owner of the house." I glanced down at the almost frantic terrier and scratched his head. "And he doesn't seem all that happy to see you."

"Neither do you," he said, voice dry. "I would have thought you'd at least have a smile for the man of your destiny."

"Destiny can bite my ass."

He laughed. It was a soft, seductive, and altogether dangerous sound. "Ah, Riley, it's nice to see you haven't changed."

"No, I'm still a guardian, and you're still interfering in Directorate business."

He raised his eyebrows. "And what business would the Directorate have with a vampire who has obviously been dead for several days?"

I opened my mouth to ask how he knew Gateway was dead then snapped it closed again. Kye was a were-wolf, so he'd smell the decay even if he couldn't see the body.

"And my questions to you would have to be: Why are you here to see him, and did you have anything to do with his death?"

His sudden smile made my stomach lurch, and it was all I could do not to drop the little dog and step into Kye's arms. They would be waiting for me, despite the outward indifference and the distance we were keeping between us.

"Vampires like him hardly ever require my style of killing." He crossed his arms and leaned casually against the door frame, the leather of his old jacket straining deliciously across his shoulders. "Besides, from what I've heard, he's been too busy drowning himself in alcohol of late to make the effort of hunting him worthwhile."

Because for men like him, the hunt was almost as important as the fee. Almost. "And how would you know he's been drinking to excess?"

He raised an eyebrow, amusement setting his golden eyes ablaze. "I can smell the booze."

"Liar." Alcohol was the one scent not present in this house. Rotting vampire, unwashed dog, and a little bit of mold, maybe, but not booze.

The smile was still flirting with his lips, and a whole lot of me ached to kiss him. "Then maybe I know he was a drunk because I do my homework when I'm following a lead."

"What sort of lead?" I glanced down at the still-squirming dog and wondered whether his intense reaction came from having another male on his turf or something more sinister. Whatever it was, scratching his head didn't seem to be calming him down. I stepped back, deposited him in the front bedroom, and quickly closed the door. He continued barking, and started scratching at the door.

"That dog seriously dislikes you," I added, crossing my arms as I faced Kye again.

He shrugged. "The alpha always defends his territory."

The steely edge in his voice suddenly had me wondering if I were one of those territories that needed defending. Was that why he'd suddenly reappeared? To reclaim what was his?

The thought made me shiver. His gaze swept me, then rose to linger on my mouth. His hunger swirled around me, thick and strong, and little droplets of sweat broke out along my spine.

I wanted him. God, how I wanted him.

I clenched my fists a little bit tighter, digging my nails into my palms, using the pain to offset my desire.

It was a useless thing to do, really, when he was a werewolf and we were connected on more than a base level.

"I'm chasing a missing person," he said softly. "Did the vamp inside kill himself, or did someone help him along?"

"I don't know. And since when did you start taking on missing persons cases?"

"I go where the cash is. And don't play games with me, Riley. You've been in the business long enough now to make an informed guess."

"It's a Directorate case, Kye. I can't discuss it."

"No, you *won't* discuss it. Not with me, anyway."

He had that right. "How long are you in town?"

"Why? Did you miss me?"

"No." *Yes.* Given the nail-digging wasn't achieving much, I flexed my fingers instead, but it didn't help release the tension rolling through me. "Why are you here, Kye?"

"As I said, I'm simply following a lead. Nothing more, nothing less." But his gaze met mine and, in those golden depths, I saw the hunter. The possessor. A wolf who hungered to control the very same things that I did. It made a mockery of his words, and it was a sight that sent a chill through my heart.

I didn't want this.

I didn't want him.

Even if my soul ached with the need of his kiss, his caress, his body.

But the wolf wasn't the sum of me, and as much as I might hunger for Kye, there was another man in my life. One I cared about, one I loved. And that part of me was what I reached for now to keep me strong.

"Whatever it is you're doing," I said, my voice harsh, "make sure you keep out of my way."

He laughed. It was a soft, cold sound that sent shivers up my spine and heat swirling through my body. "Things haven't changed, have they, Riley? Your words say one thing and your body another."

"I'm not the only one adept at playing that game."

"No," he agreed. "So what do you suggest we do?"

"Precisely what we're doing. Ignore and deny. You and I won't ever happen, Kye, and we both know it."

He uncrossed his arms and reached out, his fingers caressing my cheek. My skin tingled with the heated contact and my breath froze in my throat.

"But we will. We must. We are each other's destiny, even if neither of us particularly wishes it."

"As I said before, destiny can bite my ass." I pulled away from his caress and glanced at my watch. "Now, if you want to avoid Directorate scrutiny, I suggest you leave."

"Then Gateway *has* been murdered?"

He studied me calmly, a small smile teasing his lips, and I wondered whether he was reading my thoughts again. Kye was a siphon, which meant he could take on the psychic talents of others and use them to his own advantage. So when he was with me, he was telepathic. And despite the fact I had psychic shields strong enough to keep even the oldest vampires out, Kye seemed able to slip past them and catch any unwary thoughts.

Although if he could thread his way through the turmoil his reappearance was causing, he probably deserved to catch an unwary thought or two about the victim.

"I need to know what happened to him, Riley," he added,

Tough was my automatic response, but I knew better than to say it. I might as well wave a red rag in front of a bull. I wanted Kye out of my life, not haunting me in an attempt to gain the information he needed.

"It'll take twenty-four hours for the report to come through. Call me." I didn't bother giving him the number. I had no intention of making things easy for him.

He nodded and pushed away from the door frame. "I'll talk to you later, then."

I didn't reply, just watched as he turned and walked away.

And tried not to think about the way his jeans clung to his butt, or the loose-limbed, sexy way he walked.

Once he was through the gate and out of sight, I blew out a relieved breath and closed the door. The little dog had finally stopped barking, but the minute I opened the bedroom door, he charged out, making a beeline for his dead master. I scooped him up. "And what are we going to do with you, then?"

He glanced at me and whined. He really was a cute

little thing, and while I couldn't leave him here, I didn't particularly want to dump him at a shelter, either. Which meant either taking him with me or finding him a home.

Dogs and a pack of wolves generally weren't a good idea, and although he didn't seem to have a problem with me, his reaction to Kye suggested it would be a different matter when it came to Rhoan and his mate, Liander.

So he needed a home. It'd be nice if I could find him another vampire.

The thought stalled and I grinned.

I knew the perfect person.

To say Sal was surprised to find me standing on her doorstep would be the understatement of the year. She and I had a whole lot to do with each other on a professional level—she'd taken over my position as Jack's main assistant and generally handled a good percentage of my calls—but we weren't friends and weren't ever likely to be.

"Riley," she said, her normally sultry tones decidedly frosty. "I'm on vacation. From you *and* from the Directorate."

"I know. I just thought you might be able to help out a friend," I said, the little dog still half hidden under my jacket.

Her gaze narrowed. "And why would you think I'd be interested in helping out one of your friends?"

"Because his master's just been killed, and I don't

really want to dump him in a shelter." I pulled the little dog out from under cover and offered him to her. "His previous owner was a vamp, so he has no fear of us nonhumans."

A point he proceeded to prove with his ecstatic tail wagging and happy little panting. Obviously, it was just Kye he had a problem with.

"God, he's darling," Sal all but purred as she plucked him from my arms and snuggled him against her. Then her gaze narrowed. "What's the catch?"

"Nothing. I just figured he deserved a good home, and I knew you liked dogs."

"Thanks," she said, then added tartly. "But don't think you can start dumping any old stray you're feeling sorry for on my doorstep. I'm not a halfway house for the abandoned."

"Got it," I said, knowing that if I ever did turn up with another stray, Sal wouldn't turn him away. She might be a hardheaded bitch when she was dealing with me, but when it came to *real* dogs, she was the biggest softie around. And that made her a good person in my book—even if I'd never tell her.

"Glad we're clear about that," Sal said, tossing her caramel-colored hair out of her eyes. "Now go away."

I grinned and left. No one was home when I got there, but I knew both Rhoan and Liander would be back for dinner so I left them a note to wake me and went to bed.

It seemed that no sooner had I hit the pillow when something hard was hitting me upside the head. I opened a bleary eye and found myself staring at a shoe.

A rather grimy and sweat-drenched running shoe, to be precise.

"I know that smell and I do not appreciate it sitting on my pillow," I muttered, swatting the shoe off my bed. "Go away and leave me alone."

"You're the one that wanted to be woken for dinner," Rhoan said, his voice gratingly cheerful. "Liander's just about to serve."

"What time is it?" I tried glaring at the clock, but it was facing the window rather than me and I didn't have the energy to reach out and grab it.

"It's six-thirty," he said, suddenly appearing in my vision as he bent down to retrieve his shoe. He was wearing old sweatpants that clung to his lean, muscular legs and a blue muscle shirt that was darkened with sweat. My nose twitched, drawing in the familiar scent of him, feeling the security of it wrap around me like an old but much-loved blanket. All wolves needed their pack, but for too many years Rhoan and I had only had each other. And while we now had Liander and Quinn sharing our lives, we'd been together for so long, with no one else.

Which was why Liander now lived in our apartment, why Quinn was spending more and more time here, and why we were seriously considering getting a bigger place. With the four of us, it was getting a little cramped.

"You're not showering before you eat?" I mumbled, dragging my pillow closer in a last-ditch effort to retain some threads of sleepiness. I didn't want to get up. I felt like crap. Dreams had disturbed my sleep, and it felt like I hadn't got any rest at all.

The bed bounced as Rhoan plopped his sweaty self down. "Liander likes the odor of hard work, so no, not just yet. Did you write up your report for Jack?"

My eyes flew open and I groaned. "God, no. Totally forgot about it."

"Which would explain the irate phone call we got a few minutes ago. I don't think you're his favorite guardian right at this moment."

"Am I ever?" I muttered, and dragged myself upright. Every muscle in my body protested the movement. Anyone would think I'd gone twelve rounds in the boxing ring or had a night of rough-and-tumble sex.

"You look like shit," Rhoan said, eyeing me with a frown. "What happened last night?"

"Nothing out of the ordinary and certainly nothing strenuous." I rubbed a hand across gritty eyes. "I just feel drained and tired."

"How long were you asleep?"

"Nearly six hours."

"Maybe you're coming down with something." His gaze went to my neck, although if he was looking for bite marks, there were none to be found. I healed extraordinarily quickly these days. "Quinn's not taking too much blood again, is he?"

"Quinn's still substituting synth blood for mine a couple of days a week, so no, he's not taking too much." I yawned. "Maybe I just need coffee and food."

"Maybe." Rhoan pushed to his feet. "We've got roast lamb tonight."

Roast lamb was my one of my favorites, and it was usually something we saved for special occasions, simply because the price was so high these days. "What are we celebrating?"

"Nothing," he said, his eyes twinkling as he all but danced out the door.

I scrambled out of bed and threw on some clothes. Something was going on, and I needed to find out what. Liander was setting side plates down on the table, but he glanced up as I walked in, a smile he couldn't quite control dancing about his lips.

"Okay," I said, glancing from one to the other. "What are you two up to?"

"Nothing," Liander said. His hair was plain silver today—no garish highlights, no glitter. It sharpened his features and made his silver eyes glow. "And everything. Sit down for dinner."

He disappeared back into the kitchen, leaving me with my oddly euphoric brother. It had me stumped, because it had to be something big for them to be reacting this way, and yet there was only one thing that I knew of that could make Liander *this* happy. Only it was the one thing I'd thought my brother would never, ever do.

I met his gaze and said, "Don't tell me you've finally agreed to fully commit to the man?"

A loud snort echoed from the kitchen. Rhoan merely grinned.

"Then what the hell are you two so giddy about?"

Another reason hit me, and my stomach dropped. "God, you haven't bought a place of your own, have you?"

Some of his happiness faded. "You don't really think we'd do that to you, do you?"

I took a deep breath to calm the hammering of my heart. "No."

"Good, because we wouldn't. Ever. And don't expect that you and Quinn can get away from us, either. We're a pack now, whether he likes it or not."

"This whole pack equation doesn't come easily to a vampire," came Quinn's dry comment, "but I am slowly getting used to the idea."

My heart leapt at the sound of his softly lilting tones, and I swung around. He was standing in the doorway, one hand on the doorknob and a smile twitching his oh-so-kissable lips. His gaze met mine and, as ever, I felt myself getting lost in those gloriously dark depths. Kye might be what my wolf had hungered for, but this man—this vampire—was everything else. He was my night and my day and my heart, and I didn't want to lose him.

But that possibility was a malignancy that lingered in the background of everything we did, everything we planned.

Because of Kye.

Because none of us knew whether the pull my wolf felt for her soul mate would in the long run be stronger than the pull I felt for Quinn.

He closed the door behind him and walked toward me, a dark-haired vision of male perfection in a gray suit. I bounded toward him, wrapped my arms around his neck, and dragged his luscious lips to mine. As kisses went, it was pretty delicious.

"Missed you," he said softly, when we finally parted.

"And we're missing dinner," Rhoan said dryly, "so get over here and eat."

"You won't let him eat at the dinner table," I said, grinning as Quinn draped an arm around my neck and guided me over to the table. His fingertips brushed my breast, sending little surges of desire coursing through my body, and I momentarily debated dragging him off to the bedroom.

Then the smell of roast lamb hit my nostrils, and hunger won out.

"That's because it's not polite to get orgasmic at the dinner table if you're not sharing the sensation," Liander said, placing a plate of food down in front of me and a pack of synth blood in front of Quinn. "And Quinn keeps insisting he doesn't do guys."

"Not unless it's an absolute do-or-die situation," Quinn agreed.

I raised my eyebrows as he pulled out a chair for me. "So you have done guys?"

"As I said, it's not my preferred option." He kissed my nose before sitting down himself.

"That's not what I asked."

A smile touched the corners of his luscious lips. "Yes, I have taken blood from men. No, I have never actually had sex with them."

"But isn't that your preferred way of feeding?"

He raised his eyebrows at me, the amusement touching his lips finally reaching the dark depths of his eyes. "You prefer men, but that hasn't stopped you from kissing women, has it?"

"That's different—"

"How?" he interrupted. "We both do what we must when it's required. It doesn't mean we enjoy it."

I guess he had me there. I'd kissed Vinny solely to get information that might have helped solve a case and save lives, and he fed off people to survive. His might be more necessary than mine, but we were both doing what we had to.

His gaze flicked from me to the two men on the opposite side of the table. "Now, how about you two explaining the highly charged buzz I'm getting off you both?"

I began tucking into the lamb. The meat just about melted in my mouth and I groaned in delight. Quinn glanced at me, his thoughts reaching for mine. *You do realize I'm planning to make you groan like that later.*

Unfortunately for us both, I have to be at work by eight.

He glanced at his watch. *I can do quick.*

I leaned sideways, dropped a kiss on his cheek, and said with a mental grin, *Quick would be good.*

Liander placed the remaining plates on the table, then sat down beside Rhoan. His smile was a mile wide, and there were little crinkles of happiness lining the corners of his eyes. Rhoan was almost as bad.

"Well," my brother said, picking up his utensils and cutting into the thickly sliced lamb. "We do have an announcement to make."

"Color me surprised," I said dryly, munching down more lamb.

Rhoan's smile grew, though I wouldn't have thought it was possible. "We have decided to have children."

I just about choked on my meal. The meat lodged somewhere in my throat and I started coughing violently. Quinn gave me several hard thumps on the back, which didn't exactly help. As I wheezed and wiped the tears from my eyes, he pointed out the obvious. "You're both guys. Neither of you can actually carry a child, and one of you is sterile."

"We do realize this," Liander said, eyes twinkling. "Which is where we hope Riley comes in."

"Me?" I squeaked. "In case you've forgotten, I'm as barren as Rhoan here."

"You may be barren, but you have frozen eggs," Rhoan said. "We're twins, Riley, which means you're as close as Liander's going to get to having a kid with me."

I looked from one to the other. "You're serious, aren't you?"

Liander nodded. "My sister has agreed to carry the child for us. It's our chance to have a child, Riley. It's our chance to carry on the family name." He paused. "But if you're not comfortable with it, that's fine. We'll just pick another donor. We don't want it to seem like it's you or nothing."

"Either way," Rhoan added softly, "it leaves Liander with something to hold on to if the worst ever happens at work."

Something unfurled inside me—a desire long acknowledged and yet long forced away. My fingers began shaking—in fact, I think every part of me was shaking—so I put my knife and fork down on the table and leaned back in my chair. Quinn caught my hand, his fingers so steady and warm against mine. I squeezed his hand, more grateful than ever that he was there.

"We're different packs," I murmured, more to break the expectant silence than out of any real concern over whose name any resulting child might bear.

A child. Liander's and *mine*.

God, I wanted to get up and dance at the prospect and yet, at the same time, my stomach was churning with fear.

After everything that fate had thrown my way of late, it was hard to believe I was now being presented with this opportunity. Hell, part of me didn't *want* to believe that it might actually happen, because I didn't want to face the pain of yet more disappointment.

"Told you she'd say that," Rhoan murmured, then leaned forward, his arms crossed on the table. "We're starting a new pack. The Jenson-Moore pack, which currently consists of three werewolves and one vampire. Said vampire will be expected to play uncle and change diapers along with everyone else."

"Said vampire," Quinn said dryly, "seems to be getting the raw end of the deal. No surname involvement *and* excrement duty. Do not expect joy at the prospect."

"You did get off midnight bottle duty, even though you're usually awake," Rhoan said, glancing at me. "Well, what do you think?"

"I think I'm too shocked to actually think," I muttered, then leaned forward and studied the two of them. Though it was good to see the two of them so excited—so happy—the sick fear churning my stomach wouldn't let me give in to that same happiness. Maybe because I'd been right where they are—had my hopes up for something good, only to have it pulled out from under my feet—and I didn't want them to go through the same sort of pain.

"You do know this won't be easy," I said slowly. "My eggs are viable, but no one can say what effect, if any, the drugs Talon once gave me will have had on them."

"We're aware of that, Riley," Liander said, twining his fingers through my brother's. "We're willing to take the chance."

Yeah, but was I? Those drugs were still changing me, and no one had any idea where or if it would end. Did I have the right to put any child of mine through that sort of uncertainty?

And yet the eggs couldn't remain on ice forever. The doctors had already warned me that there were no guarantees that they would remain viable after more than a few years. If I ever *did* want children of my own, this might be my one opportunity.

But was I ready for a child? Was I ready for the heartache that might just come with it? Because, right now, those eggs represented hope. What if we went through with the surrogacy, only to discover that the eggs weren't strong enough—or had been changed too much by the drugs that had been forced on me—to ever become a living entity?

Confusion and hope and fear swirled through me. I

didn't know what to do. I really didn't. And I was clinging so hard to Quinn's hand I was probably on the verge of crushing his fingers, and yet it felt like a lifeline.

"We're not asking you to make a decision right here and now," Rhoan said softly. "We know this has probably hit you like a ton of bricks. We just want you to think about it, and let us know."

I took a deep breath and released it slowly. "Have you asked anyone else about donating eggs yet?"

"No, but we have several options. As I said, don't feel pressured into this if you're really not comfortable with it. We're okay if you say no."

Yeah, but would I be? "But another donor would make the child of your line, not yours and Rhoan's."

"In the end, the bloodline doesn't matter, only the child," Rhoan said. Then a grin split his lips. "Of course, we could imitate Talon and try the whole cloning issue, but setting up the lab and finding a willing scientist could get messy and expensive."

I smiled, as my brother had no doubt intended. "When do you need an answer?"

"My sister reckons she'll be good to go in a couple of months. Her own pups will be past the diaper stage by then, and she'll have more energy for the pregnancy."

"And you've sat her down and explained the dangers?" My gaze jumped between the two of them. "Does she really understand that this may not be a regular pregnancy in any way, shape, or form, simply because no one knows what my eggs will do once they're fertilized?"

"She knows," Liander said, face somber. "I wouldn't risk my sister's life by not giving her all the facts, Riley. But she really wants to do this for us."

Then she was a sweetheart. But I guessed I would have done the same for my brother, had I actually been capable of carrying a child.

"Okay, I'll get back to you on it soon." I hesitated, then grinned. "You do realize, of course, that a week of roast dinners could influence the outcome."

Rhoan snorted. "Have belly, can be bribed."

"Totally." I shoved some lamb in my mouth and chewed happily. "I think breakfast should come into the equation, as well."

Liander glanced at my brother. "I can see her stretching this out for as long as possible."

Rhoan gave me a warm smile, happiness in his eyes. "We can fix that easily enough. I'll just start doing the cooking."

I just about gagged at the thought. "God, no. Anything but that."

His smile gave way to an outright grin. "I cook as well as you do."

"Yeah, that's what I'm afraid of. Quinn will have to start paying for more dinners if that happens."

The vampire in question snorted softly. "Even I would struggle to support your appetite full-time."

I met his gaze, a sensual smile playing about my lips. "Oh, I don't know," I said archly. "You're doing a pretty good job of it now."

He leaned forward and kissed me. His lips were so warm, so inviting and delicious, that the kiss quickly deepened, becoming a sensuous exploration that had me aching in an instant.

"Oh, get a room, you two," Liander said dryly.

I grinned, twined my fingers through Quinn's, and stood up. "Good idea."

I dragged him to my bedroom, closed the door, and kissed him again, this time fiercely. His arms wrapped around me, pulling me closer, until my body was molded against his and I could feel the slow beat of his vampire heart and every intake of breath. He might not be human in any sense of the word, he might not be a werewolf nor the man I'd spent half my life longing for, but he was very much the man I needed in my life. The vampire I wanted to spend the rest of my life with.

And no matter what fate had planned, I would fight for this. Fight for us. It might have taken me altogether too long to realize just what this vampire meant to me, but now that I had I had no intention of letting go.

"I can see you as a mother," he murmured, his fingers sliding underneath my T-shirt, sending delicious tingles of desire scampering across my flesh as he lifted my shirt up and over my head. "I think you'd be a good one."

My gaze searched his. "But can you see yourself being one of the dads? You once said you couldn't stand children."

"Riley, this will be *your* child, and it'll be as close as I'll ever get to having one of my own. That makes the difference." He smiled. It was such a sweet, warm smile that my heart just about melted. "And you are wearing far too many clothes for my liking."

"This from the man wearing a suit," I said, tackling his shirt buttons. When they were all undone, I pressed my hands lightly against his skin, letting them rest on the hard planes of his stomach, reveling in the pleasure of simply touching him. Then I slowly slid my fingers upward, enjoying the firmness of his toned body, luxuriating in the way his muscles quivered and jumped at my caress.

My hands slid under the material at his shoulders, my thumbs hooking both shirt and coat and slowly sliding them down his arms. Only to come to a dead halt at his wrists.

"Damn," I said, raising my gaze to his, laughter bubbling through me. "I forgot about the shirt cuffs."

"It never happens in the movies, does it?" he said, amusement touching his lips as he undid the problematic cuffs.

"It's the magic of the big screen," I said, watching the play of his muscles as he pulled off his jacket and shirt. Loving the way his gaze held mine, full of promises, full of desire.

"Bet you've never seen this done on the big screen." He bent and, in one smooth motion, scooped me up into his arms.

I grinned and flung my arms lightly around his neck. "The hero carries his heroine to the bed and ravishes her senseless in all the best romances."

He arched an eyebrow, bedevilment dancing in his dark gaze. "But does he do this?"

And with that, he tossed me. I yelped as I flew through the air, then laughed in delight as I hit the bed and bounced several times. "I don't think there are many human males who could throw their women with such ease."

"And there aren't many human females who have an appetite as strong as yours."

"Know this for a fact, do you?"

"Yes. I've been around a long time, remember."

"A very, very long time," I agreed solemnly. "I'm amazed you can still manage to get it up."

He took a swipe at me, but I rolled away from it with a laugh. "And there I was about to add something very nice."

I raised an eyebrow. "Like?"

"Like every day I thank fate for putting such a stubborn, sexy, and altogether wonderful werewolf in my life."

Something inside me went mushy. "I might just let you bite my neck for that."

"I might just hold you to that." He bent over the end of the bed and reached for my jeans. I arched my hips to make the zipper easier to reach and his smile grew.

"Such an eager pup," he murmured, hooking the waist of my jeans and panties and pulling them swiftly down my legs.

"Well, I can't have you fumbling around taking forever to get down to business. I do have to go to work soon, remember."

"After being on this earth for twelve hundred years, I'd like to think I'm beyond mere fumbling."

He dropped my clothes to the floor then tackled his own. My grin grew as his body was revealed, my gaze drifting up the lean muscular planes of his legs to the rampant hardness of his erection.

This man was desire personified, and it was all I could do not to jump his bones right there and then.

"Every man fumbles," I commented dryly, "because every man sometimes lets the little head think for the big one."

On hands and knees, he walked up the bed, straddling my body but not actually touching my flesh. His scent, his desire, filled every breath, making my body burn and my heart ache.

"There have only been two times in my life that I've allowed the desire for sex to overrule my better judgment," he said softly, his dark gaze burning into my mine and his expression serious. "And in the second case, it's the best thing that has ever happened to me."

Then his lips dropped to mine and he kissed me. But it was more than just a kiss, more than just a meeting of lips and desire. It was heart if not soul, and the only place I wanted to be, now and forever.

There was no more talking from that moment on, just caressing and kissing and pleasuring. I explored his body as fully as he enjoyed mine, taking my time, letting the pleasure build and build, until it felt like every part of me was wound so tight it would surely break. Then he entered me, and everything *did* shatter, the power of my orgasm tossing me about like a leaf in the storm. When his teeth entered my neck, I came a second time, the pleasure of that one action sweeping through me like a tide.

And later, when I could think again, I realized that

for me, it would never be *just* about the bite. It was this—the hot and sweaty aftermath, lying replete and exhausted in his arms—that was the most addictive moment.

The blood whores had no idea just how much they were truly missing.

Chapter 4

"Where the hell is your report?" Jack bellowed the minute I walked through the door of the day division's rather cramped Directorate quarters.

Of course, calling ourselves the day division was something of a misnomer, given we seemed to work all hours of the clock, not just the daylight ones.

"I sent it in before I left home," I said, plucking a coffee from the cardboard tray I was holding and handing it to him.

He sniffed the coffee and looked somewhat mollified. I'd learned some time ago that while Jack could drink any sort of coffee—good or bad—it paid to get the good stuff from Beans when I was in his bad books.

"You were supposed to send it in by five," he said, slightly less loudly. "This one could get nasty, Riley. We need to keep on top of it."

"I know." I gave Kade a grin of greeting as I handed him his coffee, then plucked my own free and tossed the cardboard tray in the trash. "Did Cole come up with anything unusual in the autopsy?"

"No. The body and the saw are clean."

I frowned as I walked around my desk and sat down. "That almost suggests a professional hit."

"If we have three men beheaded in the same way, then yes, I do think we are dealing with professionals."

"So Henry Gateway's death is connected to Haven's?"

"You know, you could read the report and find out for yourself," Jack noted dryly. "But yes, Gateway was killed by the same method as Haven, although it wasn't the same saw, and we haven't yet found the one that was used on Gateway."

"It's a particularly brutal way to murder someone," Kade commented. "It seems to me that the killers are intent on attracting attention more than merely killing."

I glanced at him. The harsh fluorescent lighting gave his normally warm red-brown skin a sallow look, and there were dark shadows under his eyes. Amusement bubbled through me. Several more mares from his herd had given birth recently—meaning he now had a grand total of nine kids—but it looked as if having that many youngsters in one household was beginning to take its toll.

"If we're dealing with a gang intent on stirring up trouble between the vampires and the humans," I said, "then it's highly likely they *do* want attention."

"Which is why I've put a lock on the press for the moment." Jack took a sip of his coffee, then added, "And why I want this murder solved as soon as possible."

"Hard to track down a killer who leaves no clues," I muttered, logging on to the computer and leaning forward for the system to scan my retina. "I don't suppose you'd know if there's a connection between the three murdered men?"

I glanced at him as I said it and saw the slight hesitation. Meaning there was a connection, all right, but he wasn't revealing it. Which made me wonder if the vampire council was somehow involved. Jack might answer to his sister, but *she* answered to the council. She was on it.

"We're still checking into that possibility," he said eventually. Meaning he was still getting clearance to discuss it with the plebs.

"The sooner we know the better."

If only because, if we knew the connection, we had a chance of stopping the next murder. But Jack knew all that—he'd been at this game a lot longer than I.

Jack grunted. "Did you get anything useful from the witness?"

I restrained the urge to point out that it was in my report, and said, "Well, she wasn't really a witness, more a relayer of information. And the man who paid her to call was apparently disguised, so that's not much help."

"Did you check the security recordings?" Kade asked. "They might show something."

"Starke said he didn't use electronic security."

"Then the bastard is lying," Jack said. "Clubs like that must have full-scale security by law. Requisition the tapes."

"Requisitioning them might not be wise," Kade said. "If he wanted the Directorate to see them, he would have mentioned them. Asking for them through official channels merely gives him time to dispose of them."

I gave Kade a somewhat dirty look, which only made him raise his eyebrows and look amused. I suppose he wasn't to know that confronting Starke—or rather, confronting his overt sexuality—was *not* something I wanted right now. Not after barely escaping his presence the first time with my dignity intact.

"That's certainly possible. Go view those tapes, Riley," Jack ordered. "And if Starke tries to deny their existence, tell him I'm ready and willing to conduct a little interview with him."

"That makes it sound like there's a whole lot of history between you and Starke, boss."

"Let's just say we've had a few run-ins over the years, and leave it at that." He pushed away from the desk he'd been leaning against and added, "But before you talk to Starke, I want you and Kade to head over to Keilor. A woman named Renatta Bailey was found dead in her home a couple of days ago, and the police have called us in."

"So they suspect nonhuman involvement?" Kade asked, suddenly looking far more interested in the proceedings. Maybe it was the office work that was getting him down—something I totally understood, and the reason I tended to avoid it whenever possible.

"They have no idea what to suspect," Jack said. "They fast-tracked the autopsy and found no external or internal causes. She just died."

"People don't usually just up and die," I said. "There has to be a reason, even if it's as simple as old age."

"She was twenty and in good health, so old age and organ failure are out, as are drugs or other substances. As I said, there was no obvious reason for her death."

"So why has it been fast-tracked to us?" I asked. "And why has it suddenly got priority over the beheadings? If the autopsy couldn't find a cause of death, and the police couldn't find anything suspicious, why do they think we can solve the case?"

"It's been fast-tracked to us because the woman who died is the niece of the governor, and he wants us on it."

"Political clout is a wonderful thing when it's abused," Kade muttered, echoing my sentiments exactly.

"Abuse or not, we'll look into it. And you, dear Riley, are on the case because you're the only one who can see souls. If she's hanging about and feeling talkative, it might be a quick way to solve this one and get back to the important crimes."

As if things were *ever* that simple. I glanced at Kade as Jack walked out of the room. "You got time to head over there now?"

"Hell yeah," he said, standing and stretching. "Some fresh air would be good."

My gaze traveled up the long length of him, pausing

briefly on the washboard abs his hiked-up shirt revealed before moving on past his broad shoulders and muscular arms. Arms that could hold a girl just right, although they hadn't held me for quite a while now. Jack's no-fraternizing rule and my own commitment to my relationship with Quinn had seen to that.

"What case has Jack got you working on right now?" I pulled my gaze away from his magnificent form and called up Cole's autopsy report. I didn't bother looking at it, just redirected to my car's onboard so I could check it out later.

"Some stupid vamp is feeding on kids at Luna Park." Which was one of the local amusement parks. Kade walked around the desk and offered me his arm. "Jack wants him stopped before it goes too far. I've spent the whole fucking day going through witness reports."

I smiled and hooked my arm through his, letting him escort me to the elevator. His scent spun around me, rich and fresh, reminding me of sunshine and freshly cut grass. "Like the new aftershave," I said, then added, "So why aren't you out there talking to the witnesses yourself?"

"It'd take too long, and it's only repeating work the cops have already done."

"If the reports didn't give the cops anything, then they're unlikely to give you anything."

He shrugged. "Jack said read them, so read them I am."

Fair enough. "So this vampire hasn't killed yet?"

"No, but he's come close. Last week he attacked a

couple of nine-year-olds who'd just come out of the ghost train ride and dragged one into the shadows to feed on him. The other kid's screams attracted help, but the vamp had escaped by then."

Which explained why there was a kill order out on a vampire who hadn't actually killed yet. Any vamp stupid enough to attack little kids deserved to die.

"If all the attacks have been at Luna Park, then maybe he's holed up somewhere near there."

"I've done a thorough search of the area, and I can't find anything remotely resembling a vamp den."

"Yeah," I said, pressing the garage button as the door swished closed and zoomed us upward. "But you're running on regular senses—"

"Well, no," he interrupted. "I'm an empath, remember? I couldn't feel him, though."

"But someone has to actually be emoting for you to sense them, don't they? And if he was asleep and not emoting, you wouldn't sense him."

"True." He glanced at me. "I'm sure you're working up to some point with these questions, but I'm damned if I can figure out what."

I grinned. "It's easy. I'll help you find your attacker, and you help me find the moron hacking heads off vampires."

"Deal—though Jack may not approve."

"Jack wants this case solved fast. I doubt he's going to quibble."

"You haven't seen the backlog of cases we have, obviously."

"I try to avoid backlogs," I said, voice solemn but

amusement twitching my lips. "They're bad for the health."

"Your health will be on a downward spiral if Jack hears that."

I patted his hand lightly. "But he won't hear, will he? Because otherwise I'll have to tell Sable you've been flirting with the secretary on the ninth floor again."

"It's a stallion's job to flirt," he said with a twinkle in his eye as he opened the driver's-side door and ushered me in.

"Not when you've agreed to hold herd numbers at fifteen."

"Who said anything about adding to the herd?" His grin was mischievous. "I was merely offering to show her the advantages of being with a stallion."

Having tasted those delights myself, I couldn't help feeling a little envious. I might have Quinn, and I might have my soul mate, but that didn't stop the wolf from occasionally hungering for the pleasures to be found in the arms of others. I could have chosen to follow those desires had I wished, but only because I hadn't yet sworn my love to the moon for either man. Although there was only *one* man with whom I'd take that step, and it sure as hell wasn't my soul mate.

"You're incorrigible."

"That's why you all love me so much," he agreed, slamming the door shut and walking around to the passenger side. "And anytime you want to revisit past pleasures, just say the word."

"Jack would kill us." I started up the car and reversed

out. "And no amount of sex—no matter how brilliant—is worth facing his fury."

"He'll be even more furious if you crash the damn car again. I should be driving, you know."

"I haven't had an accident for over a month. You're perfectly safe."

He gave me a look of complete disbelief, then leaned forward and switched the onboard on. After identifying himself, he called up the police reports on Renatta Bailey. "Okay, she lives at 13 Hope Street. Head onto the freeway, and I'll direct you once we get there."

I nodded. "Nothing illuminating in the report?"

"Nothing much more than what Jack's already told us." He frowned. "They interviewed her workmates, who said she hadn't been sleeping properly for the last week. Apparently she looked tired and run-down as a result, but nothing more than that."

"So if she wasn't sick, maybe she was enjoying a little too much sex."

"Totally possible, if she'd had a lover. But according to the report, her last relationship ended six months ago and she wasn't seeing anyone."

Which didn't mean she wasn't having sex. Although I guess the report would have mentioned it if she'd tumbled anyone recently. "If she'd run herself to the ground, the autopsy would have picked it up, wouldn't it?"

"I would have thought so." He leaned back in the seat and shrugged. "Sometimes people just die. It happens."

"Yeah, but apparently it shouldn't happen to the niece of the governor."

We drove on in silence and quickly reached Hope Street. I parked in the driveway and climbed out. The air was fresh and filled with the scent of the nearby wattle trees. The house itself was nondescript—just another large, brown-brick, double-fronted house in a street filled with them. The only differences seemed to be the color of the roof tiles.

"She died four days ago," Kade said, walking up the steps and opening the screen door. "I can't see how us coming here now is going to help solve the case."

"I think the point is more us being seen. Jack may hate politicians using the Directorate like this, but those men sign the paychecks, so he does what he has to."

I held the screen door open as he got out what looked like a small black box from his pocket and pressed it against the door lock. A second later, there was a beep and the door clicked open.

"Still carrying illegal electronic lock pickers in your pocket, I see," I said, voice deadpan.

"Unlike you, I prefer not to break down doors." He stood to one side and waved me on. "After you, sweet cheeks."

I snorted and stepped past him. The hallway was dark, and the air had that slightly musty odor of rooms locked up for too long. Which was odd considering Renatta had only been dead for four days.

I looked through the first doorway. It was a bedroom,

but obviously not the main one, unless Renatta slept in a single bed. Which I doubted, because it didn't smell used. I walked on.

"Her bedroom is the next on the left," Kade said.

I glanced at him over my shoulder. "How can you tell?"

"There's an echo of ecstasy coming from it."

"Ecstasy? So she *did* have sex before she died?"

"From what I'm sensing, yes."

I walked into the room and stopped near the end of the bed. The pale sheets were rumpled and the lingering scent of humanity and death emanated from them. I couldn't smell anything else—certainly not sex or even ecstasy.

"Renatta was alone in the bed when she died. I'd smell it if it were otherwise." I looked around the room. It wasn't plush or girlie in design, but more what I'd term "beachy." Her furniture was simple and classic, in sun-bleached hues paired with natural, neutral textures. On her dresser were several stands that were full of earrings and rings, and a jewelry case was open, revealing a goodly quantity of gold chains and pendants. Whatever had happened here, it certainly hadn't involved robbery. White fingerprint dust lay over everything, even the many perfume bottles. The police had given the room a good going over.

"If the sense of ecstasy is still strong enough to linger, why wouldn't the fact that she'd had sex been picked up?" I asked, my gaze moving back to the bed.

"I don't know." He stood beside me, his hands on his hips and his gaze on the bed. "But regardless of the fact that it wasn't, I'm quite sure she was having a damn *fine* time before she passed away—and it wasn't just for the one night. It's too strong a sensation for that."

"So maybe someone cleaned her up before her death was reported?" I spotted her purse on the bedside table and moved around to take a look. "Or maybe she was a lesbian, which would explain the lack of sperm."

"It's possible, although if she was in bed with a woman, you'd be picking up the scent, wouldn't you?"

"Yeah. I'm not getting any vibrations along the clairvoyant lines, either, so her soul hasn't hung about for a chat."

"Meaning it *was* a natural death?"

I shrugged. "Maybe. Or maybe it was a death she went to willingly." Souls didn't seem to hang about in that case, either.

I opened up her purse and went through it. There was over one hundred dollars sitting in it, as well as several credit cards. There were also half a dozen business cards, all of them for vampire clubs—the higher-end ones, not clubs like Dante's. I plucked one out and showed it to Kade.

He raised an eyebrow. "The police report didn't mention that she was a blood whore."

"Maybe the governor hushed it up." It certainly wouldn't be the first time *that* had happened. "There's been enough press about them lately to make it an unpalatable connection for anyone in power."

Kade snorted. "Yeah, but he also wants her death solved, and that's hard to do if we haven't got all the facts."

"So there was no mention of vampire bite marks in the report?"

"None. If she *was* a whore, she hadn't gone to the clubs for a while."

"From what I've heard, it's as hard for a whore to give the clubs up as it is for a drug addict to give up substance abuse."

"We don't know she was an addict."

"She's got six business cards in her purse. That suggests a more-than-casual interest." I put the purse back on the bedside table. "Maybe whoever she was with found out about the addiction and found a sneaky way to get rid of her."

"Maybe." His voice was lazy, but his expression was intent as he walked around the bed. I didn't say anything, just watched him. After a moment, he added, "There *is* something else here."

I raised an eyebrow. "What?"

"I don't know. It's very faint." He hesitated, then walked across to the dresser mirror. "It came through here."

"Through the mirror?"

He glanced at me. "The sensation is strongest here."

I walked across and stopped beside him, flaring my nostrils and tasting the flavors in the air. I couldn't find anything that triggered either my mental or psychic alarms.

"Nothing," I murmured. "Whatever it is you're feeling, I'm not catching it."

"It's not really anything I can define."

He shifted the mirror to look behind it. I peeked under his arm, but there was nothing more than dust.

"Jack's going to ask you to, so you'd better try."

"It's a wisp of power, a sensation of age." His frown deepened. "What the hell sort of creature can come through mirrors and attack a person? And why wouldn't Renatta have been terrified?"

"Two good questions I can't possibly answer."

He grinned suddenly. "And here I was thinking you had an answer for everything."

"You're confusing me with Jack."

"Ah," he said, a devilish twinkle in his warm brown eyes. "But you're Jack's little protégée."

I snorted and swiped at his arm. The blow had enough power in it to rock him back on his heels. "Watch your mouth or I won't go vamp hunting with you."

"Yeah you will, because you want my help more than I want yours."

He had a point. I trailed after him as he walked from the bedroom and checked out the other rooms. The rest of the house was also done in neutral colors, with easy comfortable furniture. I couldn't feel anything out of place, and nothing seemed to have been touched or broken into.

"I don't think there's anything else to find," I commented after the last room. "What about you?"

"The only room that has the other scent is her bedroom. I'll snag one of the liaisons to do some research on mirror creatures." He glanced at me, a grin of anticipation twitching his lips. "In the meantime, let's go hunt us a vampire."

* * *

The screams and giggles of children on rides mingled with the blare of music and the scent of fried food and humanity, creating an ambience that was both intriguing and oddly nauseating.

I slammed the car door and stared up at the huge face with its open mouth that was the entrance to the park. Though the face was supposed to be laughing, I'd always thought it had a slightly maniacal edge. But maybe that was just an adult werewolf's natural distaste for anything that involved being confined in a somewhat small area with too many people.

Yet humans certainly didn't seem to have that problem. Despite the fact that it was nearly nine, the park was packed with people. And most of them seemed to be having a good time—if you ignored the high-pitched screams of the little ones who were obviously either tired or not getting what they wanted from their parents.

Something I could look forward to if I agreed to Liander and Rhoan's plans.

Depending, of course, on whether everything went according to plan and the pregnancy and birth went off without a hitch, the disbelieving side of me felt obliged to add.

And really, when had anything in my life gone off without a hitch?

I worried lightly at my bottom lip and then thrust the concern aside as I fell in step beside Kade. Now was *not* the time for these sorts of thoughts. Work first, babies later.

"So when was the last attack?" I asked, watching the roller coaster roar overhead, the screams of the people lingering in the air long after the carriages had sped by.

"Last Saturday. He seems to be active only on the weekends." Kade showed his badge to the woman at the ticket counter, but she basically waved him through without even looking at it. Which didn't mean she wasn't looking at Kade—and the amused twitch of his lips suggested he was more than a little aware of it.

"Don't tell me the ticket lady is yet another conquest," I said, voice dry. "Jack won't be pleased if you've been fooling around during investigations."

He might be all for using sex as a tool to get information from suspects, but I very much doubted he'd believe the ticket seller would have any information that couldn't be gained through less involved methods.

"There's been no fooling around as yet," he said cheerfully, "but she's been most helpful during the investigation and is definitely a possibility once this case is handled."

I shook my head in disbelief. "How can your herd not be satisfying your sexual needs?"

"They are," he said, a devilish glint in his eyes. "But there's always room for a little outside fun. Keeps the little man interested."

I snorted. "There's nothing little about your man."

"Totally true." He waggled his eyebrows at me. "Want a hot dog?"

"Nope, but you can buy me some cotton candy. The pink one, not the blue one."

He did, and I groaned in delight as I bit into the

overly sweet spun sugar. It was heaven itself. "So," I said, licking the sugary goodness from the side of my mouth. "What are we going to do? Just wander around and wait for him to attack someone? Or are we going to check out the underbelly of this place and see what we can find?"

"I've checked every ride, and I haven't been able to spot anything."

Which didn't mean that *I* couldn't, if only because I had the advantage of infrared, which could pick up body heat. And, of course, vamps *did* have body heat, despite how they were often portrayed in movies and in literature. They only got cold if they weren't feeding enough.

But Kade knew that, so I didn't bother pointing it out. "What makes you think he's made the park his home rather than simply arriving with the weekend crowds?"

"Maintenance people have reported seeing some-thing moving around after hours, but apparently whatever—whoever—it was disappeared before any-one could track it."

"None of the maintenance people has been at-tacked?" Kade shook his head, and I frowned. "That's rather odd, isn't it?"

He shrugged. "Maybe he's an older vamp who only needs to feed a couple of times a week."

Quinn was about as old as they got, and while he could go long periods without feeding, he really needed to take blood every day to keep at his optimum levels of fitness and strength. Either this vampire was on a diet—and I couldn't ever imagine a vampire going though *that* willingly—or he was getting his meals from something other than humans. Like pigeons. There were certainly enough of them around—although there'd have to be a fairly high kill ratio to satisfy a vamp. Still . . .

"Don't suppose anyone has reported an increase in the number of dead pigeons, have they?"

He blinked. "Pigeons wouldn't have enough blood to satisfy a vampire."

"No, but if we're dealing with a small vampire, then a few drained pigeons might keep him going. It might also explain why he isn't going after adults. He might be stronger than a human, but maybe the size difference intimidates him."

"Good point. I'll ask."

I nodded. "A vampire also needs protection from the sunlight, and I would have thought the only viable places like that here would be places maintenance would need to go on a regular basis." And while vampires *could* wrap themselves in shadow and effectively vanish from human sight, they didn't actually *become* shadows. If someone brushed against them, they'd feel it. "Besides, you said you hadn't been able to sense anything that obviously felt like a nest."

"Nope, but that doesn't mean it's not here. Or he might be just moving around, keeping ahead of the maintenance people."

That was possible. And I suppose old amusement parks like this—even if they had been updated with newer rides and facilities—still had enough of the older rides left to provide hidey-holes for those intent on not being found.

"So let's walk around the older rides, and I'll infrared the internals and see if there's any body heat where there shouldn't be."

"Sounds like a plan." He bit into his hot dog, looking very much at ease with the noise and the crowd.

I ate some more cotton candy and wished I could be similarly at ease. I must have been exuding some agitation, though, because the crowd tended to part around me, giving me free space and less of a hemmed-in feeling.

Until someone fell in step beside me.

Someone who made my skin tingle and my wolf want to howl.

"What the fuck are you doing here, Kye?" I said, not even bothering to glance at him.

Which *didn't* mean I wasn't aware of him. His scent wrapped around me, musky and lush, and the heat of his body prickled mine, making the little hairs on my arms stand on end. It was almost as if they were reaching for him.

"I'm following you," he said, amusement in his voice. He reached across me, not touching me and yet close enough to make no difference, and offered Kade a hand. "I'm Kye Murphy. I'm guessing you'd be the horse-shifter, Kade."

"You'd be correct," Kade rumbled, glancing at me with a slightly raised eyebrow and a dangerous glint in his eyes.

I shook my head at the unasked question. Kye's sudden appearance might be a problem in more ways than one, but I didn't want Kade involved. For a start, I very much doubted that Kade, for all his size and impressive physique, would have the strength actually to outhustle Kye, and, second, we didn't need a scene that might just alert our quarry.

"We're on Directorate business," I said, dumping the cotton candy in the nearest bin. I'd suddenly lost my taste for sweet things. Or rather, my taste buds suddenly hungered for sweetness of a different kind. The kind that involved heat and flesh and lust . . .

I wrenched my thoughts from *that* particular direction and added, "And you're definitely intruding."

"I usually am," he said, amusement so evident in his voice that it was all too easy to imagine the flit of it across his lips. But I didn't look. I didn't dare. "But I happen to think you and I might be hunting the same killer, and pairing up achieved the desired results last time."

I glanced at him sharply. Hunger lurked deep in the brightness of his eyes. But he wasn't talking about the two of us bringing down the witches. He was referring to sex.

I shivered. I might hunger for his touch, but I feared it almost as much. Feared what it could mean to me and Quinn and everything else currently so right in my world.

"And why would anyone hire a killer with your reputation to hunt down a vamp who hasn't even killed yet?" I gave him a sour look. "We both know they wouldn't, so don't lie to me, Kye."

He smiled. It was a cool, hard smile that nevertheless had my insides quivering with desire. It was the nature of the wolf to seek out the strongest mate, and Kye was certainly that. "I wasn't referring to the cretin attacking children. That is certainly not worth my while."

"Then why are you here?"

I edged a little closer to Kade, hoping his sunshiny scent would swamp the allure of Kye's presence. But it didn't even make a dent in the awareness that was swamping me.

"As I said, I've been following you. Sometimes the best way to hunt down your target is to piggyback other investigations." He glanced at me, eyebrow raised. "Besides, isn't it natural to want to be near your soul mate?"

Kade made an odd sound and started coughing. I hit him a couple of times on the back and he nodded in thanks.

Kye glanced from me to Kade and back again. "That's a little detail you obviously forgot to mention to your fellow guardian."

"She sure did," Kade wheezed.

"It's not like either of us is ecstatic about the fact," I muttered. "So why the hell should I announce it?"

"Because you've been waiting your whole life to find your mate?" Kye said, the sarcasm absent in his expression very evident in his voice.

"At least I desire something more than the next kill," I shot back.

"Oh, I desire a hell of a lot more than that," he murmured, his gaze on mine, hard and cold and yet somehow heated. "And I always get what I want."

My stomach quivered. God, how was it possible to want someone so much and yet loathe them this badly?

"Then it's about time someone made you realize that you can't always get what you want," I snapped, and yet even I couldn't help noticing the slight tremor in my voice—a tremor that arose from the breathlessness that surged through me.

He merely smiled. He didn't need to say anything. We both knew my words were little more than a flimsy facade. All he had to do was reach out and touch me, and the fight would be over. At least until sexual satisfaction was reached.

No amount of loving from Quinn would ever ease the soul-deep hunger of my wolf for her mate, and sooner or later that need was going to overwhelm all opposition, all common sense.

"As fascinating as I'm finding this conversation," Kade said, voice casual and yet holding a hint of steel, "I do believe we may have found our quarry."

I stopped. "You're picking up something?"

"Stirring hunger." He pointed to the ghost train ride. "And it's coming from there."

"Someone's about to get a real fright for a change," Kye murmured. He flexed his fingers, his excitement surging, wrapping around me as sweetly as a caress, causing my own heart to leap and race. "Shall we go find the vamp?"

I swung around sharply, meeting his hard gaze with one of my own even as I desperately tried to control the growing desire to press my lips against his.

"There is no 'we.' This is Directorate business." I glanced across my shoulder and saw that Kade was on the phone, then added in a softer tone, "Stay out of the way, Kye, or I'll arrest you. I mean it."

Something flashed through his eyes. Something dangerous and wicked. Then he grabbed my arm, dragged me toward him, and kissed me.

It wasn't a nice kiss. It was as brutal and as harsh as the man could be, and yet my heart raced and my body ached, and I found myself returning the kiss eagerly, my wolf desperate for anything she could get.

And I hated that. I really hated it.

But he released me as suddenly as he'd grabbed me, the kiss so brief I doubted that anyone had noticed. We stared at each other for a moment, still so close our harsh breaths mingled. I had no doubt that the desire and anger that raged in his eyes had its echo in mine.

He smiled. It was as bitter and as cold as the kiss we'd just shared, yet still my wolf hungered.

I forced my feet backward. The sudden distance between us didn't help the ache.

"The manager is closing down the ride, but he'll keep the lights off. Hopefully, the vamp won't realize we're on to him," Kade said, shoving his phone back into his pocket. He glanced from Kye to me and raised an eyebrow. Being an empath, he'd no doubt be picking up all sorts of crazy emotions, but all he said was "I'll make sure the vamp doesn't escape via the rear entrance. You want to go through the front and flush him out?"

I nodded, spun on my heel, and stalked toward the ride. Kye remained where he was, and I wasn't entirely sure whether I was relieved or dismayed. I might have warned him off, but at least if he'd remained with me, I could have kept an eye on him.

Or maybe that kiss had rattled me more than I'd thought, because wanting to keep an eye on Kye was insane. That man was dangerous in more ways than I could count, and keeping him close was only asking for trouble.

The ghost train ride was a stand-alone building capped by a skull wearing a top hat and holding a megaphone to his mouth. It was easy to imagine he was inviting everyone to roll up and try the ride, though no words came out of his skeletal mouth. There was a long line of people waiting out the front, although one look at the many unhappy faces in the line suggested word had gone out about the delay. I leapt over the metal railing that divided the ride from the rest of the crowds and flashed my badge at the ride supervisor. From within the building came a series of clanks, screams, moans, and a multitude of other spooky sounds, all accompanied by the rattle of carriages running on a wooden track.

"The last carriage is going through now," the supervisor said, as another carriage rattled into the station and two teenagers climbed out, both looking somewhat bored. "When that one comes out, you can walk through."

"Have all your people been given the word to clear out?"

He nodded. "Just let us know when the coast is clear."

I waited until the last of the old wooden carriages came out, then pressed the two-way stud that had been inserted into my ear long ago and said, "Heading in now, Kade."

"The employees are out," he said, his rich tones warming my inner ear. "The place is empty of life."

But maybe not empty of death. I gave the ride supervisor a tight smile, then pushed through a replica of the park's entrance—only this time the smiley face definitely had an evil look to it—and entered the shadowed confines of the ride.

The doors crashed closed behind me, but silence didn't settle in. The staff might have abandoned the building, but the effects were still running. I stood there in the darkness, listening to the noise, trying to detect a whisper of movement. Something, anything, that might indicate the vampire was on the move.

There was nothing.

Frowning, I followed the wooden track around to the right, blinking to alternate between infrared and regular sight, but there was no life to be seen in either mode. A caged piano—complete with fake chopped-off hands playing the keys—came into view. Then, as the track swung around to the left again, there came a series of weird, supposedly ghostly portraits and murals. I smiled and shook my head. It was a wonder that anyone got scared of any of these things, and yet I could remember screaming at them when I was a kid and here with my brother to celebrate our birthday.

Or maybe I'd been screaming at the thought of being trapped in the park with so many humans.

The darkness closed in again as I continued to follow the tracks. A ghostly apparition appeared on the top of a mural staircase, and it took me a heartbeat to realize that apparition wasn't the work of lights but rather the red heat of life sitting perched atop the faded artwork.

Only it wasn't human size. It was bird size.

And either that bird had weird roosting habits, or our vampire had been a shifter before he'd undergone the change. It would certainly explain why Kade had been unable to find anything when he'd done the search. A roosting bird probably wouldn't emit much in the way of emotions, and Kade certainly wouldn't have been looking for something that size.

I reached into my back pocket and pulled out my laser, flicking it on as the weapon settled into my palm. As I did so, the bird squawked and took flight. Not flying away, but coming straight at me. The vampire had balls, I had to give him that—especially given a pigeon wasn't exactly as threatening as a bird of prey.

I ducked under his swoop, then twisted around and fired. The red beam flashed out, briefly giving the shadows an eerie glow as the shot clipped the bird's wings. Feathers fluttered downward as it squawked and awkwardly tried to fly down the hall. I fired again, but the bird dropped at the wrong moment, and the laser sliced though the edges of a dancing skeleton. I swore softly and ran after the bird.

"Kade," I said, keeping the creature in sight but not firing, "he's on the run. He's also a pigeon."

"A pigeon? Good lord, that's almost as bad as a seagull. No wonder he became a vampire."

He wasn't getting an argument out of me. A seagull might be one of my alternate forms these days, but I had something of a love-hate relationship with it.

"He's going to have to shift shape to come out these doors," Kade continued. "I'm ready and waiting."

"You always are," I said, ducking under the ghostly tendrils of fake cobwebs.

Kade's laughter rolled through my inner ear. I fired the laser again. This time the bright beam clipped tail feathers before slicing into a bed that came complete with a white draped body hung with cobwebs.

The vampire squawked and fluttered to the ground, landing rather ungracefully on the old wooden track. I slid to a stop and trained the laser onto him.

"Directorate," I said, my voice edged and low. "Whoever you are, shift shape or you'll die in bird form."

He hopped around until he faced me, his beady black eyes glaring somewhat balefully.

"Your choice," I said, pressing my finger against the trigger. The whine of the weapon powering up cut through the surrounding noise, and the pigeon hopped backward in surprise.

After a moment, a shimmer rolled across his bloody feathers, hiding his form, reshaping it, until what stood in front of me was cloaked in human skin.

Only it wasn't a man but a boy. A child. A cute, cherub-cheeked child with golden hair and big blue eyes.

A kid this size could certainly survive on a diet of pigeon and seagull blood, although why had no one noticed the steady supply of dead birds?

Then the adorable image shattered when he snarled, revealing teeth that were long and pointed and every inch a vampire's. He came at me, fast and furious, and though I had my finger pressed against the laser, I didn't fire.

I couldn't.

It was a *kid,* and I couldn't shoot a kid. I didn't *want* to shoot a kid—even one that was a feral vampire attacking other children.

Surely there was hope for him. Surely there was a chance . . .

I jumped as a gunshot boomed through the darkness. The breeze of it burned past my ear, signifying the bullet was silver, then the little vampire went down. The back of his head disappeared, splattering a mess of blood and bone and gore across a somewhat macabre collection of dolls with revolving heads.

For a moment, I simply stared, disbelief and horror churning my gut. Then I swung around. Kye stood several yards behind me, his face expressionless, but cold fury in his eyes.

"Don't ever hesitate," he warned softly. "Bad things happen when you hesitate."

"It was a *kid*," I all but yelled. "Goddammit, Kye, you shot a *kid*."

"That kid was a vampire attacking other children. Remember who we're trying to save here, Riley."

The laser whined as my finger twitched against it. It was tempting, *so* tempting, just to raise the weapon and shoot the coldhearted bastard. I switched it off instead. As much as I might want to shoot Kye, a guardian who killed without reason wasn't long for this earth. Besides, he was my soul mate, and killing him meant I'd be basically killing myself. And I wasn't ready to die just yet.

"The kid hadn't killed yet," I spat. "He might have been saved."

"You can't ever chance that." His gaze swept me, followed sharply by his hunger. I half expected him to close the distance between us and kiss me, but he shook his head and stepped back instead. "You're a guardian, Riley. A protector of *humans,* not vampires."

"Don't fucking tell me how to do my job."

"Someone has to." He glanced behind me, then gave me a sketchy salute. "Consider this payment for the information you owe me. And you will meet me with whatever information you currently have tonight, or I shall be forced to take other steps."

Something went cold inside. Coming from a hired killer, those so-called steps could only mean one thing. "You touch anyone—"

"Oh," he said blandly, "I wouldn't *touch* anyone. Shooting, though, that's another matter. And we saw here today just how well a silver bullet can work against a vampire."

Sick fury filled me. I clenched my fists, digging my nails into my palms against the urge to use them against him instead.

"You wouldn't *dare*."

He merely raised an eyebrow. The fury within me got stronger.

"He's just as much my soul mate as you are, Kye. Are you willing to risk shooting him without knowing just how that will rebound to you?"

"Are you willing to bet on the fact that I'm not?"

He knew I wasn't. It was there in the victorious twitch of his lips. I hated him. I wanted him. God, did things have to get this twisted? "Where and when?"

"Five Proximity Drive, Brooklyn. One o'clock." He gave me another one of those cold half smiles. "I'll even provide an after-midnight snack."

The hungry glitter in his eyes made it clear just what type of snack he was referring to. "Don't bother, because there's nothing you could offer me that I'd actually want. Now get the hell out of here."

He stared at me for a moment longer, his gaze flat and yet so heated, sending alternating flashes of desire and annoyance surging through me. Then he turned on his heel and disappeared into the darkness.

"Why did you let him walk away?" Kade said from behind me. "You could have held him with a threat like that."

I shoved my laser into my pocket and turned around. My gaze fell on the remains of the cherub face at my feet, and all I felt was a useless sort of anger. Kye had been right about one thing—my hesitation had been fatal. Just not for me.

"I have no doubt that Kye has a herd of lawyers who could get him out of such charges inside a minute flat. It isn't worth the hassle."

"You could just have shot him. I would have backed the shoot as justifiable."

I smiled. It probably looked as thin and humorless as it felt. "He's my soul mate. I might as well take a gun and shoot myself."

Kade frowned. "I thought that whole dying-when-your-mate-dies deal happened only when wolves swear their love to the moon."

"Death is certain when that happens. There have been instances of unsworn wolves surviving the death of their mate, but right now, I'm not willing to take that chance."

"Good call. I don't think your brother would take your death too well." Which was the understatement of the century. Kade looked down at the limp little body. "And you wouldn't have been alone in hesitating."

It wasn't much, but it at least made me feel a little better. "Thanks."

He looked up and smiled. "Guardians need to do more than just shoot first and ask questions later. No matter what Jack or that dick you call a mate preaches, there will always be circumstances that cause hesitation." He hesitated himself, then added, "I guess this means we're going to have to track down his maker."

"I hope like hell someone else gets that task." If only

because I didn't think I'd be able to control my anger if I found the vampire responsible for making—and then abandoning—the youngster.

"There are laws in place that should prevent these things from occurring," Kade said, voice grim. "I don't think his maker is going to sidestep the consequences."

"Good." It was vehemently said. I took a deep breath and blew it out slowly. Though it didn't help the anger, I felt a little less rattled. But no less sad for the little vampire who never got a chance.

I glanced at my watch, then said, "I've really got to go view those tapes. Can you call the cleanup team in?"

He raised his eyebrows. "I was under the impression you wanted help with that."

"I did, but it might take a while to get a cleanup team here, and Jack will not be a happy man if I haven't viewed the tapes by midnight." I hesitated, then added, "When you get the chance, could you glance through all the reports for the beheading case? It'll get you up to speed, and you might just catch something I've missed."

He nodded. "As long as Jack doesn't hand me another case as soon as I get back."

Given the backlog of cases we had, that was likely, but I knew Kade well enough to know that he'd still look through my case files.

Which would be good. I had a bad feeling I'd need the help if I was to have any hope of solving this one.

Chapter 5

It was just before eleven when I arrived at Dante's, and the place was crowded. I slammed the car door shut and shoved the keys into my pocket as I walked toward the graffiti-covered building. A bass beat that was both heavy and seductive crawled through the night, accompanied by the scent of desire and blood. Despite my distaste for what was happening inside the building, my pulse leapt and raced. I was a wolf, and desire was a scent as sweet to us as blood was to vampires.

If it had been the Blue Moon I was walking into rather than Dante's, I would have been tempted to pander to that surge of desire. But I had no intention of pursuing such a whim here—and not just because I distrusted strange vampires.

No, in this particular case, it was more not trusting

myself if Dante made a serious attempt at seduction. The charged atmosphere, and the power of the man himself, was too dangerous a combination.

I showed my badge to the guard, and he scowled as he opened the door. I carefully invaded his thoughts as I brushed past him. Hatred burned into my mind—hatred and anger. This vamp was one of the ones not overly pleased with the Directorate's execution of several vampires charged with killing blood whores.

Which made me wonder if he'd actually come to my aid if trouble hit inside—although I couldn't imagine Starke being happy if he *didn't*. After all, given the business he was running, he'd probably prefer to keep on the Directorate's good side—no matter what he might personally think about us.

Once inside, I waited until my eyes had adjusted to the darkness, then walked across to the bar. The same gum-chewing barman ambled up to serve me—although this time the towel he was using to dry the glass looked a whole lot cleaner.

"What can I do for you, Ms. Jenson?"

"Is your boss around tonight?"

He hesitated. "He is, but he's in a meeting and doesn't want to be disturbed."

Half of me wanted to use that as an excuse just to get the hell out of the place, but that would mean coming back a third time. "I need to see the security tapes your boss reckons he doesn't have. Can you arrange that, Boris?"

He raised a pale eyebrow, his blue eyes holding more than a little hint of amusement. "The boss said you'd be back for those. He left a message that you were to be directed into the security office and given the good coffee."

I snorted softly. "As if that's going to let him off the hook for giving me the runaround."

And given the apparent history between Jack and Dante, the only legitimate reason I could think of for him doing something like that was to piss off Jack.

Boris's gum-chewing grin grew. "He also said that if you were still here after midnight, he would give you a more personal apology."

I glanced at my watch. I had fifty-eight minutes to get out of here, then. "I take it the tapes are set up and ready to go?"

He nodded. "Security is the red door at the other end of the bar. I'll buzz them to let them know you're coming. Coffee will be along in five minutes."

"Thanks." I headed down toward the red door. The darkness seemed to get deeper the farther into it I moved. Many of the humans who were in the room wandered around like vapid ghosts, their expressions either edged with anxiety or pleasure, depending on where they were within their fix cycle. The cloying scent of blood and ecstasy mingled with undertones of hunger that were coming from the many vampires in the room, and despite my distaste for everything that was going on here, my pulse surged again. Desire—be it for blood or sex—was a powerful emotion, and no wolf was immune to its effects. Several vampires who leaned up against the bar about halfway down the room stood up abruptly, their gazes swinging in my direction and teeth protruding in excitement. The scent of fresh, available blood did that to a vamp.

I got my badge out and held it up. It might be dark, but they'd see it well enough. "Sorry, boys, here on official business."

Their surge of excitement was snuffed out almost instantly. The lead vampire—a thin, brown-haired man with a boyish face and ancient hazel eyes—looked me up and down, his lip curling in distaste.

"So you're one of *those*. Shame."

"If you mean that I'm a guardian, then yes. And I totally agree with it being a shame, but hey, sometimes you've got to go with the flow."

His dour expression suggested he didn't see any humor in my reply. Apparently, neither did the other three, who all edged closer to their leader and flexed various muscles. I raised my eyebrows, wondering if they were stupid enough to seriously consider attacking a guardian.

"Lay off, boys," the bartender said, his voice holding the whip of command. Obviously, the laid-back attitude was a front.

The brown-haired man snarled, then turned around and stalked off into the shadows. His friends followed. Three seconds later they all had women on their arms.

I shook my head and glanced at the bartender. "All this freely available blood must be making them a little crazy."

He grinned. "They meant no harm. Besides, they

know the boss won't abide any trouble inside the building."

And they feared Starke more than they feared a guardian. Or maybe they simply feared that Starke would cut them off from their easy feed.

I continued on to the red door and rapped my knuckles against it loudly—although the sound was almost lost in the thump of music coming from the speakers three feet away.

But the door opened, revealing a tall black vamp with startling green eyes. "You the guardian?"

"I am." I got out my badge and flashed it again.

He stepped aside and waved me in. "The tapes have been set up to run on the end computer. The boss said you'd want to view from one o'clock onward."

One o'clock being the time Grant Haven had finished work and was walking toward Dante's, only to be met by someone wielding a saw. *Why* he'd simply let that someone hack off his head was a question I'd forgotten to ask Jack, which meant I'd actually have to read the report later.

But Mandy Jones had reported his death at one-twenty, so at least there weren't going to be mountains of tape to view.

"That's perfect." I walked over to the desk and sat down.

The vamp shut the door then ambled over. "Press this button to play, this one for slo-mo, and that one for pause. If you want to print any of the frames, just hit this one."

"Thanks."

He nodded and went back to his screens. I pressed PLAY and leaned back in the chair, watching as the computer worked its way through the various tapes. The bartender came in with my coffee about halfway through, the scent of cinnamon and hazelnut filling the small room.

"I'll have one of those," the big vamp said, not taking his eyes off the screens.

"Then you can get it yourself at shift change," the bartender said, slamming the door as he exited.

"He's such a charmer," the black guy muttered. "You do realize he only got you one because he wants to get into your pants?"

"Actually, it's your boss that wants to do that." I took a sip of the hot liquid and sighed in pleasure. "How long have you worked here?"

He shrugged. "A year and a half."

The timer was winding up to one-twenty, so I concentrated on the screen for several minutes but could see neither Mandy nor the stranger who'd apparently paid her to call the murder in. As the camera view switched, I said, "And do you enjoy it?"

"Yeah. The conditions here are pretty good."

I glanced at him. "They are? The place looks pretty run-down to me, and I imagine staff amenities are much the same."

He flashed me a grin, revealing rows of shiny white teeth but no fangs. He wasn't getting turned on by what he was watching on the screen, but then, I suppose if he was, he'd be of no use in this job.

"Most club venues have pretty crappy amenities for staff, no matter how upmarket they claim to be."

"So why not work at one with a better rep?"

"Because this one pays above-average wages."

"Why? No offense, but it doesn't exactly look like a hard job, and this place hasn't had much in the way of trouble." At least, not the sort that attracted police or Directorate intervention. Not until the recent beheading on its back doorstep, anyway.

"Maybe there's been no trouble because the boss pays us well to ensure there isn't."

Good point. I sipped my coffee for several minutes, watching the ebb and flow of blood seduction on the screen. The timer was again nearing one-twenty. I leaned forward, watching the screen closely.

Mandy suddenly appeared in camera view. A tall, dark-haired vampire escorted her into the corner shadows, lifted her arm, and bared his teeth. A look of pure ecstasy crossed her face as his teeth pierced her flesh and he began to drink.

"What's Dante like as a boss?"

He shrugged. "Keeps to himself, mostly. We only see him if there's trouble."

"What about the ladies? I imagine he's got a few of them traipsing to and from his bedroom."

He laughed. It was a surprisingly high sound—like his voice was on the edge of breaking. It made me wonder just how old he'd been when he'd turned. His gangly frame did remind me somewhat of a teenager, but not all vamps were muscle-bound. Quite the opposite, in fact.

"With his looks, and that mojo he has happening? Hell, yeah. There's practically a parade of women traipsing upstairs to be with him."

"So he picks his bedmates from the women in the club?" Dante didn't actually seem the type to go for blood whores. But then, why would he run a club like this if he wasn't?

"No." He hesitated. "But some of them seem the type. They have that look, if you know what I mean."

I did. But if Starke wasn't getting his bed partners from this club, did that necessarily mean that he was getting them from others? And if that was the case, why would he bring them back here?

Was it some weird method of gaining more customers for his club, or was something else going on?

On a whim, I took out my phone, accessed my car's computer, and called up the photo of Renatta Bailey. "This wouldn't happen to be one of the women, would it?"

I turned the screen around so he could see it. He took a quick glance, then shook his head. "Not that I've seen, although I'm not on shift twenty-four hours a day. But she looks a little too classy to be visiting a place like this."

"And Starke's ladies don't?"

"No. They might not have all been whores, but they looked like the ladies do here. Trashy."

I wondered how Mandy Jones would react to being called trashy. Then I remembered the desperate awareness in her eyes and realized she'd probably agree.

On the screen, Mandy's shadow-bound tryst with

her vampire ended. He bowed lightly then disappeared offscreen, obviously intent on finding his next mark. Another man approached. He was wearing a black trench coat that concealed the shape of his body, but his shoulders were broad and he walked with a long-legged grace that not only reminded me of a cat on the prowl but also seemed a little too familiar.

My gaze flicked up to the hair. It was blond, not the dark red I'd been half expecting, but that didn't mean anything. The face underneath the hair was dominated by a bulbous nose and sharp cheeks. But Kye had proven to be amazingly adept at disguising himself in the past.

The stranger approached Mandy and began talking to her. He kept his back to the camera, and I wasn't able to see if any money changed hands. He left, and three seconds later, another blond man approached her, this one also broad-shouldered, but walking with a heavier gait and a slight limp. Again, the camera was at the wrong angle to fully see what was going on, but he also left as quickly as he'd approached.

I rewound the tape, printed out snapshots of both men, then glanced at my watch. Nine minutes to spare. Brilliant.

"I think that's it," I said, retrieving the printouts. "Thanks for your help."

He nodded. "Tell that lazy bastard tending bar I'm still waiting for my coffee."

"I believe he told you to get it yourself."

"He always tells me that." He flashed me a grin that was decidedly boyish. "But he's almost as keen on men as he is women, and he wants to get into my pants something bad, too. He always comes up with the goods in the end."

"Meaning you'll probably have to reciprocate in the long run."

"Oh, I will. But I also believe in making them wait. Keeps them keen."

I grinned. "Waiting isn't something we wolves worry about."

"Well, it's not exactly something I practice when it comes to blood, but a relationship is different." He gave me a sketchy wave and turned his attention back to his screens.

I closed the door and headed back to the bar. The barkeep—minus his tea towel for a change—ambled up. "All done?"

I slid the now-empty coffee mug over to him, then folded the printouts and tucked them into my pocket. "Yes. Thank your boss for me."

"If you wait a few minutes, you can thank him yourself."

I grinned. "A pleasure I shall forgo."

His own smile grew. "You'd need to say that with a little less sarcasm if you want me to believe you."

"Next time I want you to believe me, I might give it a try."

He snorted softly, then gave me a nod and walked over to serve another customer. I headed out. The bouncer wasn't at the door when I exited, which was unusual. Maybe there'd been some trouble inside somewhere. I hadn't noticed anything, but that was probably why Starke kept so many guards on staff—to put out the flames of a fight before they got too hot.

I was about a dozen steps away from my car when I realized I was no longer alone. Two figures appeared out of the shadows of the house ahead. The back of my neck tingled, warning that there were two more men behind me. Four men in total—the same four men who'd confronted me inside the club earlier.

I flared my nostrils, tasting the anger in their rancid scents.

These guys *were* as stupid as they'd seemed.

I stopped and held up my hands. The footsteps of the two men behind me were whisper soft, and with the breeze flowing past me, it was difficult to judge how close they actually were. But I had more than just regular senses at my call, and it was those I relied on now. They were still out of kicking range. "Guys, you really don't want to do this."

The hazel-eyed leader gave a slight sneer. "It's four vampires against one woman, guardian. I'm thinking the odds might be in our favor."

"And I'm thinking you're all fucking idiots." I shifted my feet a little, adjusting my weight so that most of it was balanced on my right leg. The men behind me were almost close enough. Almost. "Attacking a guardian will get you into more trouble than you could ever imagine. You really don't want to do this."

He flexed his fingers and gave me a grin that was all teeth. "You guardians killed a blood brother. His only crime was obeying the wishes of a whore, and he was punished for it."

"It's against the law to suck a human dry. You may not like it, but it's the law and we have to enforce it." As my skin began to burn with the closeness of the two vampires, I twisted, sweeping my leg up and around. The blow took the first vampire on the chin and the second in the chest, pushing them both backward. I followed through with a punch, smashing the first vampire's nose, sending blood and snot and God knows what else flying. He dropped like a stone to the pavement and I spun around, looking for the second vamp. He was already out of reach.

Still, three against one was better odds by far.

But I had little time to appreciate it as the other two attacked. They were fast and strong and coming from different directions, and I found myself backing up against the onslaught of their fists and feet. I barely missed connecting with a one-two punch to my face, felt the breezy approach of another and ducked, only to see the blur of an oncoming boot. I threw myself backward, twisting as I did so, landing on all fours and launching myself upright. One of them landed on my back, his spindly arms and legs wrapping around my body as his teeth tore into my shoulder. A scream rolled up my throat but I gritted my teeth against it, forcing myself to concentrate as the other two vamps came at me.

I dropped, sweeping with one leg—the movement somewhat awkward and cramped thanks to the moron stuck to my back. The vampire avoided the blow then launched himself toward me. I twisted, punching upward, wishing like hell I was wearing my wooden stilettos right now. They sure would have been handy—

although a blow to the privates nevertheless took another attacker out. It just wasn't as satisfyingly painful to him as a stake would have been.

Then a fist connected with my chin and knocked me sideways. I crashed down onto all fours, the rough road surface tearing at my palms as I skidded along for several feet. I shook my head, trying to clear it, trying to ignore the pain and just get up. The vampire on my back was still clinging like a leech and the smell of blood tainted the air, intensifying the whole situation.

The footsteps of another approaching vampire loomed large. I had to move or this whole situation could get *really* bad.

Then another scent hit me—orange blossom and dark spices.

Starke.

The footsteps of the third vampire abruptly stopped, and a heartbeat later, bones cracked. I grabbed the thumbs of the leech on my back, pushing them backward—hard. As he screamed, I threw myself onto the ground, smashing his head against the roadside and crushing him beneath me.

Starke appeared before me, his golden eyes burning with so much fury that they glowed.

"Please accept my apologies," he said, holding out a hand. "The guard at the door is supposed to prevent things like this from occurring and has been appropriately dealt with for his lapse."

I untangled myself from the arms and legs that were still wrapped around me, then placed my hand in

Starke's and let him haul me upright. He did so with little effort and, surprisingly, released me straightaway.

Which didn't mean the ever-so-brief touch had no effect. Quite the opposite, in fact. "It's hardly your fault these four decided to be morons." I barely resisted the urge to wipe the lingering heat of his flesh onto my jeans. He'd basically saved my life, so the least I could do was not insult him by showing such an outwardly adverse reaction to his touch. "Or that the bouncer values his hatred more than his job."

He smiled, but there was nothing warm about it, and I was suddenly damn glad that look hadn't been aimed my way. Jack might not have a very high opinion of this vampire, but I suspected he was *way* more dangerous than he was letting on.

"Whether or not he has specific grudges against guardians should never have come into it. He was employed to do a job and I expected him to do it."

I couldn't really argue with that. I looked past him. The vampire he'd stopped—who happened to be the leader of this little band of morons—was lying on the ground, his back twisted at an odd angle. Meaning it was broken. While this wasn't a fatal wound for vampires, it sure as hell put them through a slow and painful recovery. I can't say I was sorry about that. Although if his friends didn't get him out of the street before dawn, he wouldn't have to worry about the pain. He'd be burnt to a crisp by the sunlight.

Couldn't say I'd be sorry about that, either.

I looked back at Dante. Anger still burned in his golden eyes, but the heat of it had been tamped down a little, its force replaced by a heat that was more sexual in nature. Surprisingly, there was no spark of blood hunger lighting the deeper depths—an oddity given the blood that still poured down my back. But maybe he'd just fed. The meeting the bartender had mentioned could very well have been code for feeding.

I wondered if he fed during sex, like Quinn. I couldn't actually smell sex on him, just the delicious aroma of desire. It was a wave of heat that caressed my skin as sensually as any touch, and it sent little prickles of longing shuddering through my body.

This vampire was dangerous, all right—and not just in the way I'd presumed moments ago.

I stepped away, trying to deflate the intensity of my awareness, suddenly glad that not every vampire had sexual glamor. Nonhumans and humans alike would have been in deep trouble if they had.

He smiled and closed the distance between us again.

"How badly did the vamp on your back wound you?" he asked, his golden gaze flicking to the vampire behind me. It was just as well he was still unconscious, because if that look was anything to go by, he would have suffered a fate deadlier than a broken back.

"I've had worse." Which was true enough. Even so, I'd have to shift shape soon or Quinn would have to forgo his feeding the next time we made love. I stepped farther away, but it didn't ease my hunger for the golden vampire.

Amusement played about his lush mouth. "Why not come back to the club and clean yourself up? I promise not to peek while you strip down."

Yeah, I believed *that*. "I'm afraid I'm expected back at the Directorate—"

"And you wouldn't stay anyway, even if I offered you your favorite coffee." He paused, studying me. "I find it odd that a werewolf is so reluctant to pursue such an obvious attraction."

"And we both know that this *isn't* an attraction but the sexual glamor you're using on me."

"Ah. You know about that."

"Yeah, so stop it."

He waved his hands and somehow managed to look woebegone. "If only I could. But alas, it is part of my makeup and therefore uncontrollable."

"Other women might buy that. I don't." I took the printouts from my pocket. "Don't suppose you know either of these men, do you?"

He took the photos from me, his fingers somehow managing to brush mine and send yet another delicious shiver of desire skating through me.

"That one, no," he said, giving me back the one I suspected was Kye in disguise. "This man isn't a regular, but I have seen him around before. I believe his name is Luke. Luke Johnson."

"Is he a vamp?"

"Human. The few times he was in the club, he was fed on, not feeding." He handed me back the printout. "If you'd like, I can ask around and see if any of my staff know of him."

"I'd like." I folded the pictures up and shoved them back into my pocket. "If you do happen to find anything, just call the Directorate."

"If I find anything, I shall insist you come and get it. After all, I just saved your life, so you can hardly deprive me of another glimpse of your beauty."

I snorted softly. "Do shitty pickup lines like that often work for you?"

His sudden grin had my hormones racing about excitedly. "Totally. In fact, it's working now—only you won't acknowledge it."

He had that right. "Again, thanks for your help."

"My pleasure," he said. Then, moving with lightning speed, he caught my hand and dragged me against his long, strong body. His free hand slid under my sweater, caressing skin, sending delighted shivers up my spine. "Are you sure you don't want to come back? That wound is bleeding profusely and really should be tended to."

His lips were so close that his breath burned mine, and suddenly it was all I could do *not* to stand on my tippy-toes and kiss him. "Starke, release me or I'll kick you in the balls."

And that would *hurt,* given the current rock-hard state of that area.

"I'm only trying to help—"

"Bullshit. Now release me."

He sighed dramatically and did as I asked. I stepped back and tried to ignore the hammering of my heart. And the urge to step right back into the hard warmth of his embrace.

"Don't try that again, Starke, or there will be trouble."

Amusement glittered in his bright eyes. "Trouble

and I are old companions. I enjoy its taste." His gaze swept down me then rose to meet mine again. His desire was stronger than ever before, scorching my skin. "As I will eventually enjoy tasting you."

He gave me a slight bow then walked away before I could say anything, his gait effortless and sexy.

Lord. I mentally slapped the lusty image away, then shifted shape and trotted to the car. Once back in human form, I took off my blood-sodden sweater and shredded bra, chucked them in the trunk, and retrieved the spare T-shirt I kept there for emergencies.

As I climbed into the car, my phone rang. I turned the key in the ignition to warm the engine, then answered the call. "Riley here."

"Riley? Liander. Rhoan's just been shot."

My heart just about stopped. For several minutes, I couldn't think, couldn't speak, couldn't do anything. Rhoan had been shot. And *I* hadn't felt it. Hadn't even known he was in trouble.

"He's okay," Liander added quickly. "The bullet winged him, nothing more. They've almost finished stitching the wound and it looks fine."

If he was in a hospital, then it was more than just a graze. I needed to get there. "Where is he?"

"At the Albert Hospital. But there's no need to come here—meet us at home."

"Liander, I can't—"

"Riley," Liander interrupted, tone stern. "He's okay. He's being released, but it'll take us at least another hour to finish up here and get home, so you might as well meet us there."

I took a deep, shuddering breath. He was right, I knew that, but the urge to run to my twin's side was an instinct I couldn't easily shake. "Okay, I'll see you there."

"Good."

I hit the END button, then glanced down as the phone beeped again. This time it was a text. I opened the message.

How's your brother? it said. *Silver bullets can cause such nasty wounds.*

Just that. Nothing more.

But I didn't need anything more, because I knew exactly who it was from.

Kye was a dead man.

$\mathcal{W}$ith Rhoan safe and Liander advising me to meet them at home rather than the hospital, it was an easy decision to go after Kye. I already had an appointment set up with the man, and the attempt on Rhoan's life made me eager to keep it.

Which was probably the reason he'd shot Rhoan in the first place.

Proximity Drive in Brooklyn turned out to be a road filled with hulking warehouses. Number five was caged by wire, but unlike the others in the street, it wasn't surrounded by tower lights. It sat in the shadows—a long, slender building that seemed out of place among its beefier peers.

I drove up to the gates, but before I could wind down the window and press the intercom button, the gates began to open. I leaned forward and spotted the camera perched atop the posts. Kye must have been watching for me. No surprise there.

I sucked in a breath that did little to control anger still roiling inside, then lifted my foot off the brake and drove forward. A solitary light gleamed about halfway down the long white building, illuminating a heavy steel door.

I parked in a bay near the door, then transferred Cole's report from the computer to my phone and climbed out. There was another camera perched above the doorway, and the door clicked open as I approached it.

"Follow the hallway" came Kye's instructions, seemingly out of nowhere because I couldn't see a speaker. "I'm in the second room on the right."

The door swung shut behind me. The only light in the place seemed to be coming from a semishut doorway down the far end of the hall. The air was crisp and cold, and my nipples puckered in response. I crossed my arms—though it didn't do a lot to alleviate the chill—and walked forward.

It took all my control not to run.

Unsurprisingly, the second doorway on the right was the one emitting the light into the hall. I pressed my fingertips against the cool metal and slowly opened it. I wasn't sure what to expect, but it sure as hell wasn't a rifle range.

Kye was shooting at a target set far down at the other end of the room, but the minute I walked in, he swung around. The gun was long and mean-looking, and it was aimed squarely at my heart.

I stopped. I might want to kill him, but I didn't want to die in the process. "You shot my brother."

The gun didn't waver. Neither did the waves of cool amusement that were coming off him. He was dressed in jeans and a tight-fitting black T-shirt, and part of me couldn't help admiring the way it defined his back and clung to the top of his biceps.

Obviously, my wolf was as insane as the man she was admiring.

"I thought," he said, his voice flat and oh so controlled, "you might need a little reminder about our meeting tonight."

"He's a guardian, Kye. You just committed an arrestable offense."

"Arrest me, and both your brother and that mate of his will be dead within the hour."

Fury boiled through me, but it was accompanied by bitter confusion. "Why do this? He's my *twin*— anything you do to him might just rebound back through me to you."

He raised an eyebrow. "And you think I care?"

I didn't know *what* to think. "I was coming here anyway. You didn't have to shoot him to make your point."

"You and I both know you'd forgotten about our meeting."

He was right—I had. But how the hell had he known that? He could sometimes read my thoughts, but up until now, I hadn't realized it was a long-distance occurrence. "I'll damn well kill you if you try anything like that again."

He finally looked up from the rifle's sights and gave me a cold, hard smile. "No you won't. The difference between me and you, Riley, is that you have people you care about. I don't."

Not even me, the woman who was his soul mate.

And while that should have made me happy, it only increased the anger. At him, at me, and at this whole, twisted situation.

I flexed my fingers, trying to ease the tension in my body. It didn't help. Nothing would. Not when it came to dealing with this man and his perverse games.

The worst of it was, there was *nothing* I could do about any of it. He was right about one thing—I had people I cared about, and I would *not* risk their lives. Even if that meant having to accept this man into my life.

"Care for a little shooting practice?" he said, and the intensity of his gaze had my stomach doing flip-flops. "I've always wondered which one of us was better. And faster."

"Giving me a gun might not be the wisest of moves right now," I said, desperately trying to hold on to the anger. To not give in to the urge to walk to this man and claim what my body craved. Damn it, he *shot* my brother.

But right now, my wolf didn't seem to care.

"Why were you at Dante's the night Grant Haven was killed?"

He raised an eyebrow, then proceeded to break the rifle apart, quickly cleaning the various parts before putting them away in a luxuriously padded case. Only when everything was safe did he answer.

"Why do you smell like you've been covered in blood?"

"I asked my question first." Which sounded decidedly childish, but this man made it extremely easy to act that way.

But there was nothing childish about the way he was looking at me. Nothing childish about the effect it had on me.

His lush lips twisted into a half smile as he walked forward. On any other man, that smile would have been seriously sexy. On Kye, it was simply dangerous.

"I was there following a lead. Nothing more, nothing less."

He stopped an arm's length from me. Close enough that his heat and scent surrounded me. Close enough to reach out and touch if I wanted to.

I didn't touch, but that didn't mean I didn't want to.

I licked my lips, saw his gaze drop to follow the movement. Smelled the sweet surge of his desire. Clenched my fists against the urge to claim the kiss we both hungered for.

"What did you talk to Mandy Jones about?" Surprisingly, my voice sounded near to normal. Given the desire rolling through me, I'd expected husky.

"We talked about several of the men she'd been with. She didn't provide any useful information."

"So you didn't talk to her about the vampire beheaded outside the club?"

"No, I did not."

"I will check, you know."

"Check all you want. I'm not lying." His gaze swept down me then rose, pinning me. "Your turn."

I shrugged. "Four vamps felt the need to attempt a little retribution."

"You obviously beat them."

"Not without a little help. It happened outside Dante's, and the owner came to my rescue."

"Did he now?" There was an edge in his voice that surprised me. It almost seemed as if he were angry. Furious, even. "Did he kiss you?"

I frowned. "Why?"

"Because I've heard him boast that once he kisses a woman, she is his unto death."

And I could hardly be Dante's when I was *his*. I snorted. This wolf was a control freak. "He tried to, but I threatened to knock his balls through his ass, and that seemed to do the trick."

Although if he *had* really tried, would I have been so resistant? Somehow, I didn't think so.

He seemed to relax a little. "How badly were you hurt?"

"One of them had something of a flesh fetish. He took a chunk out of my shoulder before he started feeding." I shrugged again. "It's just another scar to add to the list."

"Show me."

"Kye, it's fine. I shifted shape—"

He moved, his right arm slashing downward, something sharp and silver glittering in his hand. A heartbeat later, the front of my T-shirt fell open, the knife slicing through it like butter but never touching my skin.

"If you don't want the rest of the shirt sliced up, you'll show me the wound."

His voice was hard and cold, the total opposite of his eyes. I returned his gaze, wishing I could just smash the arrogance from his face and walk out, yet unable to do it. I might hate him, but I needed this. Needed *him*. Not just sexually, but in a deeper, more fundamental way. After six months apart, it suddenly seemed as if he were as vital to my wolf as air.

Without a word, I shucked off the remains of my T-shirt and turned around. I didn't hear a step, but the scent of him swirled more strongly around me—a sensual and heated caress that had my nostrils flaring and body burning.

Then his fingers brushed my skin and it was all I could do not to press back into his caress.

"It's going to leave one hell of a nasty scar," he murmured, his voice flat and emotionless as he slid his fingers slowly down my spine. "And your pants are soaked with blood. Best not to let the vampire bite you for a few days."

"What the vampire and I do is none of your business." I spun around before the knife could flash and my jeans met the same fate as the T-shirt. "Where the fuck did you pull that from?"

"This?" He rolled the weapon through his fingertips, the blade a blur of silver fire. "Sheath at the small of my back. And you'd be wrong about it being none of my business."

I ignored the latter part of his comment, and said, "That blade is silver, so I take it the sheath is lead-lined?"

He raised an eyebrow. "Why would you care one way or the other?"

"I don't." I was just curious. Silver was deadly to a wolf, and it was extremely unusual for one of us to carry it so close. But then, he also used silver bullets in his gun. Obviously, he wasn't worried about his own weapons being used against him. I retrieved the phone from my pocket. "Give me your phone number, and I'll transfer the file you wanted."

"Why don't you just tell me the important bits." The blade disappeared as quickly as it had appeared. This wolf was frighteningly fast.

"You know, as much as I'd really love to stand here and chat about the case—" My voice was dry and a smile touched the corners of his mouth. "—the fact is I haven't actually read the file."

"Sarcasm is something of a fallback for you, isn't it?"

"Much the same as murder is for you. Do you want the file or not?"

"I want the file." His voice was soft, and the smile still played about his mouth. I tried to ignore it, but my damn gaze kept dropping. "I also want this."

His hand snaked out and wrapped around the back of my neck, dragging me to the lips I'd been desperately trying to avoid.

His kiss was heated and hard, and it was everything I craved, everything I wanted. I gave in to the power of it, wrapping my arms around his neck, clinging to him, tasting him as fully as he tasted me.

He gave a low growl in the back of his throat and suddenly I was being pushed backward. My back hit the wall and I grunted at the force of it, yet still I kissed him, my wolf desperate for his taste and his touch after such a long absence.

His hands cupped my breasts, squeezing and teasing as his lips left mine, kissing my face, my neck, my throat. I shuddered, my legs suddenly weak, my knees threatening to buckle at the force of pleasure rolling through me.

I grabbed his T-shirt and ripped it up the middle, exposing the beauty of his chest and stomach. I slid my hands up his abs, feeling the quiver in his muscles, reveling at the intensity of desire so evident there.

He undid the button and the zipper on my jeans, then his hand was sliding past the elastic of my panties, down to the place that was so wet and eager for his touch. I moaned as he touched my clit, arching forward into his touch, wanting more. He chuckled softly and thrust his fingers deep inside me.

But as good as it felt—as desperately as I wanted that and more—sanity sparked somewhere deep inside.

No matter how much I might crave this, I couldn't let it go any further. It would only strengthen the ties that bound us.

So I shoved my hands against his chest and pushed him away from me as hard as I could.

He flew backward, but all too quickly regained his

balance, his hand instinctively reaching for the knife sheathed at his back. I shifted my stance, ready for anything, my breathing little more than pants of air.

Then his gaze met mine and his hand dropped. But he didn't relax, and neither did I.

This wolf was an explosion waiting to happen.

"I didn't come here for sex, Kye. And I will *not* give in to this."

"You have no choice." His voice was rough with the urgency that still burned between us. "Neither of us does."

"We're not animals, Kye, and I *will* control this." I bent and retrieved my phone from the floor, though I couldn't remember even dropping it. "Phone number?"

He spat the numbers out. I transferred the file, then shoved the phone into my pocket and did up my jeans. "I'll be going now. Don't bother walking me out."

He smiled. It was a cold, hard thing. "Don't think you're going to get away that easily."

I didn't even look at him, just turned and walked toward the door.

"I want to see you again, Riley."

I ignored him and kept walking. It was the hardest thing I've ever done in my life.

"Lunch tomorrow, at Franklin's on La Trobe Street. Wear something nice. They have a strict dress code for entry."

I spun around at that. I couldn't help it. "You want a fucking *date*? Why, when neither of us wants this relationship?"

"I may not want the relationship, but I want you, and I also want information about this case. And I always get want I want, Riley. One way or another."

I stared at him, hating him more than ever and yet fearing what he could do. He was a killer without conscience, and the threat he posed to those I loved loomed large in my mind.

"That's blackmail on top of attempted murder, Kye. I can now officially kill you."

He moved with frightening speed. One minute his hand was empty, the next there was a gun in it. I think he pulled it from an ankle holster, but I wasn't one hundred percent certain. "And this is loaded with silver bullets. Don't think I won't hesitate to shoot if I need to, Riley."

My hands were clenched so hard my fingernails were digging into my palms. I forced myself to relax and gave one short, sharp nod. "Franklin's at lunchtime, then."

I turned and walked out. But I was barely through the door when he added, "And Riley? Stay away from Starke."

I didn't ask why. I just got the hell out of there.

Chapter 6

*R*hoan and Liander were both home when I got there.

"I'm fine, sis," Rhoan said, the minute I opened the door. "Really, it's just a shoulder wound."

"Doesn't mean I wasn't scared." I wrapped my arms around him and hugged him tight, soaking myself in the scent and strength of him. "Maybe you and Liander need to take a holiday somewhere nice while you recover."

Part of me wanted to warn him about Kye and the threat he posed, but I knew the minute I did that, Rhoan would go on the offensive. And *that* could get damn dangerous for us all. Right now, the better option seemed to be silence. As long as I kept playing Kye's games, everyone I cared about should be safe.

Rhoan snorted. "And you think Jack's going to let

me do that?" He waved his bandaged limb about. "It'll be fine in a day."

"I know, but—"

He placed a finger on my lips, quieting me. "I'm fine. In fact, I look a whole lot better than you. Why is that?"

"I got into a fight with some vamps." I stepped back, not wanting to get into the details of events at Dante's or the warehouse. Too much had happened in too short a time, and I just needed time to sort it all out. To figure out what the hell I was going to do. "And now I need a long hot bath."

"Then go. We'll have the coffee waiting when you've finished."

I leaned forward, dropped a kiss on his cheek, then headed for the bathroom. An hour later, feeling a whole lot cleaner but actually no wiser, I twisted around in front of the mirror, trying to look at the wound the vampire had given me. Though it was already healing, it was going to leave a nasty mark. Give me another year in this job, and I probably wouldn't have any unscarred skin left.

Yet short of leaving the job—an option I didn't have—there wasn't anything I could do about it. The more I fought bad guys, the more things would go wrong. And one of these days, that wrong would mean death.

Which was a good reason to say yes to Liander and Rhoan's request. At least part of me would live on.

But then, there were also people out there who'd be more than willing to use any offspring as a pawn against me. Hell, Kye was showing no qualms about using Liander and Rhoan's safety as a means to secure my obedience, and he was my damn soul mate.

I blew out a frustrated breath then tossed my towel in the laundry basket, collected my coffee, walked into my bedroom, and climbed between the sheets.

Once again, my sleep was uneasy, but this time the mix of worry and desire blossomed into unbridled pleasure. This time, the dreams were sharp and real rather than just restless sensations. I dreamed of being caressed and kissed, of hands sliding and teasing, of heated flesh pressing against mine, taking me, bringing me to fulfillment, again and again.

My dream lover had no face and no smell. My dream man could have been Quinn, it could have been Kye, or maybe it was both all mashed up into one. It didn't matter. I just enjoyed, even if somewhere deep inside I wished it were real rather than imaginary.

And then it *did* become real.

Quinn's scent filled my lungs as he slid in beside me, his hands moving down my body to where it was warm and wet.

I moaned softly, arching into his caress as I reached out sleepily and drew him closer. I kissed him, my lips soft on his as my hands began to roam the warm, hard expanse of his body.

And just like the dream, his body pressed against mine, his flesh joining mine, so heated and hard. It felt so damn good that I wanted to cry. Then the pleasure intensified and I came, as did he, my name on his lips moments before his teeth entered my neck, taking the substance that was a vital part of the act for him and giving me yet more pleasure.

As the soft haze of sated exhaustion rolled over me, he moved to one side and gathered me in his arms. I snuggled against his bare chest, breathing in the scent of him, wishing the day and the problems that would come with it would just all fade away and let me lie here forever.

His fingers brushed the sweaty strands of hair away from my forehead, then his lips lightly took their place. "Good morning, sweetheart."

"The only good thing about this morning is your sudden appearance in my bed," I muttered, wishing I could go back to sleep.

His smile held a warmth I felt deep inside, even if I couldn't see it. "You did look as if you'd had a bitch of a night."

"Understatement of the year." I gave up on any attempt to sleep and stretched, my body pressed warmly against his. "I don't suppose there's coffee anywhere near, is there?"

"Only a mug of congealed muck I presume you forgot to drink last night. But I did put the coffeemaker on before I came into the bedroom."

"What a clever vampire you are." I shifted and kissed him lightly. "You worked late."

"I wasn't working. An old friend arrived in town, and we went out for drinks."

I raised my eyebrows. "An old friend? Should I be jealous?"

"I wish you would be." Though he grinned, there

was more than a little sadness in his eyes. He might have gotten used to my werewolf ways, but part of him still hungered for a truly one-on-one relationship. It was something I could never give him, especially now that my wolf soul mate was on the scene. "Tell me about your dream."

"It revolved around sex."

He laughed. "That explains why you were so wet and ready when I climbed into bed."

I grinned. "I'm a werewolf. We're always wet and ready."

"So who was your dream lover? Or is that a question that's likely to make me jealous?"

"He didn't have a face or a smell. He could have been anyone." I wrinkled my nose. "It was weird, really."

If only because I felt as if I had spent the entire night making love rather than just dreaming it. My body felt drained and lethargic—although that could have been a result of Quinn feeding so soon after I'd lost so much blood from the attack.

"Is there any reason why you should be dreaming about sex?" He shifted upright, his shoulder lightly pressing against mine. I could feel the sudden tension in him. It was almost as if he knew something vital had happened.

Which he probably did.

He was linked to me in much the same way as Kye, and while the connection might not be as strong as the werewolf bond, it was still there. It probably gave him insights I couldn't even begin to guess at.

And there was no easy way to tell him about Kye, so I just up and said it. "Kye's back in town."

He was silent for a moment, then asked, his voice softer, "And you've seen him?"

"Seen him, yes. Had sex with him, no."

He glanced at me, his dark gaze exploring my features, as if searching for a lie. "But you will."

It wasn't a question. "I'm trying not to, but denying my nature is the hardest thing I've ever had to do. I can't promise it won't happen, Quinn. I really can't."

He looked away. His chest moved as he breathed deep, though a vampire didn't really need air to survive. He released it slowly, a silent sigh that somehow conveyed so much tension and anguish. "I'm asking too much, aren't I?"

I reached out and clasped my hand through his. His fingers curled around mine, warm and steady. "It's the same as me asking you to restrain your urge to take blood after sex."

"Restrain, not stop. There is a difference."

He was wrong, but I didn't bother saying it. It wasn't a point worth arguing.

"We both knew this moment would arrive eventually," he continued. "I will fight for us, but at the same time, you can't continue to fight what you are. I shouldn't have ever asked you to."

Relief swirled through me, the force of it so strong tears stung my eyes. Yet there was also frustration. Kye was going to force a relationship, I had no doubt about that. Just as I had no doubt that whenever we made love, the ties that bound us would get deeper and stronger. How could that *not* affect my relationship with Quinn? I had no idea if the bond I had with him was deep enough to withstand the onslaught of binding with my wolf soul mate.

It was an answer I probably would uncover sooner rather than later, and it was one that filled me with fear. "Quinn—"

I wasn't entirely sure what I intended to say, and it didn't matter, because he raised a hand and pressed it against my lips. "When it happens, I don't want to know about it. And if I see him, I will beat him to a pulp."

"As long as you promise to give him a whack or two from me, I'm fine with that."

He laughed softly, then looked around at a knock at the door.

"Sorry to interrupt," Rhoan said, opening the door and peeking around it, "but Jack's on the phone. He's pissed off again. Apparently you have your phone off."

I swore softly. I'd meant to switch it back on once I'd gotten home, but I'd been so shaken by Rhoan's injury and my close encounter with Kye that it had totally slipped my mind. I kissed Quinn softly, then scrambled out of bed, grabbed the phone, and made a mad dash for the bathroom.

"I'm on my way, boss," I said, flicking on the shower and waiting impatiently for the hot water to appear.

"I swear, Riley, one of these days you'll push me too fucking far."

I raised my eyebrows at the curt tension in his voice. "What's happened?"

"If you'd keep up with local news, you'd fucking know."

"Boss, I did work late—"

"And turned off your phone and com-link in the process. How many times do I have to tell you about that?"

The water finally got hot. I flicked the phone to speaker, shoved it on the basin, and stepped into the shower. "I'm sorry. It won't happen again."

He snorted. Obviously he believed it about as much as he believed in Santa Claus and the Easter Bunny. "We've got another woman dead for no apparent reason. I want you to meet Kade over there ASAP."

"I'll be out the door in five minutes." I hesitated, wondering if it was wise to poke the bear, but decided I needed an answer. "Something other than this new death has gotten up your nose, hasn't it?"

"Some damn fool reporter has gotten wind of the vampire beheadings, and now it's all over the news. The headline reads 'Vigilante gang hunts down vampires.' "

"Which it may well be."

"Yeah, but we don't need the vampires thinking that, and we certainly don't need the humans thinking they need to arm themselves against retaliatory attacks. Trust me, there's already been some talk about that."

"I gather Director Hunter is keeping the vampire council well informed on the situation?" And surely the council would be able to keep a lid on the reactions of the general vampire population? At least for a little bit longer.

"Of course, but with the tension already in the ranks over our handling of the blood whore situation, this is going to add more fuel to the fire."

"And won't that make the streets a fun place to be."

"Yeah. Be careful out there, Riley."

If Jack was adding a warning like that, then he was really worried. Which meant my gun and I were going to become very close companions. Once I had never wanted to use the damn thing, but I'd learned the hard way that sometimes strength and speed just weren't enough.

"I've got a possible lead on the beheading case," I said, and quickly updated him about Luke Johnson and the information I'd gathered from the security tape—although I didn't tell him the other man seen talking to our so-called witness was Kye. He wasn't likely ever to trace the image back to Kye, and the fewer people who knew he was back in town, the better for my sanity. "I'll send through the pictures now so someone can chase up some information on them."

"I'll get Benson on it the minute he gets here."

Benson was one of the newer liaisons, and while he was every bit as efficient as Sal, he was far less fun to goad.

"Thanks, Jack," I said, and he hung up.

I quickly finished my shower then ran into the bedroom to get dressed. Quinn wasn't there, but the smell of man and coffee led me into the kitchen, where I found both. He handed me a steaming travel mug, then kissed me lightly on the lips. "Be careful out there. It could get nasty."

I raised my eyebrows. "You overheard my conversation with Jack?"

He shook his head. "I'm an advisor to the council, much the same as Jack is."

"Two facts I wasn't aware of until now." I studied him for a moment, wondering if I'd ever uncover all there was to know about him. "I can understand Jack being an advisor, given he's in charge of the guardian division and his sister is on the council, but why are you?"

"I was once a cazador, and I'm one of the few who survived the experience." He shrugged. "I'm the one they call for advice when things go bad."

Cazadors were basically vampire hit men. From the little Quinn had said about them, they worked for the council and took out anyone who broke the council's rules or those who went *really* bad. As in more than the Directorate could handle, and we handled some pretty nasty shit.

"So they haven't called you for advice yet?"

"No." His expression sobered. "And pray that they don't, because that would probably mean we are on the verge of war."

"Do you think things will get that bad?"

He hesitated. "If the Directorate can quash the speculation in the press and catch whoever is behind these beheadings quickly enough, then the council will be able to control the situation, vampirewise."

"But what about the unrest over the Directorate's handling of blood whores?"

"The council is about to issue an edict regarding that, and it will basically back the law as it currently stands." He shrugged. "They have no other choice, really, though the decision was not unanimous."

If he knew how the voting was going on council decisions, then he was something more than a mere advisor. "So you agreed with the vote?"

He smiled and tapped a finger against my nose. "I didn't vote, if that's what you want to know. As an advisor, I can't."

"But you were there to witness it."

"Yes, but simply because I'm also fairly far up in the hierarchy. It is my right—and often my duty—to witness all council decisions."

"So how come you're not on the council itself? I gather you could be?"

"Yes, I could. I just have no wish to be."

"Why not?"

"Didn't Jack tell you to hurry to some murder scene?"

So much for him not listening to my conversation. "Yes, but if I leave now, I may never get an answer to my questions."

"The problem with you and questions is the fact that you never seem to run out of them."

I grinned. "You shouldn't be such a damn mystery then, and we wouldn't have that problem. And seeing that you avoided my last question, I'm owed one more. Then I'll leave."

He rolled his eyes. "Okay."

"How did you attend council meetings when you were living full-time in Sydney? I was under the impression that the council met every day."

"Every state has it own council, and they handle the day-to-day governing of the vampire population. The highest-ranking members from each of these make up the greater council, which presides in Melbourne. These are the meetings I attend, and they're generally once a month, unless problems arise."

"Is there some sort of worldwide übercouncil?"

He smiled. "I can't say."

Meaning he wouldn't say but that there was. "So the greater council would handle things like the discontent over the Directorate's handling of the blood whore killers and the beheadings."

"Yes. The man I went out with last night came to town specifically to attend the greater council meeting. We went for drinks afterward."

"Will I ever get to meet this friend?"

"That is a second question."

"You are such a pain in the ass, vampire." I leaned forward and kissed him. Lightly. Sweetly. "I have no idea what time I'm going to be home."

He smiled. "Nor do I. Julien has expressed a desire to visit some wolf clubs to see just what it is that has me so engrossed with the culture."

Something inside me twinged. Jealousy? God, I hoped not. And yet . . .

I couldn't deny that some small part of me didn't want him going to the clubs without me.

Which was totally stupid, given the odds of my date with Kye *not* ending in sex weren't great.

Still . . .

"But you hate the culture."

"True. So perhaps he hopes to capture his own luscious redhead." He leaned forward and kissed me again. "I don't have the heart to tell him my redhead is a rare and precious jewel that I'm never going to give up."

His words made my heart do a giddy little dance. I chuckled softly. "Just for that, I might let you bite me again tonight."

"I'll bite you now if you don't get your pretty ass in gear." He slapped said rear lightly. "Go, before Jack starts calling again."

I sighed dramatically but spun around and walked out the door.

The new murder scene was in Craigieburn, which was on the northern outskirts of Melbourne. I was going against the main flow of traffic, so it didn't take me long to get there via the ring road and the freeway.

Kade was already there when I arrived. I pulled up behind his car and killed the engine, then grabbed the laser from its hidey-hole under the seat and climbed out.

"A laser?" Amusement twitched his lips and his chocolate-colored eyes sparkled with mirth. "So you think a ghost might jump out and start hassling you?"

"I'm making a point not to go anywhere unarmed at the moment."

"Ah, the fuss the papers are making about the so-called gang responsible for the beheadings." He paused. "You don't think the vamp population is going to get antsy about it, do you?"

"I had two very old vampires warning me to be careful this morning. This is me being careful. I haven't got telekinesis as a weapon, like you." I shoved the weapon in my back pocket and waved him forward. "Has Jack filled you in on the details?"

He'd sent me the file, but the computer's metallic tones had annoyed the crap out of me, so I'd switched it off and concentrated instead on the road and drinking my coffee.

"Yeah, it appears to be the same MO as the last one," Kade said, opening the front gate and ushering me through. "The victim's name is Janette Crowley. A divorcée in her midforties—no kids, no family, no lovers. The woman she shares the house with found her body last night."

"So an autopsy hasn't been performed yet?"

He shook his head. "But the police report said there were no obvious signs of a struggle in the room or on the body, and no sign of forced entry into the house. Because we were already handling the Renatta Bailey case, they threw this one straight to us."

"Even though it may not be related?"

"The cause of death may not be known, but everything else is the same." He shrugged. "I guess they're not taking chances."

I grunted and opened the screen door. Kade rapped his knuckles on the sturdy-looking front door. The sound echoed inside, suggesting the house was empty. He knocked a second time, then dug out his electronic lock pick. The door clicked open, and the air that rushed out was filled with the stench of death and decay.

I wrinkled my nose and tried breathing through my mouth. "I'm guessing that not only isn't the housemate staying here, but she didn't find her straightaway?"

"No. She'd just come back from a two-month holiday. Initial reports suggest Crowley died at least a month ago."

"Well before Renatta Bailey, then."

I followed Kade inside but didn't shut the door behind us. The house desperately needed some fresh air. We made our way down through the living room and small kitchen area to the back of the house, following the smell. It led us into a small hall at the rear of the house, past a large bedroom and bathroom, before dumping us into a second, smaller bedroom.

Janette Crowley's taste in furnishings was the polar opposite to Renatta Bailey's. Her bed was a single, and the rumpled sheets and blankets looked threadbare and worn. The dresser and side tables were teak, but both had seen better days, as had the small writing desk that sat underneath the half-window. The smell of decay had permeated the room, and I very much doubted there'd be much in the way of emotions lingering, let alone a soul.

I stopped near the doorway, desperately trying to ignore the smell as I watched Kade move through the room, his large form dominating the space.

"Nothing," he said after a moment. He glanced over his shoulder. "You?"

I shook my head. "It's been a month. Most souls tend to lose energy after a few days, so even if she was here, I might not be able to sense her."

He frowned and turned around, his gaze sweeping the room. "Jack would have known that, so why bother sending you in the first place?"

"Because I keep doing the unexpected, and he's hoping for an easy way to solve the puzzle." I shrugged— a movement he wouldn't have seen because he was walking toward a mirror on the wall.

"It's opposite the bed, just like the one at Renatta Bailey's," I commented.

"That was my thinking." He lifted the mirror and looked behind it. "I can't sense anything, but as you said, it's been a month."

My gaze swept the room, spotting a purse on the dresser. Wrinkling my nose against the overwhelming stench of death, I walked across and picked it up. Surprise, surprise, more vampire club business cards inside.

"We have a connection," I said, holding up the cards. "You know, it seems a little odd that blood whores have now come up as a connection in two apparently separate cases."

Kade dropped the mirror and walked over. He plucked the cards from my fingers and examined them critically. "The beheadings just happened near a whore club. And none of these women appears to have gone near Dante's."

"Just because they haven't got a card doesn't mean they haven't visited. And at least two of the beheading victims serviced 'clients' at Dante's." Given the propensity of cases to intertwine in the past, I wasn't about to ignore a possible link now. Not if it meant a quick end to one or both of the cases.

Of course, to discover if either of the women had gone to Dante's, I'd have to go question the man himself—and that wasn't something I wanted to do. The man was sexual dynamite, and I really didn't want to take my chances with him any more than necessary.

"I can't sense any sort of magical or emotional tag on the cards, so I don't think they're connected." Kade handed them back to me, then shoved his hands in his pockets, his expression one of frustration. "There has to be more of a connection between these women than just the clubs."

My gaze went to the bed, and I frowned. "Maybe there is. Let's presume Crowley died the exact same way as Bailey. So if she'd been found early enough, there would have been a feeling of ecstasy in the room, would there not?"

"Yes."

"Well, emo vampires feed off that sort of emotion, don't they?"

He frowned. "Yeah, but emo vampires can't travel through mirrors."

"That we know of." I met the warm chocolate of his gaze. "Even if they can't, they're still vampires and still territorial. The first murder was on Vinny's turf. She'd surely be aware of someone encroaching."

I'd discovered Vinny's existence a while back, and she was currently under observation, thanks to the fact her wealth was growing extraordinarily fast and because she had several underage, unidentified, newly turned vampires under her care. The Directorate—and the council, apparently—didn't like having unknowns in their midst.

"Then we'd best go talk to her."

I grinned. "And wouldn't Vinny just love you? Which is why we'd better split up. I'll talk to Vinny. You go investigate these clubs." I waved the business cards at him.

He raised his eyebrows. "You don't trust my control?"

"No, I don't trust Vinny. Her aura is so powerful she had me kissing her, and I'm definitely *not* attracted to women. You'd be putty in her hands."

His lips twisted cheekily. "I'm never putty when I'm in someone's hands. As you should know."

My grin widened. "I do remember that fact quite fondly."

He stepped forward, wrapping a hand around my waist and dragged me against his long, strong body. "Care for a refresher?"

The stallion was already half rampant. I sighed wistfully then shook my head. "I'm afraid I have enough men on my plate at the moment."

"Such a shame," he murmured, and bent to give me a quick kiss on the lips. It was a friend's kiss, not one shared by lovers. He was teasing, not actively trying to seduce.

Still, it wouldn't have taken much to flare into something more serious, so I pulled free of his grip and stepped back. "I'll meet you back at the Directorate, then."

"One of these days, I'm going to break down those barriers and enjoy that luscious body of yours once more."

"In your dreams, my friend."

"Oh, you don't want to know about my dreams, trust me on that." Kade walked past me and headed for the front door.

I trailed along behind, enjoying the view. I might not be able to touch, but that didn't mean I couldn't look. And he always did wear jeans *extremely* well.

Once in my car, I zoomed into the main road traffic, then clicked the com-link in my ear and said, "Hello, hello, anyone there?"

"Unlike some who shall not be named, I do not slack off." Benson's deep tones were dry. He'd obviously been taking lessons from Sal. "What can I do for you, Riley?"

"Did Jack pass on a request for an information search on a Luke Johnson?"

"Yes, and I've done it. He's human."

"He's also a possible source of information. I need his details."

"Patching them through now. Anything else?"

The onboard beeped as the information came through. I glanced at it briefly, then said, "Did you get any hits on the other man?"

"Nothing yet. We're currently going through license information."

"Thanks, Benson."

"My pleasure," he said, and signed off.

I transferred Johnson's address to the nav computer and drove across town to his place.

Luke Johnson, it turned out, was a dead end in more ways than one. He opened the door naked, and his scrawny body stank of booze, cigarettes, and sex. His neck was littered with the scars of old vampire bites and there was an unhealthy, sallow look to his skin— suggesting he was indulging in his drug of choice a little *too* often.

"Yeah," he said, squinting blue eyes and leaning forward slightly, as if he were having trouble seeing me.

"Luke Johnson?" I flashed my badge. "Did you visit Dante's club two nights ago?"

He frowned and gripped the door frame a little tighter, though it didn't seem to help stop his swaying. "I think so. Why?"

"Do you remember talking to this woman?"

I took out a photo of Mandy and held it up. He leaned forward, squinting harder. "Yeah. She's not a vamp."

"No, she isn't. What did you talk to her about?"

"Thought she was a vamp, didn't I?" He teetered backward, his viselike grip on the door and the frame the only things holding him upright. "She wasn't."

"Did you talk to her about anything else?"

"No. Found me a vamp, didn't I?"

Which left me with Kye, and he'd already denied

talking to the woman about the vampire found dead outside the club.

So why would he lie? Because he obviously was. I'd seen the cash in Mandy Jones's wallet and had found no lie—or psychic interference—in her thoughts or memories.

"Thanks for your help, Mr. Johnson."

He nodded and closed the door. His footsteps meandered away, going back to whoever was sharing his bed. I could only feel sorry for them.

I went back to my car and headed over to Vinny's.

She still lived in one of those high-rise brick-and-glass buildings that the government had insisted on building some fifty years ago. The intention had been to relieve the low-income housing crisis, but the resulting buildings were neither pretty nor truly functional. Add tenants who hadn't really given a damn about the place, and you were basically left with a large hovel. One with many smashed windows and doors, and decorated by multicolored graffiti.

Vinny's building had been vacated by both the government and the real tenants years ago, and according to recent Directorate records, she'd bought it outright. It was interesting to note that the broken glass and graffiti that had once decorated this place were now gone.

I walked up to the front door. As before, the stink of vampire grew stronger with every step, until the cloying, unhealthy smell all but surrounded me.

Obviously, she still hadn't got the water running properly in the downstairs area.

I opened the glass front doors and stepped inside. Footsteps whispered through the shadows—the sounds so soft regular hearing wouldn't have caught it.

"Riley Jenson from the Directorate," I said, raising my voice just a little. "I'm here to see Vinny."

A young woman in her late teens emerged from the shadows to the right. Her plump face was smeared with dirt, but otherwise she was extremely pretty—and very healthy looking. Which was a vast change from the scrawny, half-starved figures I'd seen on these lower levels when I first visited. Vinny was obviously feeding well if the lower levels were looking this good.

"She is expecting you," the vamp said, her voice a low hum of excitement.

Which was worrying. Rising excitement among a nest of emo vampires might not be good for my health. Just as well I was still carrying a laser. And that I could fly, and they couldn't.

"You can use the elevators," the girl continued. "They're working now."

"Thanks, but I prefer to walk." If only because I didn't trust Vinny not to trap me inside one of the damn things. She and I had something of a volatile relationship—although calling it a relationship was also something of a misnomer. It was little more than a wary connection—one formed when I'd uncovered her lair while working a case.

She was useful and so far had seemed reasonably happy to help the Directorate when asked, but I had no doubt she would double-cross us if it suited her purpose. The only thing Vinny worried about was Vinny.

I grabbed the handrail and began climbing. The un-washed scent of vampire faded the farther I went up, so that by the time I reached the eighth floor, it had all but disappeared. In its place was the rich freshness of springtime—a scent provided by the series of red candles that sat in the stylized, rose-shaped sconces that lined the hall.

Down at the far end, a woman waited. Like most of the vampires on the floors below, she was young and gangly. But unlike them, her blond hair had been recently washed and shone like pale gold in the flickering candlelight.

She wasn't a stranger. She'd been the door guard on several of the occasions I'd had to come here for the Directorate. She didn't talk much, but I'd gleaned a name—Rose.

She was one of the ones we couldn't identify.

"Morning, Rose," I said, as I strolled toward her.

She nodded, her dark gaze sweeping the length of me. "You armed?"

"Yes, and this time I will remain so."

She opened her mouth but didn't get a chance to protest as I added, "Vinny, if I wanted to fucking shoot you, I could do so quite easily from here."

Something flickered through the girl's eyes, and a moment later she opened the door. Unlike the squalor in which the majority of her nest lived, Vinny enjoyed her comforts. The room beyond could only be described as lush. The walls were covered by thick velvet drapes that were a dark, dramatic red, and the carpet was the color of rich sand, thick enough to lose your toes in. Two big chandeliers hung from the ceiling, sending rainbow-colored sprays of light though the shadows.

I stepped inside and looked beyond the thickly stuffed black leather chairs and sensuous-looking chaise sofas to the small circle of people at the far end of the room.

Half a dozen toga-clad boys and girls—I always refused to think of them as anything else, because not one of them looked to be older than seventeen—stood around a mahogany and leather chaise longue. In it sat Vinny.

Power and sensuality oozed from her and, as ever, the force of it caused me to hesitate, however briefly.

Then her lush lips twitched and annoyance swept through me. She'd been warned often enough not to try her tricks on Directorate personnel, but she liked to push. And given that she was currently more of a help than a hindrance, there was nothing I could do about it.

I strode forward. Vinny watched me. She was an ordinary-looking brown-haired, brown-eyed woman of medium height and build, but there was nothing ordinary about what she could do. As an emo vampire in charge of a huge nest—which was the only one we knew of in Melbourne—she was more dangerous than she looked. She had an aura similar to a werewolf's, and was totally capable of seducing anyone she chose, willing or unwilling. She'd come damn close to seducing me, and had even won a kiss from me—although *that* was more from a desperate need to get information than any emo geis.

The scent of blossom and springtime got stronger the closer I got to her chaise, and it mixed warmly with the heavy scent of desire stirring the air. The toga-clad teenagers watched me with languorous expressions, their pupils dilated. Meaning they'd recently fed, and were now sending the vibes out to the rest of the nest. Which explained the hum of excitement I'd felt downstairs.

I stopped when there was still a good ten feet between us. This close, Vinny's skin looked almost luminous, as if the richness of the moon itself glowed from deep within her . . .

I blinked. Damn it, she was doing it again.

"Vinny," I warned softly.

She laughed—a rich sound that sent warm shivers up my spine—and unfurled her legs from the hem of her long dress. Her shoes were red and glittery, reminding me of Dorothy and the Wizard of Oz. "What can I do for you, Riley?"

"We've two dead women on our hands," I said without preamble. "Both died of unknown causes, and in both cases, desire and lust lingered in the room."

"Meaning they had sex before they died." She paused, mirth sparkling in her chocolate eyes. "Lucky them. But why do I need to know about these deaths?"

"Because we suspect an emo vampire might be at-large."

"And I have the only known nest in Melbourne."

"Exactly."

She rose unhurriedly, her movements grace itself.

Her long skirt billowed briefly around her—a cloud of pale organza that seemed to catch the flickering sprays of rainbow light from the chandeliers and gleam like the inside of an oyster shell. Those same sprays of light danced across her skin, leaving a luminosity . . .

I dug my fingers into my palms, using the pain to battle the caress of her aura, however light it might be at the moment.

"It is a waste to kill a lover," she said softly, moving around me, her body so close I could feel the heat of her. "A dead lover is of no use to the nest."

"They are if they bequeath you their estate."

She laughed, and her breath stirred the hairs at the back of my neck. I forced myself to remain still, and she reappeared on my left side. Her skirt swirled around my leg. It felt as sweet as a caress.

I flexed my fingers and ignored the urge to get out of there.

"I can get that without killing them," she said. "All I have to do is ask."

"It's against the law to use your abilities for monetary gain, Vinny."

She laughed again and stopped in front of me. "Everyone who has bequeathed me their possessions or money has done so willingly. Just ask them."

"We have."

Something flickered in her eyes. Annoyance, perhaps. "Then you know I have done no wrong. So why are you here?"

"Are there any other emo vampires or nests in Melbourne? Nests that we don't know about?"

"No."

It was flatly said, and I could sense no lie in her words. Of course, Vinny was such an accomplished liar that I probably wouldn't. And while in any other situation I would have tried to read her mind, telepathy was useless in this place. This room acted like a big hole when it came to psychic energy. There were no deadeners involved, nor did it appear to be any kind of natural psychic shield. It was just a hole. Or maybe it was more like a black hole, because it seemed to suck away any sort of mental resonance.

Jack had theorized that it had something to do with an emo's control over energy, but Vinny certainly wasn't about to confirm or deny that.

"Would you know if there was another emo or nest in the city?"

"Yes."

"Would you tell us if there was?"

She smiled. "Perhaps."

Meaning only if there was something in it for her. I stepped back into cooler air. "If you do hear anything, let us know."

"If I hear anything and let you know, I expect something for my troubles." She cocked her head slightly. "Why do you taste so tense?"

"It's the company, I'm afraid."

She waved the comment away. "*That* tension is all part of the fun of having you here. This is different." She considered me for a moment. "Your soul is weary. It fights, and yet it tires of the fight. There is a tension in you I have not felt before."

And wouldn't feel again, as long as I could figure a way to get Kye safely out of my life. "I don't know what you're talking about."

She smiled again. "You lie, guardian, but I appreciate the effort. Its taste is sweet."

Great. Now she was feeding off my emotional vibes, no matter how little I was trying to put out there. "Time for me to go," I said briskly, backing away farther. "Remember; contact us if you hear anything."

She merely smiled so I turned and got the hell out of there.

I'd barely made it down to the ground floor when my phone rang. I knew without looking that it would be Jack. It was that sort of day.

I plucked it free from my pocket and said, "What's up, boss?"

"I want you to get over to Dante's straightaway."

My stomach sank. "Not another beheaded vampire?"

"Nope. This time it's a human. A drained human and a very ugly crowd of onlookers." His voice was grim. "The shit has hit the fan big-time."

Chapter 7

he shit, as Jack had so aptly put it, really did look nasty.

I parked half a street away from Dante's, but even so, as I climbed out of the car, the noise hit me. It was voices and anger and nastiness all rolled into one, and I hoped like hell they had more than one cop down there. Cole and his team might be able to protect themselves, but they shouldn't have to. They were only doing their job.

As was I.

But that didn't stop some fool from lobbing an empty beer can straight at my head as the cops hastily cleared a way through the thirty-strong crowd for me. I caught it with one hand and met the gaze of the drunken fool who'd thrown it. His blue eyes were full of anger, his expression daring me to throw the can back. I raised it but crushed it one-handed instead—lengthwise, not through the middle. His eyes widened a little. Obviously he hadn't thought a woman could be that strong. The cops opened the barriers to let me through and I walked across to the three figures huddled around a small, forlorn-looking body.

Cole looked up as I joined them. There were shadows under his eyes, and I very much doubted they were from spending time with his new lady love. "It's not a vampire kill."

"What? But Jack said—"

"Yeah, I know. It was reported as that, but it's not." He reached out and shifted the dead man's neck, revealing two neat holes.

"It sure as hell looks like a bite to me." I hesitated, and leaned closer. "Except that there's no redness, and no skin reaction."

"Exactly," Cole said heavily. "This is an imitation. A damn fine one, but an imitation all the same."

I squatted down beside him. "Meaning we'll find another wound somewhere on the body."

"Probably. We can't be sure until we get him back for an autopsy."

I studied the frail old man for a moment, wondering if he'd been selected simply because the sight of him would garner more anger and sympathy than someone in his prime. My gaze came to rest on his left leg. A faint hint of blood rode the air, and there seemed to be something bulky wrapped around the upper part of his thigh under his pants. I was betting on a bandage. "Strip him here."

Cole looked at me like I was mad. "The crowd is going to love that."

"The crowd is the reason I'm suggesting it. Do it."

Cole shared a look with both Dusty and Dobbs, then nodded abruptly. As they started stripping him, I rose and stalked over to the mob. They weren't pressing against the barricades just yet, but they were hurling abuse and litter at the cops who stood behind them. It wouldn't take much for this whole situation to explode.

"You, you, and you," I said, pointing to three of the men who appeared to be the ringleaders of this nasty little crowd. "Get over here."

They pushed forward belligerently—big, handsome men with ugly attitudes.

"What?" the middle one said. He was the tallest of them by about three inches, and towered over me by a good five.

"You think vampires did this?"

"We know it. Like we told those men over there, we saw the car. It was a vamp car."

Meaning the windows had been fully shielded against sunlight. "And you know for certain that it was a vamp either driving or being driven in it?"

He frowned. "Who else would fucking drive one of those things?"

"I see." I stepped forward, grabbed him by the shirt, thrust my other hand on his crotch, and none too elegantly hauled him up and over the barrier. He wasn't a small man and it was a huge effort, but it had the desired effect. The crowd fell silent.

"You two," I said, dumping the stranger back on his feet and pointing to his two friends, "join us."

They did. Fast.

With my grip still on the big man's shirt, I dragged him over toward the body. The other two followed without being asked.

Cole and his team had stripped the body and were in the process of unraveling the bandage as we arrived.

"What the fuck?" the big man said, his face an angry red. I couldn't actually tell if it was anger over my treatment of him or at being dragged so close to a corpse. Some people were funny about things like that. "We don't need to see this."

"Ah, but you do, because we don't need your sort spreading rumors."

I hauled him to a stop as Cole pulled the final bit of bandage free. The wound on the old man's leg was obvious—a clean, crisp stroke that sliced from the top of his thigh to down near his knee. The skin split as Cole moved the old man's leg, revealing the layers of fat and muscle and then bone. There were small clots inside the wound, and the skin had a slightly darkened appearance, as if someone had hastily washed the area.

"What do you think that is?" I said to the man.

"A knife wound," he muttered.

"A knife wound that sliced through major arteries and would have caused him to bleed to death," I retorted. "Now, I can't imagine a vampire wasting blood like that. Can you?"

"Maybe whoever did it wanted us to think it wasn't

a vampire," one of the men behind him said, his voice aggressive.

I released the tall man and grabbed his buddy. He squawked as I yanked him forward, moving around the body until we stood near his head. Cole obligingly moved the dead man's neck so that the bite was more evident. I could feel the waves of amusement coming from him, yet you'd never know it from his expression. Dusty and Dobbs were studiously avoiding looking at anyone.

"Do they look like real vampire bites to you?"

"I don't know," he muttered, his gray eyes darting between the body and the crowd, as if he couldn't bear looking at the old man for more than a second. "I'm no expert on vampire bites."

"Well, these men are. Do you care to hear what they have to say, or are you merely interested in stirring up unfounded trouble?"

"I don't want no trouble. None of us do."

"Sure as hell could have fooled me." The crowd behind us was still very silent. "Cole?"

Cole cleared his throat, a brief twitch of his lips the only indication of the amusement I could still feel. "When a vampire bites into flesh, analgesic elements in the saliva react with the skin, causing a swelling around the wound. On the dead, this swelling does not abate. These wounds were very likely punched into the skin by a thick needle or the end of a knife. An autopsy will provide the answer either way."

"Meaning," I said, giving the man a bit of a shake,

"that someone wanted idiots like you to think this man was killed by a vampire."

"Well, we weren't to know he wasn't," the bigger man whined belligerently.

His voice was loud, carrying easily, and a murmur went through the crowd. The tension and anger, which had already begun to dissipate, subsided still further.

"Which is why it's always dangerous to jump to conclusions," I said. "Now, why don't you all leave, before I decide to arrest your asses?"

"What?" someone said. "You can't do that!"

Which was true enough. I couldn't, because they were all human, and the rules that applied to nonhumans certainly didn't apply to them. But they obviously weren't the sharpest tools in the shed, so a little twisting of the truth wasn't going to hurt. Not if it got them to restrain themselves the next time they saw a body being dumped in the street.

"The Directorate has a whole lot more power than the police, and you three were inciting violence against both the police and Directorate personnel. Consider yourselves damn lucky I'm feeling generous today."

They slunk off. By the time they'd gotten over the barriers, the crowd had begun to disperse. I blew out a relieved breath.

"That was very well done," Cole said softly, giving me a grin that reached his cool blue eyes. "Even if a lot of it could be considered stretching the truth."

"Hey, better that than getting your head kicked in by an aggrieved crowd."

"Too right," Dusty muttered, then gave me a smile

and a wink. He had a nice smile on the rare occasions that he flashed it. "Although the heads getting kicked in would be theirs, not ours, and the boss hates that."

I grinned and glanced at my watch. It was nearly eleven-thirty, which meant if I didn't get my butt into gear, I'd be late for my meeting with Kye.

I refused to call it a date. Not when he was basically blackmailing me to be there.

I glanced at Cole. "Could you send me the details of the car once it's traced? I'm betting it's stolen, but Jack will still want me to follow it up."

He nodded. "I sent the details in to headquarters, so it shouldn't take long."

"Thanks."

He nodded and got back to work. I rose and walked back to my car. Time to head home and get changed, because jeans and a top would never be classified as "something nice." Although I refused to wear something sexy, because the damn man didn't deserve that, either.

Of course, finding something that could be classified as nice without being overtly sexy was another matter entirely. I was a werewolf. Sexy was my thing.

In the end I chose a very basic floral sundress, and teamed it with a warm winter cardigan and a black leather belt, which nicely matched the black and white print. Classy and neat, even if the floral print was last year's style. Not that Kye would care.

So why did I?

I grimaced at my own fussiness and, ignoring a

small tremor of excitement, grabbed a change of clothes, then headed out.

Franklin's turned out to be at the top end of La Trobe Street, just down from Exhibition. It was a pretty, blue two-story building with lots of lovely fretwork and arched windows. The glass was mirrored, suggesting it was one-way, and there was very little signage out front—which left me wondering what sort of restaurant this place was, beyond the fact that it was obviously one that didn't want to be easily found.

I parked in one of the spots down the road then walked back, my heels clicking quickly against the concrete—a rhythm that matched my pulse.

There was no handle on the double doors out front, just a discreet buzzer. That had wariness flaring.

It was very tempting just to turn around and walk away, but I didn't trust Kye not to follow through with his threat.

Besides, part of me wanted to know what this place was. A dark and utterly *stupid* part.

I pressed the buzzer lightly and a moment later, a sultry female voice said, "Franklin's. How may we help you?"

"Riley Jenson. I have an appointment with Kye Murphy."

"Ah yes, Mr. Murphy has been waiting for you. Please come in."

The door softly clicked open, and I went through into a small foyer that was all dark marble and gold fittings. A small desk sat to the right, and a plush gold sofa and several potted plants to the left. The petite blonde behind the desk gave me a warm smile.

"Good afternoon, Ms. Jenson," she said, and waved an elegant hand to another door. "If you'll just go through there, Christine will show you to your table."

I did as bidden, but the second I went through that other door, I knew this place wasn't just a restaurant.

The soft music that caressed the air was sensual and erotic—a melody designed to relax and seduce the senses. The air was as heated as the music and rich with the scent of lust and sex and rich, spicy food. Despite my misgivings, I breathed deep, allowing the ambience to soak through my pores, right into my very bones. An answering tremor of excitement coursed through me.

Franklin's was a wolf club—a very *discreet* wolf club. One that obviously catered only to certain levels of clientele. Certainly I'd never heard of this type of club before, but I guess that was no surprise because they weren't targeting the likes of me. It *was* surprising they allowed the likes of Kye, but I guess he could probably afford whatever this place cost. He *was* one of the top hit men in the country, after all.

The door swung shut behind me, and another petite blonde appeared. "Riley Jenson?"

I nodded, my gaze roaming past her, studying the dark wine walls. No cameras, no deadeners, nothing security related that I could see, but I imagined it would all be there. If this place was catering to upper-class clientele, it couldn't afford not to be careful.

The blonde gave me a smile that lit up her brown eyes. A woman who enjoyed her job, obviously. "Mr.

Murphy awaits you in the green room. This way, please."

She escorted me down a long hallway that was all pale gold and green. It wasn't trying to be sexy, just warm and welcoming, and in that it succeeded. There were doors to the left and the right, and the scents coming from them were a mix of food, alcohol, and lust. But not sex. That scent seemed to be drifting down from above, though I could hear no noise that suggested mating. They obviously had good soundproofing.

The blonde stopped at the second to last door to the right, just before a sweeping gold and glass staircase. As she swiped a card through the reader slot, I leaned forward and looked up the stairs. Two oversize doors waited at the top. A grand entrance to a grand dance floor, perhaps.

"There you are, Ms. Jenson."

I gave her a somewhat tense smile and walked in. The room was on the small side, but lushly furnished. The walls were a rich, dark cream and covered on three sides with oil paintings that depicted various forest scenes in which naked people ran about. The fourth was covered by green velvet curtains, and in front of it sat a leather sofa so well padded it looked as if it would envelop you once you sat down. A black table dominated the rest of the room, the chairs well padded and the same rich green as the curtains and the sofa. The far end had been set for two, although the table looked able to seat at least eight.

Kye was leaning against a mantel, although the fire

wasn't lit. Which was just as well, given the warmth in the room. But the air was nothing compared to the heat that flashed between us when his gaze met mine. It hit like a punch to the gut and I stopped, momentarily breathless.

He looked good. *So* good. His black pants fit his long, strong legs superbly and made the most of his well-toned butt. His shirt was roughly rolled up at the sleeves, revealed his muscular arms. The color was dark green, and contrasted richly against the gold of his eyes, making them seem even brighter.

Or maybe that was just the heat in them. The desire.

His gaze swept my body—a caress that left me hot and sweating. I clenched my hands, digging my fingernails into my palms, using the sharp sting as a buffer against need.

I didn't *want* to want this man, but fate had taken that choice from me. But I'd be damned if I'd step into his arms without a fight.

"Why the pretense of a meal, Kye? Why not just save some money and attempt this seduction at one of the regular clubs?"

"Because I rarely go anywhere public these days. In my line of business, that can be dangerous."

"Meaning there's a contract out on your head?"

"Not yet, but I don't believe in taking chances."

"Then use a disguise. You're well versed in the art." I walked across to the table, poured myself wine, then added a little acidly, "Actually, you're pretty damn good at lying, too."

He raised an eyebrow. "And why would you say that?"

"Because it's true." I took a sip of the wine and almost sighed in pleasure at the sweet taste. Brown Brothers really did make a decent white.

Though I *didn't* want to know whether he'd known it was one of my favorites.

"It may be true, but I'm curious as to why you've suddenly mentioned it now."

"Because you lied to me about your discussion with Mandy Jones."

He smiled. The heat of it burned deep inside of me. "I asked her to report the dead vampire simply because, if I'd reported it, you wouldn't have come."

"It could have been any guardian who was sent there."

"Then I would have missed out on seeing your sweet face, wouldn't I?"

I snorted softly. "Cut the crap, Kye." I took off my cardigan, then grabbed the back of the chair and pulled it out to sit down. "What do you want?"

"You."

"You can't have me."

He merely smiled, and this time there was nothing sensual or heated about it. A shiver crawled across my skin.

It didn't abate the need, though. Far from it. My wolf was entranced and she wanted him—heat, ice, danger, and all.

"You would do well to remember, Riley"—his voice was soft and without inflection. The wolf at his deadliest—"that you have people you care about and I do not. I will get what I want, one way or another."

"You hurt anyone I love, and I will kill you."

"No, you won't. You couldn't even shoot that baby vampire." His expression was mocking. "Besides, you love life too much to ever shoot your soul mate."

Yeah, I loved life, but if he hurt Rhoan or Liander or Quinn, then I *would* shoot the bastard and worry about surviving the effects afterward. That he didn't know that showed how little he really understood me.

"I *will* have you," he added softly.

Why? was the question that surged to my lips, but I didn't give it voice because I very much suspected I already knew the answer.

It was the challenge I represented. Nothing more, nothing less.

Which meant that maybe my best option would be to give in to this heat and hope that once he'd gotten what he wanted, he'd leave me in peace.

Of course, giving in might just cause additional problems, and I didn't really need that right now.

"You may get me physically. I certainly can't deny the burn is there." I studied him for a moment, noting the lazy half smile teasing his lips, the determined glint in his eyes. And I suddenly realized the challenge I represented went even deeper than I'd realized.

"But you don't just want my body, do you, Kye?" I added slowly. "You want the complete package. You want what I'm giving Quinn."

He didn't say anything, but I knew I'd guessed right. I gave him a smile that held a nasty edge. "I'm telling you now, no matter what you do, you won't ever have *that*. You may have my soul, but that's all you'll ever get."

Anger flared briefly in his eyes but was just as quickly gone. Control was this man's forte, and he wasn't about to lose it over a well-aimed barb. He pushed away from the mantel and strolled over to the table. I shifted as he sat, crossing my legs and pointing them away from him so that there was no danger of our knees meeting. I wasn't sure my hormones could stand such a touch, however light or accidental.

But he was close enough that his delicious scent and the heat of his body swirled around me, teasing my senses and making my pulse race. I took a large gulp of the wine. It didn't do anything to help lessen the fires.

"I thought you might be hungry after your efforts outside Dante's this morning, so I've already ordered lunch," he said conversationally. "I do hope you like roast lamb."

I leaned back in my chair and wondered who he'd been talking to. Two of my favorite things appearing on the menu was one coincidence too many. "Why were you at Dante's this morning?"

He gave me a smile that was all sharkish charm. "Following a lead."

"Yeah, and tomorrow armies across the world will throw down their arms and live in peace."

"Let's hope not. If everyone lived in peace, I'd be out of a job."

"So what *is* your job this time?"

"Causing problems for you." He glanced around as

the door opened and a waiter entered. "Ah, excellent timing. Thank you, Joseph."

Obviously he came here a *lot* if he was on first-name terms with the waiters, because they certainly weren't wearing name tags. "You didn't answer the question."

"Yes, I did."

Frustration swirled through me, but I bit back my retort and gave the waiter a smile as he placed a plate in front of me. The rich smell of lamb wafted upward, and despite my annoyance, my mouth watered.

I picked up my knife and fork and dug in. I might not want to be there, but I sure as hell wasn't going to waste a delicious meal. Especially when I wasn't paying for it.

Not with money, anyway.

The silence stretched between us. The only sounds stirring the air were soft music and the clink of cutlery against fine china. But while we may not have been talking, I was all too aware of his every move. Of the way his gaze rested on me as he ate. Of my own heart racing and the deepening ache in my body.

Eventually I finished and slid the plate away with a sigh that was part pleasure and part regret. The meal was finished. That just left the rest of it.

"Okay," I said, picking up the wine and filling my glass again. "What is it you really want, Kye?"

He smiled and leaned back in his chair. "Have you got any leads on the beheadings?"

I countered his question by repeating one of my own. "Why were you at Dante's this morning?"

He raised an eyebrow, his gaze briefly sweeping me, coming to rest on my crossed legs. He reached out and snagged one foot before I could react, then slid off the shoe and tossed it to one side. His quick, clever fingers began to knead my instep, and tremors of delight shot up my leg. I licked my lips, torn between the desire to enjoy and the knowledge that *that* would only lead to complications I'd been fighting to avoid.

"I've been employed by a desperate husband," he said softly, his gaze on mine as he continued to rub and stroke my foot. "His wife is a blood whore, and it is endangering his reputation. He's hired me to track her down and take care of her."

"By take care, you mean kill."

"Not directly, as that would do as much damage to his reputation as having a whore for a wife. So I shall arrange an accident that she will not survive."

He said it so flatly, so casually—and I don't know why I was surprised, but I was. Maybe something deep inside—the stupid dark part of me that wanted this man so badly it ached—kept blindly hoping that there was some spark of humanity in him. It would have made this thing between us seem a little more palatable.

But I might as well pray for snow in the middle of a desert.

I tore my foot from his grasp and shifted my legs farther away from him. Amusement glinted in his eyes. So did determination.

"You've just admitted to planning a murder. It happens, and your ass will be in jail quicker than I could say 'thank God.' "

He chuckled. It was a rich, mellow sound that ran across my skin. "There are, at last count, at least a dozen rich young things attending that club of Dante's. I know of eight who are married and cuckolding their husbands, and three of those drink so much they are accidents waiting to happen. You'll never know my target from a real accident."

Which wouldn't stop me from trying if there was a sudden run of accidents among the upper class. "Technically, they're not cuckolding their husbands. Blood whores get off on vampires taking their blood. The clubs cater to that, not sex."

"Most clubs *do* adhere to the rules. Some, like Dante's, do not. Half the upstairs is given over to private rooms, and the whores pay a hefty price to be fully serviced."

"And that's how you're hoping to catch your client's wife? You have the rooms bugged and are recording events?" It also explained why he was so horny. Voyeurism was a part of the wolf culture—and a huge turn-on for most of us.

"Yes, but she hasn't been there for a few days, hence my hanging about catching all your activities."

"So you were there on stakeout when Grant Haven was beheaded?"

"You already know I was. I reported—or got that woman to report—the crime."

"And yet you claim you didn't see anything."

He picked up his empty wineglass and toyed with it

idly, twirling it around his fingers as he had the knife in
the warehouse. "You've never actually *asked* me what I
saw that night."

Fucking hell . . . "Kye," I said acerbically, "what the
hell did you see that night?"

He was silent for a moment, continuing to toy with
his glass. I watched the movements, the quickness of
his fingers, and wondered what those fingers could do
if they played across my flesh.

"Perhaps," he said softly, "it's not so much a matter
of what I saw but what I know."

"What *I* know is I'm barely resisting the urge to haul
your ass downtown, find some nasty murder to pin on
you, and throw your smart mouth in jail."

He merely smiled. "Grant Haven was a member of
the Melbourne vamp council. The rumor is that the
vampire who was beheaded and incinerated two days
before Haven was also a council member."

"And Henry Gateway?"

"I haven't been able to find confirmation one way or
another, but I suspect he might have been, too."

I frowned considering him, considering the information. "Why would three men from the local council
be visiting a place like Dante's when there are more upmarket venues available?"

He smiled. It was a luscious, hungry thing that
swept across my senses as warmly as a caress. "As much
as there are humans who do not wish their addiction
known, there are also vampires who feel the same. Besides, Dante himself is a member of the council. Maybe
they felt safer there."

Yet they obviously weren't. But I guess being on the council at a time when the general vampire population was extremely unhappy about the clubs and the laws surrounding them *might* just make them targets, especially if they were seen as hypocrites for patronizing the blood whore clubs. So was that what was going on here? A bit of retribution from the ranks?

Maybe the fact that all three murders happened near Dante's was some sort of warning to him. Maybe he'd pissed the wrong person off—which, according to Jack, wouldn't have been hard.

Still, if that were the case, why attack the other councilors in the first place? Why not go after him directly?

"How could you know all this?" I said, taking another sip of wine and feeling the mellowness grow. A dangerous situation, given the company. I put down the glass and added, "And why were you even there in the first place? We both know your monitoring equipment wouldn't be anywhere near Dante's."

And even if he'd cut into the feed from Dante's own security cameras, none of them had been pointing into the parking lot.

"I'm interviewing all Dante's regular clientele in an effort to get a clearer picture of my target's behavior." He shrugged, a casual movement that didn't match the intensity of his gaze.

"From what I saw in the club, that's a pretty useless exercise. The whores care for nothing more than their next fix."

He shrugged again. "Leaving nothing to chance is a rule I live by."

And something I'd do well to remember. "How can you be sure the three victims and Dante are—were—members of the local council?"

"I'm a siphon, remember, and stakeouts are boring. Let's just say that, when I'm in the club, I amuse myself by seeing how much information I can steal from a vamp's mind before he becomes aware." He contemplated me for a moment. "Haven's shields were nowhere near as strong as yours."

Starke had told me that Haven had been on vacation and that his first night back was the night he'd been murdered. Meaning either Kye or Starke was lying. But which one? Right now, I had no flaming idea.

"Did you actually see anything the night Haven died?"

"A car taking off in a hurry. A blue Ford, tinted windows. Couldn't see the driver but I did get the plate number." He reached into his pocket, pulled out a slip of paper, and slid it across the table to me.

I ignored it for a moment, meeting his gaze, holding it. "Did you kill Grant Haven?"

"No, I did not." There wasn't a flicker in the amber of his eyes. Nothing to indicate a lie. Part of me wanted to believe him—did believe him—yet I knew this man was a professional killer who probably could lie his way out of hell itself.

There was one way to find out for sure, and yet I couldn't force myself to take that step. Aside from the fact that he was a siphon and able to steal the use of my shields, I didn't really want to get into his thoughts and discover what he really felt about me.

I was too much of a coward to face the reality of *that*. It was far better for my own emotional stability to keep thinking that this was nothing more than a challenge—a game—to him.

The waiter came in through the side door and began clearing the table. I picked up the paper, taking care not to touch Kye's fingers. His writing was neat, careful—much like the man himself. I folded it up and slipped it into my purse.

"Do you wish dessert?" the waiter asked, once he'd finished clearing the dishes.

Kye glanced at me, eyebrow raised. I shook my head. "No, thanks. I really have to go."

A smile twitched Kye's lush lips, but all he said was "Just make it the usual. Thanks, Joseph."

"Very good, sir." The waiter departed, closing the door softly behind him. Music drifted through the silence, its beat shifting from the gentle, erotic melodies that had accompanied our dinner to something more upbeat and danceable. I found my foot tapping, and stilled it abruptly.

"Anything else I should know about?" As a dangerous—and sexy—glint sparked in his eyes, I added hastily, "Anything else you might have seen or heard and forgot to mention?"

"Nothing I can think of."

"Then I need to go."

I rose and walked over to retrieve my shoe. But as I bent to pick it up, he slipped up behind me, his hand clamping around my hip and drawing me back against his long, strong body.

"Dance with me," he murmured, his breath stirring my hair and tickling my neck.

"No," I said, but it came out breathy as his other hand came around my hip and rested on the flat of my stomach. His touch was so hot it felt like he was branding me, and the fires that had been on slow burn during the meal exploded into life.

Slowly, rhythmically, he began to sway in time to the music, his body pressed against mine, guiding me, teasing me. I closed my eyes, knowing I needed to break away if I didn't want this to go any further and yet unable to stop myself from moving in time with the music and his body.

The sensible part of my nature might not want this, but my wolf wasn't always sensible, and she needed his touch as badly as I needed regular doses of coffee.

His lips brushed the nape of my neck and my breath caught. He kissed me again, his mouth butterfly light and yet searing deep. *Don't, don't, don't,* part of me was screaming. And yet I just didn't have the will to pull away.

His right hand eased upward, skimming the soft material of my dress until it rested underneath the swell of my breast. He paused, his breath quickening against my neck, matching the rhythm of my own. For several seconds, we moved to the music, my body trembling, waiting for his caress to rise, *needing* it to rise. But instead, he moved his hand down again. The shudder that rolled through me was unfulfilled longing and relief and disappointment all mixed into one.

His fingertips brushed down my belly, over the hand that held me against him so firmly, then continued on, skimming my pubic mound, sending another shudder of delight coursing through my body. But his caress didn't linger, sliding on down my thigh. When he could reach no farther, his fingers began gathering the material, hitching up the hem of the dress until he could caress skin. Slowly, surely, he began making his way upward again, his fingertips brushing my inner thigh, the heat of his touch branding me, making me ache, quiver. A moan escaped as he cupped my mound and let his clever fingers play along the silk of my panties.

And still we danced, moving to the music, our bodies molded together, his erection pressed against my butt, as heated as the rest of his flesh. I wanted that heat. Needed it.

No, the inner voice screamed, *don't do this.* But the voice of resistance was weaker, drowning under the myriad of sensations flooding through me.

I wanted this. I'd come here for this.

And we both knew it.

Even if I hadn't actually admitted it until right now.

The hand resting on the flat of my stomach moved upward. His fingers found the edge of my dress top and slid underneath, brushing lightly across my erect nipple. I shuddered and arched back against him. He chuckled softly, and kissed my ear, my neck, my shoulder. His teeth caught skin, nipping lightly, playfully. A tremor ran through me and the deep ache increased.

If you can't walk away, that inner voice said, *then seduce him. Don't let him be the aggressor. That way, he wins.*

And I couldn't let him win even this small battle. Not on his terms, anyway.

I shifted, drawing his hands away from my body then turning in his arms. Cupping his face in my hands, I brushed my lips against his, tasting him, teasing him. A shudder went through him and his arms tightened around me, dragging me closer, his crotch grinding against mine. I deepened the kiss, exploring his mouth with my tongue, pressing him backward toward the table.

The backs of his knees hit a chair, and I pushed him down into it. I leaned over him, claiming another kiss as I brushed my fingers down his body to the top of his pants then went farther, scraping them down his fly, feeling his cock jump under the restriction of the material. I did it again, harder this time, and heard the hiss of air escape his lips as his body tensed in reaction.

The third time I did it, he moaned. With a satisfied smile, I quickly undid the top button, then the zipper. His cock leapt free, thick and hard, the tip shiny with pre-cum. I ran my hands along its length, watching his eyes, enjoying the shudders that racked him, the urgency I could sense growing in him.

When it neared the point of no return, I smiled and stepped back, my gaze holding his as I reached for the dress zipper and slowly undid it. He watched me

avidly, hungrily. Heat and lust swirled all around me—
his *and* mine—making my body tremble and little
beads of sweat prickle across my skin.

I slid off the dress then hooked my fingers under the
elastic of my panties and slowly slid them down, my
body moving in tune to the music. His breathing
quickened and his fingers flexed, as if he were fighting
the urge to reach for me.

I smiled and tossed my panties next to my dress, then
stepped forward and straddled him. I wrapped my
arms around his neck then slowly lowered, until the tip
of his cock was barely inside.

"Is this what you want?" I said softly, my lips brushing his as I spoke.

"Yes. God yes," he groaned, his hands going to my
waist in an effort to push me down.

"How badly do you want it?" My thighs were trembling with the effort of resisting the fierce pressure of
his grip and remaining above him. Especially when all
I wanted to do was plunge down on him.

"Very." It came out as little more than a hiss of air. It
tore at my lips, tasting of hunger and desire and need.
Everything I felt, everything I wanted. "God, please."

Those two words tasted very sweet. The man who
controlled every little aspect of his world was begging
me to finish what he'd started. The turnaround was an
incredible turn-on.

I slowly pressed down, shuddering at the sheer
pleasure of it. The heat of him filled me, completed me,
and yet it wasn't just flesh. As I'd feared, it also became a
meeting of souls, a strengthening of the ties between us.

Part of me just wanted to get up and run, but it was already too late for that. So I tried to ignore the heat of him in my mind, concentrating instead on the heat of his flesh and on spiraling pleasure. His breathing was short, sharp, his body rearing under mine. I rode him hard, grinding into him, enjoying the urgency, feeling the pleasurable tautness grow and grow, until my whole body was shaking with the force of it. Then it shattered and I came, shuddering and shaking and moaning at the sheer depth of it—a depth that was body *and* soul. A heartbeat later he followed me into that sweet oblivion, his body fierce in mine as he came, hard.

Then it was over.

For a moment I did nothing more than simply sit there. My body was replete, satisfied, and yet my heart was torn. I wanted this, I *needed* this—needed him— and yet at the same time, I hated it. Hated the need— hated him.

Hated *myself* for not being strong enough to resist what my soul craved.

I pushed away from him, grabbed my clothes, and walked to the door. My hand was on the doorknob when he said, "Same time tomorrow, then."

I didn't say anything, just opened the door and walked out.

And yet I knew that, come tomorrow, I'd be back.

Chapter 8

$\mathcal{I}$ found a bathroom and quickly cleaned myself up, then got dressed. The receptionist bade me a cheery good-bye as I left, and I somehow managed to drag up a smile and a nod as I went out the door.

Once in the car, the shaking began, and for several seconds I could do nothing more than grip the steering wheel against the reaction. God, how was I going to get past this and not have it destroy everything I held dear? I really didn't know, and that frightened me more than anything fate had thrown at me so far.

I needed someone to talk to. Someone who stood outside my own little circle but who knew me well enough to understand. And there was only one person who fit the criteria.

Dia.

I grabbed my phone and quickly dialed her number.

She didn't answer, but her phone clicked over to voicemail, and her sultry tone said, "I'm with a client at the moment, so please leave a message. Riley, if you need to talk, I'll meet you at the usual place at five-thirty."

I smiled as I hung up. Dia was a powerful—and famous—psychic, and this *wasn't* the first time she'd anticipated my need to talk to her. Obviously, whatever vibes I'd been sending out into the universe were strong enough for her to pick up.

I threw my phone back into my handbag, then started up the car and headed for the Directorate.

Kade did something of a double-take when I walked into the office. "Well," he said, leaning back in his chair and giving me a wide grin. "Don't you look delicious. Who'd you dress up for?"

"No one special." I dumped my bag on the desk and plopped down on the chair. "How did it go at the clubs?"

He shrugged, his gaze lingering on my legs as I crossed them and slid forward toward my desk. "It seems that neither woman was a patron at the same club. Crowley preferred Shades, and Bailey was a regular at Indigo Desires and Dark Arts."

None of which I'd heard of, but then, I wasn't a part of that desperate little world. I leaned forward so the scanner could check my eye, then clicked into the system to do a search on the plate number Kye had given me. "I suppose the managers didn't notice anything unusual about either woman in the week leading up to their deaths?"

"Got it in one." He shifted, clicking the mouse, then added, "I went to Dante's, too. The owner wasn't in but I talked to the bartender. He's never seen either woman."

"Which doesn't mean there isn't a connection between your case and mine."

"I still think it's a coincidence, nothing more." He glanced at the screen again. "How'd it go with Vinny?"

"She claims to know nothing about the deaths and states that killing her energy sources like that is nothing more than wasting seduction time and effort."

He raised an eyebrow. "And you believe her?"

I hesitated, and wrinkled my nose. "I don't know. That woman is a consummate liar, and I can't use telepathy in her den."

"So we keep a watch on her?"

"Yeah, though I've got to clear it with Jack first."

"Clear what with me?" Jack said as he stalked into the room.

His expression was dark and my stomach sank. It surely meant another murder had occurred, and we really didn't need that right now.

"I want the current observation on Vinny expanded to a full-time watch. She claims she's not connected with the unsolved deaths, but I'm not sure if I believe her. I think we need to see who is coming in and out of her den." Because she might be a vampire, and might have the usual daylight restrictions, but those restrictions didn't mean she couldn't be involved in some way with these killings. "Even if the murders aren't Vinny's handiwork, they're happening on her turf, and I can't believe she doesn't know about them."

Or that she wouldn't be using that knowledge to her own advantage. Vinny, after all, was all about climbing the financial ladder. And if someone was here with her permission, they'd be paying for the privilege.

"You'll have to arrange the day-shift watch between you, Kade, and Iktar. Rhoan's on another case right now, and we can't afford to have him off it. And make sure your watch is not at the expense of the other investigations." He stopped in front of the coffeemaker, grabbed a cup, and began filling it up. The smell of semiburned beans filled the air and I wrinkled my nose again. Jack didn't seem to care as he took a sip then turned around to face us. "What sort of progress have we got on the beheading cases?"

"I have another possible witness. He gave me the license plate number of a car he saw taking off from the area at the time of the murder."

"That's a start." Jack paused, his gaze meeting mine. "Cole told me about the mess at Dante's this morning. Well done on that."

"Thanks." I glanced at the computer as the search finally spat out the name and address of the car owner. I transferred the information across to police records and started a cross-check search, just to see whether my hunch that the car had been stolen was correct. "I did hear that our beheading victims—*and* Dante Starke—are all members of the Melbourne vampire council. Is that true?"

He studied me for a second, his green eyes giving little away. "Where did you hear that?"

I raised my eyebrows. "The source doesn't really matter, does it?"

"Did Quinn tell you this?"

"No. He gave me a general background on the council, but not specifics. I know he's an advisor, like you."

"You are?" Kade said, surprise in his voice.

"In my capacity as director of the guardian division, yes." Jack's gaze flicked from Kade back to me. "Who sits on either the local or greater council is not something we advertise. There are few outside those two circles who know."

"As you said, the councilors themselves know, and that information is available in their minds for those who know how to grab it."

"So who stole it and told you?"

I hesitated, knowing the answer wasn't going to make him any happier. "Kye."

"Well, that explains the party dress," Kade murmured.

I gave him a dirty look, but the damn man gave me an unrepentant grin, and I knew I was going to be subjected to an interrogation later.

"And what the hell was he doing hanging around Dante's?"

"He's working for a man who's not too happy about the fact that his wife is a blood whore."

"You warned him off killing the woman?"

"I did."

"Good. If the kill proceeds, we'll nab him. At least it'll mean one less monster on the streets."

I didn't say anything. I hadn't told Jack that Kye was my soul mate, but it was interesting that he used "nab" instead of "kill." Maybe Quinn had mentioned it.

"That still doesn't explain how the bastard knew our victims—and Dante—are councilors," Jack continued.

I shrugged. "Apparently he got bored during the stakeout and started reading vampire minds. Haven's was one of them."

"And you believe that's all he did? Because it's a bit of a damn coincidence that we have a hired killer hanging about Dante's at the same time we have a rash of beheadings."

"He denied beheading them. I believe him."

"And you confirmed his denial by reading his thoughts?"

I hesitated. "I actually can't. He's a siphon, remember, so he basically steals the strength of my own shields."

I didn't mention that I didn't even try—that I'd been too scared to try. Jack would never have understood reasoning like that.

"Meaning you can't be one hundred percent certain." Jack shook his head. "I want to know his movements. Grab a skin-tracker from research and place it on him."

"He'll find it—"

"Not these he won't."

I wouldn't bet on it, but I wasn't about to argue about the point. Not when Jack had that look in his eyes. "If our victims were councilors, why weren't we told? Surely it has some relevance?"

"Why would it? No one knows who the councilors are just so they can't become targets."

I frowned. "So how does the daily council business get run? There has to be some sort of public face for the council, doesn't there?"

"There's a general office if people wish to bring something to the council's notice. All decisions are filtered down the ranks via telepathy from the old ones."

Quinn was an old one. Was he one of the relayers of information? Somehow, I just couldn't see it. It seemed too passive for someone who'd once been a cazador.

"But it wasn't just Haven and Gateway. There's the other one—"

"Who we believe is Norman Garrent. He didn't report to the meeting last night, and hasn't been sighted for several nights."

"So, we *do* have three dead councilors. That suggests a pattern to me."

"Now that another one of them—Harvey Bastiel— has also been found beheaded, I suspect you're right." He took a sip of his drink and grimaced. But not, I suspected, because of the taste of the coffee. After all, while he might prefer the top-shelf stuff, he didn't care what it tasted like, as long as it was hot. "Cole and his team are on their way there now. I want you to follow. Bastiel's housekeeper was killed, as well."

Meaning it was possible her soul was hanging about for a chat. "I gather you—or the greater council—is currently in the process of warning the remaining members of the Melbourne council that there could be a psycho after them?"

"They knew after the first beheading."

It was a damn shame *we* hadn't. I blew out a breath, then glanced down as the computer beeped. The car *had* been stolen. The owner probably wouldn't be able to tell me much more than what was already in the police report, but I guess it still had to be chased up. I grabbed a pen and wrote down her name and address. "After Bastiel's, I'll head over to Vinny's and start the watch, but I've got a meeting with Dia at five-thirty. Can we get one of the night-shift guys to take over after five?"

He frowned. "I'm not sure that this is the sort of case Dia can help us with."

"Right now, with no solid leads, I'm willing to give it a go."

"Just don't sit there on my time drinking coffee and chatting about the weather," he said heavily. "Or I will take it out of your salary."

I grinned. "As if I would do that."

He harrumphed and walked out. I glanced at Kade. "You available to do some watching tomorrow?"

He grimaced. "It's not my favorite thing, you know that. Besides, I thought you wanted help with the beheadings. I can't do both."

He could if he really wanted to—but even as that thought crossed my mind, I knew I wasn't really being fair. He had just as many unsolved cases on his plate as I did, and Jack would be all over him if he dropped everything to help me.

Plus he had a family and babies to go home to, and I didn't.

Not yet, anyway, I thought with an inner shiver.

God, how would *that* change my life? How would it change my attitude to this job and the risks it involved?

It had taken me a long time to admit I actually enjoyed being a guardian, but the chase and the danger were extremely addictive. It was in my blood now, and giving it up would not be easy.

But giving up one dream after another hadn't been easy, either, and having a baby was the last one left. The only one that I really had any chance of fulfilling.

It should have been an easy choice, a simple one. But it wasn't.

I liked what I did. *Loved* what I did. We made a difference, and that made the risks and the dangers worthwhile. And however much I might have fought becoming a guardian, it made me feel like I'd finally found something I was meant to do.

And yet, I didn't want any child of mine growing up without the love of a pack around him—or her—and that pack *had* to be more than just Liander, however much he might cherish our offspring if the worst happened. Rhoan and I only ever had our mother growing up, and however much she might have loved us, it wasn't a pack. We were never considered a pack, and that isolation had echoed through our relationships both as children and as grown-ups.

I didn't want that loneliness—that feeling of never really belonging—for any child of mine.

"Earth to Riley. Come in, Riley."

I blinked and glanced at Kade. "What?"

"I said I'll do a couple of hours, but that's all I can manage."

"Great. What about around lunchtime?"

He raised an eyebrow. "Another hot date with a certain werewolf?"

"It's not a date." More a battle of wills. "I don't want anyone killed, Kade, so I'll play his games until he gets tired of them or I can find something to pin on his ass and get him out of my hair."

"I'm sure if you tell Jack about the threat, he'll handle the situation appropriately."

"Maybe, but I'd prefer to handle it myself."

"Then I'll just hope that no one you care about ends up getting hurt, because I do not trust that man."

"Don't worry, neither do I." I collected my purse, then walked across to his desk and kissed his cheek. "Don't suppose you'd like to help me out with one more thing?"

His gaze slid from my face to my breasts, which were on view thanks to the fact that the dress top had gaped forward when I bent over. "If it involves handling the beautiful ladies hanging in front of me, most definitely."

I grinned and handed him the paper with Harriet Morgan's address on it. "Would you mind going to talk to this woman for me? Her car was seen leaving the beheading scene, but she reported it stolen the day before. Someone needs to talk to her and check her story."

He barely even glanced at the paper before putting it down on the desk. His big hands cupped my breasts, holding them almost reverently. "Are you sure these beauties don't need a good massage?"

I chuckled and gently pulled back. "I'm sure."

He sighed dramatically. "I do miss them, you know."

"You didn't have them—or me—that often."

"I know. That's the most regrettable aspect of this whole situation."

I shook my head and grabbed my keys. "You're incorrigible."

"Totally." He gave me a smile that was both cheeky and sexy. "I will get you back into my arms one day. You know that, don't you?"

"When hell freezes over, or Jack gives us the go-ahead. And you know which one is more likely to happen first," I said, then waved and headed out the door and down to research.

Harvey Bastiel lived in Hampton—a beachside suburb one down from Brighton, but without Brighton's high-end reputation or price tag. Which meant the properties near the beach here went for a lowly one million rather than two or more.

Bastiel's house was actually several streets back from the beach, but it was a beautiful old California bungalow located in what was known as the "period precinct," so the price tag was right up there with houses that possessed a beach view.

I parked behind Cole's van and climbed out. The sea air spun around me, crisp and salty, and I breathed deep. It didn't do much to wash the tiredness from my system, but then, getting a good night's sleep was probably the only cure for that.

I swung open the picket gate and walked up a path lined with cream jonquils. Their sweet scent spun around me, but it was laced with the aroma of fresh blood and death emanations from the open front door. There were dusted fingerprints on both the door and the frame, and Dobbs knelt several feet inside, carefully removing what looked like bits of flesh from the shiny wooden floor. He looked up as I entered and gave me a tight smile.

"The housekeeper was shot, but Bastiel was killed the same way as the others."

"Any sign of forced entry?"

He shook his head. "It looks like the housekeeper came into the house, saw what was happening, and made a run for it. She was shot in the living room."

"Why run into the living room? Why not run straight for the door?"

He shrugged. "People don't always think straight when someone is trying to kill them."

I guess that was true. And being confronted with a gunman in your workplace wasn't the same everyday occurrence for most folk that it was for us. "What time was she killed?"

"We're estimating somewhere between five and seven this morning, but we won't know for sure until we get back to the lab."

Five was awfully early for a housekeeper to arrive, I would have thought. "And Bastiel? Where was he killed?"

"In his bed." He indicated the hallway with his chin. "Cole's down there now."

I carefully stepped around the little globules, then headed down the hallway, my footsteps echoing sharply on the floorboards. The master bedroom was the third doorway along.

Cole glanced up as I stepped into the room. His craggy face showed signs of exhaustion. "I'm getting a weird sense of déjà vu."

"Why?" My gaze went past him to the body in the bed. If it wasn't for the fact that the white sheets were stained crimson, it would almost be easy to believe that Bastiel was asleep rather than dead.

"Because of this." Cole waved a hand at the body on the bed. "Vampires lying still while someone hacks away at their necks. We had another case like this a few months back, remember?"

How could I forget? That case had brought me Kye, and all the inherent heartache that came with him. "But I thought you said there was nothing in the toxicology reports or the tissue samples of the other victims that suggests drugs of any kind. Wouldn't the witch dust show up in the lab?"

"*That* stuff would, because we've analyzed it and know its contents. But what if it's something similar, consisting of ingredients we haven't come across? If they were natural, they wouldn't necessarily be flagged."

"I guess that's possible." And it suggested that *these* murders had been planned well ahead of time. It wasn't easy to find a witch in this city—not one who dealt with the dark arts, anyway.

I flared my nostrils and cast aside both the rich metallic tang of blood and Cole's deeper, spicier aroma. The undernotes swirling though the air ran rich with the scent of vampire, human, furniture polish, and wood smoke. And there was something else—something that was little more than a nebulous foulness that tickled the back of my throat and made me want to cough.

"There *is* something odd here." I took a deeper breath, but the scent remained annoyingly elusive and undefined. The room itself held no hints as to what it might be. My gaze fell on the light layer of dust sitting behind the bedside lamp. "You might want to get some dust samples from the room, just in case."

"I already have." He paused, picking up what looked like a piece of lint and putting it into a plastic bag. "This odd scent you mentioned—did you smell it at either of the other murders?"

I frowned, thinking back. I *had* smelled something odd at Gateway's—something just as nebulous and out of place. But Kye had arrived not long after I'd scented it and had basically blown any memory of it out of the water.

Until now.

"There was a similar scent at Gateway's."

"Why didn't you mention it in your report?"

"Because I couldn't be sure that it wasn't just due to the mold in the bathroom."

And if I *had* gone back into the bathroom, it probably wouldn't have sparked any memories anyway, because it just didn't smell the same as the other witch dust.

I glanced around the room again. Nothing seemed to have been disturbed. There was a huge gold watch and a wallet filled with cash on the dresser, and several expensively framed paintings on the walls. The only link between the three—now four—beheaded men seemed to be the fact that they were all on the Melbourne council.

So what I needed to find out was who, exactly, the council had pissed off lately. And I very much doubted that it was going to be an easy task. I had no idea who the members were—besides Dante, that is, and I really *didn't* want to go talk to that man again—and Jack had showed no inclination to share information about the rest of them. Maybe he figured I didn't need to know any more than I already did, or maybe it was just the simple fact that he wasn't allowed to tell me. He was an advisor, after all. Maybe he had to get permission from the greater council before he could reveal that sort of information. And ruling bodies the world over never made it easy for anyone to get to them.

Although killers never seemed to have a problem.

My only real option was talking to Quinn. He might not have told me much about the councils, but he'd said a whole lot more than Jack, so he just might be persuaded to give me another name. If I could talk to someone—someone who wasn't sex on legs—I might just have a real chance of cracking this damn case.

I returned my attention to Cole. "Any indication on how our killer got into the house?"

"Back door was jimmied. The killer must have moved extraordinarily fast, because it appeared Bastiel had gotten no further than flipping the sheet off his face."

I frowned. "The only race who can move that fast is another vampire."

"There are several shifters who can move almost as quickly as a vampire, and almost would be fast enough in this case. A vampire's reactions tend to be slightly slower when they're waking from daytime slumber."

Which was why, throughout human history, those suspected of being vampires were staked during the daylight hours. If the staker was human, it gave them a fighting chance. Of course, opening any younger vamp's den to sunlight would have done just as good a job, but humans seemed to prefer the one-two punch, just to be sure.

"It doesn't explain how the others were caught, though. They were both awake and aware."

Cole grimaced. "You've seen the witch dust in action, so you tell me—does it act fast enough to stop a vampire reacting against an attack?"

I wrinkled my nose, remembering the zombie throwing the dust in my face and just how quickly it sucked away resistance. I'd been lucky—that lot of dust had been targeted toward vamps, not dhampires, and my werewolf blood had saved me. "Yeah, it does."

"Then that's your answer. We just have to pin down the ingredients for future reference." He gave me a weary smile. "If you could remember to grab a sample when you catch the killer, that would be of great help."

I snorted softly and waved a hand at the body. "I guess the murderer has to be nonhuman. It can't be easy to hack someone's head off like that."

"A nonhuman would definitely manage it more easily than a human, no matter how strong that human was."

"So, basically, I'm looking for a nonhuman with a grudge against the vampire council. That should be easy to pin down."

Cole raised his eyebrows. "All the victims are Melbourne council members?"

"Yes. And Jack thinks the vampire who was incinerated *before* the first beheading was also a council member." I paused. "Why wouldn't he tell you that?"

Cole snorted. "The councils are a secretive bunch of bastards, that's why. I doubt Jack would be able even to hint he knows who's who without seeking their permission first."

Which was basically what I'd figured. "It doesn't make our job any easier, though."

"I would hazard a guess that it wouldn't be a major concern for them." He sniffed—a disdainful sound. "They might pay lip service to the Directorate and human rules in general, but I daresay they have their own methods of dealing with situations like this."

Yeah, and they used to be called cazadors. What they were called now was anyone's guess.

"But as it's us dealing with the bodies and the press and the public, you'd think they'd be a little more helpful—especially given that they want this killer caught as much as we do."

"When have vampires ever been overly helpful if it doesn't suit them?" Cole snorted softly. "Director Hunter, Jack, and Quinn are the exceptions, not the rule."

I studied him keenly for a moment, then said, "That's a pretty fierce attitude, considering who we work for and with."

He shrugged. "Just because I think the majority are arrogant sods doesn't belittle what we do at the Directorate. We make a difference, and we stand between what are basically predators and their prey. That more than makes up for any quibbles I might have about who I have to work with at times."

"So the attitude you gave me when I first started working as a guardian was because I'm just as much a vampire as a werewolf?"

He grinned. It wiped the weariness from his face and sparkled in his bright eyes. "It certainly was. But you're actually not half bad, considering you've got two lots of bad blood."

I clapped a hand to my chest. "Be still my heart— that almost sounded like a compliment."

"As if." His smile faded a little, but the remnants still warmed the corners of his eyes, and some of the tension in him seemed to have faded. "Now, if you don't mind, I have work to do, so move those distractingly long legs of yours into another room."

"Now, that sounds more like the Cole I know and love." I gave him a sketchy salute good-bye and obeyed.

The rest of the house didn't reveal much. Bastiel

might have been on the council, but his study didn't hold any clues as to when or where they met. Maybe all such information was sent via a general telepathic broadcast to the appropriate members. I broke open a locked drawer in his desk, but it didn't hold much more than several checkbooks and a netbook. The latter had fingerprint locks installed, so while it might have held the information I was looking for, it was more Cole's field than mine. The kitchen and dining area at the back of the house didn't hold anything in the way of revelations, either—other than the fact Bastiel was something of a neat freak. Everything gleamed, and there wasn't a speck of dust anywhere.

I was walking back up the hall to the study when the air suddenly became chilled.

It was a sensation I was all too familiar with. There was a soul here, and it wanted to speak.

Goose bumps crawled across my skin as I walked forward slowly. Dusty knelt near the body of the woman, carefully plucking a hair from her blue woolen cardigan. He glanced up as I walked into the living room, then his gaze intensified and he straightened abruptly. "You sense something?"

"Her soul is here."

"You want me to leave?"

"No." I paused, trying to pinpoint where the chill seemed to be coming from. Surprisingly, it wasn't near her body but rather over near the big bay window. "What was the housekeeper's name?"

"Helen Hills."

"Helen," I said softly, "why do you linger here? What do you need to say or do?"

My ability to communicate with the dead had gotten a lot stronger in recent months, and their ability to gain shape and materialize long enough actually to speak in my presence had grown. So it seemed Cole's theory that they were likewise using my strength to take shape was true—and these days the mere act of talking to the spirit world left me a whole lot weaker than I liked to admit.

The chill in the air got fiercer, until it felt like fingers of ice were creeping into my bones. No one could really explain why it felt like these souls brought the chill of the underworld with them, but the general consensus was that it had something to do with them being in between—neither here nor in heaven nor hell, or wherever else it was that souls went to.

Something stirred against the sunlight streaming in through the window. A wisp of thicker air that held no shape and couldn't even be defined as smoke.

"Helen?" I repeated. "Do you need to speak to me? Have you got anything you want to say?"

Her soul was little more than a barely visible wisp of white vapor, with no features and no body. But her thoughts reached out all the same.

Why? she said. *Why did we need to die?*

"I can't tell you that, Helen. Not until I catch whoever did this to you and your boss."

For a moment there was no answer, but the chill got stronger, until my fingers and nose ached with the fierceness of it. Energy flowed around me, out of me, building in the air, giving the soul the strength to speak.

But it makes no sense. Mr. Bastiel was a nice man, even if he was a vampire.

"Nice people die all the time, Helen. It often doesn't make sense or seem right." I paused as a sliver of weakness pulled at my muscles. She seemed to be sucking more energy than the souls of the past, and that meant I'd better hurry before she drained me too greatly. That was the one fear I had about doing this—that these souls would drag me into the shadow depths with them if I wasn't careful. "What can you tell me about the man who broke into the house and killed you both?"

It wasn't one man. It was two.

Surprise rippled through me. Up until now, there'd been no hint that two men had been involved in these murders. But then, we had very little in the way of hard clues. "Are you sure?"

Yes. One was standing back, his arms crossed. He had a camera in his hand, but he wasn't using it. The other had a saw. She paused, and if she'd had a physical body, she would have shuddered. As it was, her horror rolled through my mind, stark and brutal. *He was hacking at Mr. Bastiel's neck. There was blood . . .*

I cut in, not sure I could stand another roll of horror through my mind. "Can you describe either of the men, Helen?"

She didn't answer for several seconds, her energy sucking at mine until she added, *One was a vampire. I can sense them, you know? I don't know about the other one, because I wasn't near enough to catch his scent. But he was tall and fit-looking. Both of them were.*

None of which was particularly helpful when it came to tracking down these killers. "And you can't tell me anything else about them?"

The energy in the air climbed another notch, making the small hairs along the nape of my neck and along my arms stand on end. The trembling in my muscles was getting stronger.

Finally, she said, *The vampire wasn't the type who took blood. They smell a little different from what this one did.*

Meaning we were dealing with an emo vamp? In this case as well as the other? What were the goddamn chances of that happening without there being some sort of connection?

Which meant that my watch on Vinny had just become more important than ever. She might not be involved in either of these killings, but she surely had to know who was. Vampires—whatever the make— were very territorial. If there was another emo working on Vinny's patch, she'd know about it. And be profiting by it in some way.

"There's nothing else you can tell me?"

Well, they were both extremely good-looking. And well dressed. Her voice seemed softer, but maybe that was a result of my growing fatigue. *But it all happened so quick, you know? I saw them, and ran. I tried getting to the phone in the living room to ring the police, but there was a gunshot. Then this . . .*

"Can you give me a description of them?"

There was no response. The energy flowing around

me was ebbing along with my strength. Maybe she no longer *could* answer.

"Thank you for your help, Helen." I hesitated, then added, "You can move on now, if you want to."

Her sigh echoed through my mind, then her fragile form disintegrated and the remaining energy burning though the air disappeared with it.

I grabbed at the bookcase as my knees threatened to give way and took several deep breaths in an effort to clear the tension and fatigue still rolling through me. It didn't help much.

"Here," Dusty said roughly, and shoved a steaming mug of coffee at me. "We figured you might need this if you did connect with the soul."

"I think I love you." I wrapped my hands around the mug, trying to get some warmth back into my fingers. "Was Helen Hills a werewolf?"

"We haven't checked. Why?"

"Because she spoke of smelling people." I glanced around as Cole walked into the room, his expression one of concern as his gaze swept me. He seemed to relax a little when he saw that I'd suffered no outward damage from my communication with the soul, and that warmed me more than the drink. "Our soul said there were two men involved. One of them was a vampire."

"And the other?"

"She said she wasn't close enough to catch his scent, but he was carrying a camera he didn't use. The vampire was doing the beheading."

"Well, that's going to put a cat among our vampire

pigeons, isn't it?" He frowned. "Why in the hell would they bring a camera and not use it?"

"I'll ask the bad guys that when I catch them." I took a sip of coffee. The heat of it slid right down to my belly and I had to resist the urge to sigh in pleasure. I took another sip, then added, "At least this might ease the tension on the streets. It isn't humans doing this, so the vamp population can stop getting so uppity."

"My natural response would be to state that vamps are reborn uppity, but I know a fair few humans who could be classified that way, too."

"Yeah, and more than a few of them are journalists."

He grinned. "Seems I'm not the only one with an unsavory attitude. Jack would not approve."

"Jack himself is not fond of the way some reporters tend to oversensationalize these types of events. And if they hadn't disobeyed the media blackout, we would not have been confronted by that lynch mob."

"True." Cole grimaced and scrubbed a hand through his hair. "And whoever our two killers are, they're damn good, because we're not finding much in the way of clues."

Which meant it was more important than ever that I got to talk to someone on the council.

"Well, we have a vampire involved in the killings, and we have council members as the victims, so it's not hard to guess what the connection is. All we have to do is find the why *behind* that connection."

"I wish you luck with that," Dusty muttered.

"I'm going to need it." I drained the coffee in several gulps, just about scalding my mouth. I didn't care, because its heat burned all the way down, chasing the last of the chill from my flesh.

If only I could get rid of the weakness as easily.

I pushed away from the bookcase. The room spun a little, but my knees held up just fine, even if my muscles were still trembling.

"Go get a burger before you do anything else," Cole commented. "You're still looking rather pale."

"It'll be my first port of call, Dr. Reece."

"Idiot," he said, and walked out of the room.

I gave a grinning Dusty a nod good-bye and headed out to my car. Which took more out of me than I cared to admit. With my hands still shaking, I dug my phone out of my bag, hit the vid button, and dialed Quinn.

He answered on the second ring, but the call remained voice only. Which meant he was somewhere other than his office. "Hey, lovely lady, this is a nice surprise."

"I couldn't go another second without hearing your dulcet Irish tones," I replied, a smile twitching my lips.

"As much as I wish that were true, I know it's not. What can I do for you?"

"Besides take me out for dinner, you mean?"

"I shall have the helicopter prepared and take you somewhere exotic."

My smile grew. There were benefits to having an extremely rich boyfriend. "I thought you had a date with your friend Julien tonight?"

"But not until eleven. He doesn't believe in hitting the clubs any earlier, because he doesn't believe they really start getting interesting before then."

"Then he really does need to visit a wolf club." They were interesting *any* time, day or night. "And I'm actually calling because I need your help with a case."

He didn't answer immediately. In the background, doors swished open, then came the echo of his quick steps. I knew that sound—he was just entering his office building. "What sort of help?"

"The three vampires beheaded are all on the Melbourne council. I need to talk to one of the councilors to see what decision they might have made recently that could have pissed someone off this much."

He hesitated. "That won't be easy."

"As I gathered when Jack didn't actually suggest it."

More doors swished closed, and an electronic voice started giving floor numbers. He was more than likely in the express to the fiftieth floor—an elevator I hated. The damn thing moved too fast for my liking.

"For the very good reason that he's probably doing it himself."

"Maybe he is, but I'd still prefer to talk to someone myself. He has to be respectful. I don't."

"You will if you want to get anywhere near the councilors. They tend to be even more old-fashioned than I am."

"Yeah," I said dryly. "They're so old-fashioned they attend clubs to service blood whores."

"Bastiel didn't."

I raised my eyebrows. "You've already heard about that?"

"Bad news always travels fast." His voice was as dry

as mine. "I'm gathering you know about Dante already?"

"Yeah, and I want to avoid him as much as possible. That man is a sexual predator."

"A werewolf backing away from another predator?" Surprise and amusement ran through his voice. "I never thought I'd live to see the day."

"Meaning you want me to go see the man?"

He laughed. "No. I'll talk to one of the other councilors and see if he'll agree to a meeting. More than that I can't promise."

"Thanks for trying."

"As I said, no promises. I'll be finished with work at six. Where do you want me to meet you?"

"I'm meeting Dia at our usual place in Brunswick at five-thirty."

"For work or pleasure?"

"Mainly pleasure, but I'm on Jack's time so I'll ask her an official question or two."

"Then I'll meet you at Essendon at seven-thirty," he said. "That should give you enough time after the meeting to get home, get changed, and meet me."

With a silly grin of anticipation on my face, I hung up then started the car and headed over to Vinny's. I grabbed a couple of burgers at the local McDonald's, then drove around until I found a spot that was reasonably inconspicuous but allowed me to watch the front door, and settled in for the wait.

It ended up being a very long wait.

Nothing happened. No one went in, and no one went out. Some kid with scruffy blond hair and a bored expression tried to key my car until my growl notified him of the fact I was actually inside. His expression and subsequent flight eased the boredom a little.

As five o'clock neared, I began to get a little restless, wondering if Jack had forgotten to get someone in to replace me. The thought had barely crossed my mind when my phone rang.

"Riley," Benson said, "Jack says if you don't start leaving the com-link on when you're working, he'll replace it with one you can't turn off."

I hurriedly pressed said com-link but didn't bother apologizing. "What's the problem?"

"Nothing. Talvin's in place at Vinny's if you want to leave for your meeting with Dia."

"Thanks for letting me know."

"You don't have to thank me for doing my job."

But his tone suggested he appreciated it. I hung up, then tossed the phone into my bag and headed for Brunswick. I found parking several streets away from the restaurant and walked back. The sidewalk tables were all full and Dia wasn't at any of them. Meaning she more than likely had Risa with her, as the restaurant boasted a secure children's play area at the back of the main room. I'd barely walked through the door when the little girl in question came bounding out of the shadows, her white pigtails flying as she flung herself into my arms.

"Hey, monkey," I said, grinning as her chubby little arms wound themselves around my neck and she planted a slobbery kiss on my cheek. She smelled of soap and powder and everything that was good in this world. "How was swimming today?"

Her amazingly bright violet eyes twinkled with mischief. "Swimming sucked!"

I just about choked on my own laughter. Dia was going to kill me for teaching her *that* particular expression.

"I thought you loved the water?"

"Water sucks."

I bit down my grin as I walked through the restaurant. Dia was in the far corner, sitting in a booth near the large play area. She was, as usual, both immaculate and stunning. Her hair, like her daughter's, was a pure whitish silver that shone with an almost unnatural brilliance, and when combined with the luminous blue of her eyes and the matching brightness of her dress, she was hard to miss.

Of course, neither the blue of Dia's eyes nor her silver hair was natural. Dia wasn't only a psychic but a clone with Helki shape-shifting genes, and she could subtly alter her appearance as easily as I could become a wolf. The silver and blue suited her psychic business better—and enabled her to use her true form when she didn't want to be noticed.

Little Risa's coloring was natural, and had obviously come from her father, although Dia never talked about him. Nor was there mention of him on Risa's birth certificate.

Dia's gaze met mine as I neared the table. Few would have guessed she was blind, because there was an amazing directness in her gaze. Of course, despite her blindness, she *could* see, thanks to the presence of a creature known as a Fravardin—an unseen guardian spirit that was by her side whenever she went outside the confines of her house. By linking lightly to the creature's mind, Dia was able to move with a serenity and grace that belied her handicap. I had no idea where the creature was right now, but given she was looking directly at me, it had to be somewhere close.

"You," she said heavily, "have created a monster."

"Who knew she'd take the word up with such gusto?" I slid into the U-shaped booth and untwined Risa's arms from around my neck, putting her on the seat beside me.

"Coke?" she said hopefully.

"I don't think your mom would approve," I said. Especially not right now.

I half expected the little girl to come out with the immortal "Mommy sucks," but she leaned forward on the table and gave Dia the sweetest of smiles. "Please, Mommy?" she said, the bottom lip quivering ever so slightly.

The child really knew how to work it. I grinned and leaned back in the seat, watching Dia struggle to control her smile.

"A small one," she said, "and only if you go play for a while."

Risa flung herself at Dia, gave her a big slobbery kiss, then scrambled over her and ran for the play equipment.

"That child is going to be *so* dangerous to the male

population when she gets older," I said, shoving my handbag onto the seat beside me.

"Especially given she seems to think you're a brilliant role model," Dia said dryly.

"Well, let's face it, she could do far worse as role models go. At least I work on the side of the angels."

"Yes." Dia's expression darkened. "I'm not sure she will, though."

I frowned. "You've had a vision about her future?"

She nodded. "It was a little confused. There were angels and demons and goodness knows what else."

"Angels?" I had no trouble believing that demons existed—after all, I'd crossed paths with hellhounds on several occasions, and they were apparently classified as low-level demons—but for some reason, I couldn't quite believe that angels really existed. But maybe it was simply a lack of solid proof. I hadn't really believed in demons, either—until one of them had tried to rip me to shreds.

But angel-like creatures *had* existed, and they'd been called the Aedh. Quinn's father had been a priest of the Aedh, and while Quinn might not have gotten the wings, he did have many of their abilities. Although just how many—and what they were—was something he'd never really explained.

Still, no surprise there. He might have opened up a whole lot more in recent months, but my sexy old vampire still had many, many secrets.

"Which is why I needed to talk to you," Dia said.

"Me?" I glanced up as the waitress appeared at our

table. Once we'd placed our orders, I added, "I don't know a whole lot about men with wings, I'm afraid."

She smiled. "You know more than me, though. Or, rather, Quinn does."

I raised an eyebrow. "So Risa's father was an Aedh?"

"If that's what you call one of those men with wings, then yes."

"I didn't even know they still existed," I murmured. "How the hell did you meet him?"

She smiled again, but suddenly there was something haunted in her eyes. "Sometimes there are personal bonuses when you talk to the spirit world."

"And personal costs?" I said softly.

"Yeah." She grimaced. "I might have gotten my daughter, but I saw my death. It's not pretty."

"But you have the Fravardin to protect you."

"There are some things that not even the Fravardin can conquer."

As evidenced by the fact that Misha—Dia's clone brother—had been murdered despite the protection of his own Fravardin.

I studied her for a moment, concerned. "It's not going to be soon, is it?"

"No. Risa will be well grown by the time it happens."

"At least that's something." Although it would be hell to live with that knowledge. Personally, I'd rather not know. "So how does one go about meeting one of the elusive Aedh?"

"I met mine in a bar." She shrugged. "One night, and I was pregnant."

"And you haven't seen him since?"

"No, but Risa's talents are growing at an extraordinary rate. She needs more guidance than I can give her."

"Which is where Quinn comes in."

"Yes." Her gaze swept my face. "Do you think he will mind?"

I didn't think kids were on Quinn's list of top ten things to experience, but he hadn't actually been adverse to the idea of my kid coming into his life, so maybe my vampire was getting accustomed to the idea. "I'll ask and find out."

"Thank you." She squeezed my hand, and some of the tension riding her shoulders seemed to dissipate. "Now, how can I help you?"

Now that the moment had arrived to talk about Kye, I suddenly found myself reluctant to do so. As *if* keeping him secret would make the situation any better. With a wry smile at my own stupid avoidance, I said, "You know about the beheadings?"

"I think you'd have to be living in a sealed box not to know about them." She crossed her arms on the table. "That's the case you're investigating?"

"Yes, unfortunately." I smiled a thank-you up at the waitress as she deposited our drinks and banana cake.

Risa appeared from nowhere, clambering over her mother in her haste to get to her Coke. With the straw in her mouth and her chubby cheeks glowing, she looked a picture of bliss as she downed her drink.

I spooned a mouthful of the luscious cake and probably had a similar look of bliss on my face. "We really haven't got a lot to go on, but we need to get this case solved—and fast."

"Before the vampires and the humans start taking aim at one another, no doubt."

"Preferably, yes. Although it's not actually humans doing the killing but another vampire."

Dia raised a pale eyebrow. "Really? That's not what the papers are saying."

"Which is why you should never believe everything you read."

She frowned. "Why hasn't the information been released? It would surely diffuse the situation."

"We only just discovered it. I daresay Jack will make a press conference his next priority."

"But you still need a quick solve, just in case the public decides not to believe what is printed?"

"Exactly." I took another bite of cake. "Right now, I have no concrete clues and I'm willing to give anything a try."

Surprise flitted through her bright eyes. "Meaning you're willing to let me give you a reading?"

I hesitated. I might be discussing the case, but I'd really come here to sound her out about Kye. And letting her do a reading just might reveal a whole lot more about my soul mate than I really wanted to know. And yet, what choice did I have? If she could find something useful to stop these murders, then uncovering more about Kye was a small price to pay. "Usual restrictions apply. I do not want to know what the future holds."

"You know I can't always control where the visions go."

"I know. I just don't want to hear the nitty-gritty details of just what might happen to my love life in my future." I waved the spoon at her. "I'd rather muddle along at my own speed."

"I can understand, given the future I've been shown." She took a sip of coffee, then pushed it to one side. "Give me your hand."

She held out a hand, palm up. I took a large gulp of coffee to fortify myself, then placed my hand in hers. Her eyes closed and her fingers wrapped around mine. Her skin was cool initially, but electricity soon surged, jumping from her skin to mine and spreading up my arm like wildfire. It made the hairs on my arms stand on end and my pulse race, and it felt like her essence was somehow entwining around mine. It was a merging that was both metaphysical and ghostly, and stronger than anything she'd done before. The wolf inside instinctively bared her teeth, ready to fight against the intruder, but this was a force I'd invited in, and I couldn't back away from it now.

She shuddered. "I see the murders. The papers didn't report half of it, did they?"

"No." My reply was soft. I knew from experience that if I spoke too loudly, it seemed to jar her out of the moment.

"There is a lot of hatred in those killings. And a fair bit of revenge." She paused. "Look to the vampire council, to old decisions. This began seven months ago. It is not a recent thing."

"You can't tell who or what sparked this?"

"No." She tilted her head slightly and added, "You need to be careful."

"Dia, don't—"

Her grip on my fingers tightened, even though I made no move to pull my hand from hers. "There is a player in your life at the moment. He is more dangerous than you think or know."

No prizes for guessing who *that* was. "I know—"

"No, you don't," she said, voice suddenly fierce. "He is a man without heart, without conscience, and he threatens people you care about. He *will* kill. You need to tread softly around him, and never, *ever* trust him."

"I don't. Believe me on that."

Her bright gaze flew open and pinned me. "You need to walk away from him. Now, before it is too late."

She actually sounded scared, and that was scaring the *hell* out of me. What on earth had she seen? I might have said I didn't want to know, but was the not knowing any better? Suddenly, I didn't think so.

"I can't, Dia. He's my wolf soul mate."

"Oh, God." Her fingers were clasped tightly around mine now, this time free of energy beyond the tension I could feel in her. "Fate really does have it in for you, doesn't she?"

I laughed. I couldn't help it. I'd said it so often myself that it just sounded funny hearing it on someone else's lips. "Yeah, she really does."

Dia's smile didn't quite reach her eyes. "Cling to what you have with Quinn. Use that link to fight the wolf one. It will give you a strength most other wolves would not have in this situation."

I raised my eyebrows. "Are there actually other wolves out there who hate their soul mates?"

"Not hate, perhaps, but there are certainly those who are disappointed." She shrugged. "We all have our dreams and desires, and fate doesn't always deliver."

As I'd discovered time and again. I hesitated, and then asked the question that I feared the most. "Who does he kill?"

Her gaze darkened. "I didn't see. You just need to be very careful around him. He is playing a game, and while I can't see his end goal, I sense it is a dangerous one for you." Her fingers crushed mine. "Please, *please*, be careful."

"I will. I promise."

"Good." She squeezed my fingers a final time, then released them and picked up her coffee. It was frightening to see her hand was still shaking in reaction to whatever she'd seen.

Meaning she'd seen a whole lot more than she'd ever admit.

I suddenly lost my appetite for cake and picked up my coffee. It didn't do a whole lot to warm the sudden chill.

Still, I'd known the moment I agreed to the reading that this could happen. And she warned me often enough that she would not hold back on what she saw.

And yet she was, and that was the scariest thing of all.

I glanced at my watch and saw it was nearing six.

Time for me to get going, or I'd be late for my date with Quinn. I gulped down the rest of my coffee, scalding my insides for the second time that day, then retrieved my credit card from my purse.

"I need to go," I said, swiping the card through the slot and punching in our table number. "I've got dinner with Quinn, so I'll ask him about taking Risa under his wing."

The little girl looked up at the sound of her name and gave me a cheeky smile. "Risa doesn't suck."

Dia rolled her eyes. "Indeed not."

I laughed and stood up. "Usual time next Thursday?"

"Yes. And this time, my treat. You pay enough, and I know it doesn't always go on the Directorate account."

I shrugged and leaned across the table to give Risa a quick kiss on the top of her head. "Bye, monkey."

"Bye," she said, enthusiastically waving for all of three seconds before she grabbed her straw and began a final assault on her Coke.

I grinned and slid out of the booth. But I'd barely taken a step when Dia said softly, "Riley, make sure that when you shoot, you shoot to kill."

It was an echo of the warning Kye had given me, and it chilled me to the bone.

But I didn't stop to ask why. I just got the hell out of there before she said anything else.

Chapter 9

Quinn was leaning against the side of a black Porsche when I arrived at Essendon airport. He was dressed casually—in blue jeans and a white shirt with the sleeves roughly rolled up—but casual on that man was as hot as hell.

But it meant we weren't going anywhere flash, so it was just as well I'd opted for a smart but casual look rather than a glam one.

I parked beside his car, then walked around to him. His arms wrapped around me and drew me close, his kiss warm and welcoming.

"Hmmmm," I said after a while. "That was nice."

"It was," he agreed, dark eyes shining down at me. "And you look very pretty."

"Thanks." I looked past him, studying the black

rooftop. "What happened to the red Ferrari? I was rather partial to that one."

His sexy grin had my knees going all weak and funny. "Or partial to the things we did in it?"

"Damn right."

He laughed and let his grip slip down to my arm before entwining his fingers through mine. "The six-month lease was up," he said, leading me toward a waiting helicopter. "I decided a change was in order so you didn't get bored."

"Not even I could get bored with making love in the seat of a red Ferrari."

"Ah, but if you've never made love in the seat of a black Porsche, how do you know you won't like that better?"

I grinned. "And to think I used to believe you were a staid old vampire when it came to sex."

"Not staid. Just not too adventurous until I know and trust my partner." He hesitated, and his expression became a little more serious. "I talked to one of the councilors. He reluctantly agreed to a meeting, but only under certain circumstances."

Having to meet set conditions was annoying, but I guess I could understand his caution given someone out there seemed intent on wiping out the Melbourne council. "And what might those circumstances be?"

"That it happens tonight, and it takes place somewhere outside of Melbourne."

Disappointment fluttered through me. But I could hardly complain about our dinner date being compromised when I'd asked him to arrange this. "So why his rush?"

"Because many of the remaining councilors have decided to hightail it out of the state until this has all been sorted out."

But not Dante, I'd bet. He just didn't seem the type who would flee at the first sign of trouble. "A mass evacuation might only succeed in driving our killer underground."

"A point I argued when it was mentioned. His retort was that he preferred his head remain attached to his body."

"What is the greater council saying about it?"

"I doubt they know just yet, but they wouldn't approve." His gaze swept me, a heat I felt rather than saw. "You look tired."

"I am a little," I admitted. "It's been a stressful few days."

"Workwise? Or is there another reason you're stressed?"

It was lightly said, but we both knew what he was really asking. Just as we both knew if I gave him the answer he was seeking, it would spoil our evening.

"Working on two cases that have the potential to blow up in my face is reason enough to stress," I said honestly enough. "And you said you didn't want to know how things might—or might not—be progressing with Kye."

His smile was rueful. "I'm discovering that not knowing is almost as hard as knowing. It appears I have a very vivid imagination when it comes to you and that wolf."

I stopped and swung him around to face me. "When I do something with Kye, it'll be because I have to, not because I want to. Fixate on that—and the fact that you have my heart—rather than anything else."

"Easy for you to say." He leaned forward and kissed me again, softly and quickly. "I fell in love with a were-wolf once before, and she broke my heart when she met her soul mate."

"But as you keep reminding me, I'm half vampire. The two halves of my soul have very different needs." I touched a hand to his face, letting my thumb brush lightly over his sun-warmed lips. "And I don't want to think about Kye any more than I need to, so can we please get into the helicopter and get something to eat? I'm starved."

He laughed, and the tension in him eased as suddenly as it had risen. He tugged me forward again. "Just as well I ordered a large picnic basket, then."

"So where are we going?" Not that I really cared, given that no matter where we ended up, I'd still be in the company of a seriously sexy man.

"A friend of mine owns a large plot of land in the Mountain Bay area, and it has views right out over Eildon Dam. It's stunning at sunset, and perfect for a picnic."

"Lovely."

"If everything goes according to plan, it should be." He stopped next to the helicopter and helped me in, then climbed in beside me. After making sure my belt was done up right and handing me the ear protectors, he signaled for the pilot to take off.

I might still have my stupid fear of heights, but it was an exhilarating ride nonetheless—even if I spent half of it with my eyes squeezed shut. And I was damn glad when we landed safely and I was able to get out onto solid ground.

The view made it all worthwhile.

His friend's property was situated on a hill, and had stunning views right across the water and the mountains beyond. And the silence—it was almost eerie after having grown so used to the constant hum of the city.

Quinn grabbed the picnic basket and a blanket from the back of the helicopter, then walked down the hill a little. I took off my stilettos and followed him. As he spread the blanket over the grass, the helicopter took off.

"It's going to pick up Leon," he said, obviously noticing my surprise. He glanced at his watch. "We have just over an hour to eat and chat."

Which is exactly what we did. I even remembered to ask him about Risa.

"Certainly." His response was so quick I raised my eyebrows. He smiled. "I sensed her power the very first time I saw her. She needs training, and there's few enough of us around these days to do it."

"You told me the Aedh were extinct."

"I lied."

Surprise, surprise. "Bet you didn't think it would come back to bite you on the butt."

"The minute I saw Risa, I knew it would." He shrugged, then gave me a cheeky smile that wiped away the wisps of my annoyance. "The priests no longer exist. The Aedh do, however, although they are scarce and scattered. But there have always been more males than females, so there are more of us half-breeds than full-bloods."

"So why don't the fathers hang around to teach their offspring?"

His smile was almost cold. "Because the Aedh are not human in *any* sense of the word. Family is an alien concept to them. They sow their seed, then leave. It is done out of necessity rather than desire."

My eyebrows rose again. "Necessity?"

"When the Aedh's life span is coming near its end, they become fertile and will breed. If there is no female Aedh available, they find another source."

Meaning anything female, human or nonhuman, obviously. "So if the dads don't hang around, how do their offspring learn? How did you?"

"The priests used to gather the offspring to raise and instruct. While they are no longer around, there are still teachers. Most are half-breeds like myself."

And yet his dad had been a priest, so he'd not only known him, but his sister. I frowned. "If your dad was at the end of his life span when he conceived you and your sister, then how did he teach you?"

"Because an Aedh's life span can be measured in centuries, not mere years. I was ten when he died. The other priests taught me after that." He hesitated. "It is quite possible that Risa will live for several hundred years, although the human part of her will ensure she ages normally until she hits her mid to late twenties."

Then Risa was one lucky girl. Imagine being naturally stuck at that age? Humans would kill for that sort of DNA. "So why haven't the Aedh teachers been in contact with Dia?"

"Because I'm here, and it falls to me."

"Meaning Aedh don't trespass on another's patch?"

He hesitated. "There are other half-Aedh in this city—I believe there might even be a few full-bloods. But I am the oldest, and I've trained as a priest. The task is mine."

Huh. And here I was wondering how he'd cope with the possibility of a child in the house, and all along *he'd* been waiting to step into Risa's life to help raise—and teach—her. "Will Dia ever find her Aedh? Or is he more than likely dead?"

"That I can't tell you." He motioned to the plates in front of us. "How about you concentrate on eating rather than giving me the inquisition?"

I'd rather keep asking questions, but I knew him well enough to realize I wasn't going to get any more out of him right now. So I did as he asked. Once the food was gone, I filled my wineglass and rested back against his chest, watching the sun fill the sky with ribbons of red and gold as it set over the hills. It was one of the most peaceful and restful moments I'd had in ages.

So, naturally, fate threw a spanner in the works.

The sharp ring of the sat phone made me jump. "Someone has less than perfect timing," I muttered, scooting away from Quinn so he could dig the phone out of his pocket.

He glanced at the number, then said, "It's Jacques," before answering it.

Jacques was the helicopter pilot. I frowned and glanced at my watch. It was nearly nine, so ideally he and the helicopter should have been almost back here by now. Maybe our reluctant councilor had decided to back out of the arrangement at the last moment.

Quinn made a few short sharp comments, then hung up.

"What's wrong?" I asked, even though I had a fair idea from listening to his side of the conversation.

"Leon just became the victim of a drive-by beheading." His voice was grim. "Jacques saw the attack and immediately called the Directorate, but it happened so fast he wasn't able to help the councilor out."

I raised my eyebrows. "If it was a vampire who took him out, then we're dealing with someone fairly old. The sun isn't fully down yet."

"Jacques said it was definitely a vamp who killed Leon—his skin went pink when he opened the side door of the van. There was someone else driving, but he couldn't see who." Quinn shoved the phone back into his pocket. "From what I can gather, the vamp wasn't in the sunlight for long."

"But hacking someone's head off with a saw isn't quick."

"The killer used a sword, not a saw. Apparently Leon was walking toward the helicopter when the van appeared. He jumped out of its way, but the van stopped. The next thing Jacques saw was Leon on the ground and the sword swinging. Jacques got the plate number."

Which was probably useless, given that the van would more than likely be stolen or rented. And the renter would no doubt have used a false ID—unless he was a complete moron, but these killers seemed way too intelligent. "If he was taken just before he climbed into the helicopter, that suggests he was already being watched."

"Or that they're monitoring phone conversations and knew about the meet." He drained his wine and glanced at his watch. "Jacques is only five minutes away. I wouldn't mind betting Jack will call soon."

That was a bet I wasn't about to take. The clatter of the approaching helicopter began to invade the serenity. Quinn rose and offered me a hand. I clasped his fingers and let him pull me to my feet.

"You know there's no chance of any of the councilors agreeing to talk to you now," he said, tugging me closer then wrapping his arms around my waist. "I very much doubt they'll even talk to me after this."

I knew one councilor who'd be *more* than willing to talk to me, but I had a fair suspicion Dante would require payback of the sexual kind, and I really didn't want to indulge him that way. There was something about the man that irritated me. But maybe it was just the fact that he used his sexual glamor without restrictions while we werewolves were threatened with all sorts of punishments if we even *flirted* with the idea of using our auras.

I wrapped my arms around Quinn's neck and

pressed even closer. His body was warm and hard against mine, and despite my tiredness, a little part of me wished we'd done more than simply eat and talk. "Why would the councilors refuse to talk to you? It's not like you murdered Leon or anything."

"No, but the mere fact he took my call and then a few hours later wound up as the next victim will spook the rest."

"But how would they know about the call? And why would they think you're involved anyway?" I shook my head at the thought. "I guess, given the situation, that they'd be viewing molehills and seeing mountains, but surely they'd realize a cazador could probably find less obvious ways of killing."

He smiled and pressed me a little closer, so that I could feel the smallest of muscle movements. It was a very pleasant sensation. "Most of those on the Melbourne council don't know my history. Only those on the greater council do."

The clatter of the helicopter was louder and, over his shoulder, a black speck was becoming visible. My brief time of peace was coming to an end, and right now I resented that.

I hated the thought of having to go back to the long hours of investigation and the freaks who killed. But most of all, I resented having to go back and face Kye.

Because I very much doubted he'd wait until tomorrow's lunch to see me again.

I pushed the tremor that was part anger, part anticipation aside and said, "You're not going to get into trouble with the greater council for helping me out, are you?"

His smile was warm, yet there was something very cold in his gaze. It was a quick reminder that my luscious, warmhearted vampire was a very old—and very dangerous—being. "There are only three who would—or could—reprimand me. And given the situation, I doubt they would dare."

I didn't think it was the situation that would stop them. It was more likely the man. Or rather, what he'd once been.

He leaned forward and kissed me, his lips still gentle. Like all the other kisses we'd shared tonight, it was a sweet thing, yet oddly filled with emotion. And while it lacked the instant burn of desire, that very fact was oddly comforting. We'd gone beyond mere lust, and these kisses reflected that.

The helicopter landed, creating a whirl of wind that tore at our hair and clothes before the blades slowed down. Quinn gathered the basket and blanket then escorted me to the bird.

We'd barely landed in Melbourne when my phone rang. Surprise, surprise, it was Jack.

"I know about Leon's beheading," I said, shivering a little as I stepped out of the helicopter. A sea breeze was coming in off the bay, and even through Essendon airport wasn't actually anywhere near the sea or the bay, the temperature still seemed several degrees cooler than it had been up in the hills.

"Well, fantastic, but I'm not calling about that."

"Then what's the problem? Not more dead women?"

"No, thankfully. It's the watch you put on Vinny."

"Has it turned up something?" I watched Quinn walk toward the car and toss the basket in the front seat. Half of me wished he'd throw me there instead and take me somewhere well out of phone range.

It wasn't so much that I was tired of the job, just that I was simply tired. Now that the night had swept in, my tiredness seemed to have gotten worse. I needed to sleep and yet, at the same time, I feared it. Or rather, I feared dreaming again.

Feared that it might just mean the bonds drawing me to Kye were getting stronger.

"No, nothing's happened over at the emo camp," Jack said, "but I'm pulling guardians off all nonessential duty and bringing them in for a debriefing on these killings. The number-one priority of the night shift is now the search for this killer, so Vinny has lost her watcher."

At least the three of us on day shift had escaped the debriefing. For tonight, anyway. "So if I want the watch, I have to do it myself?"

"I'm afraid so. Sorry, Riley. I know you're due to go home, but we've really got to find whoever is behind the beheadings."

"What if there is a connection between the two sets of murders?"

He paused, then said warily, "What makes you think there's a connection?"

Oh, shit. I hadn't put in a report yet, so he didn't

know. And Cole couldn't have mentioned it, because all I'd actually told him was that one of them was a vampire. "Cole's initial report mentioned me talking to the soul, right?"

"It was mentioned in the notes." His voice was full of censure. "I've been waiting for your report, however."

"I was going to send it in from home." Which was a lie, and we both knew it. Truth was, I'd totally forgotten about it.

"I would suggest you do it ASAP."

"I will." After all, I had to do something to keep myself awake during the watch. "But the thing is, the soul mentioned the fact that the vampire doing the beheading didn't smell like an ordinary vampire. I don't know how many different types of vampires there are, but I figure it's unlikely to be a coincidence that we possibly have emos involved in two different types of murders."

"We're not certain emos are involved in the murder of the women."

We weren't certain of *anything* on *either* case right now, and that was damn frustrating. "But given the circumstances, it's the most likely."

He grunted—whether in agreement or not was anyone's guess. "Emo vamps tend to live in clusters, not as single entities like us blood vamps do. They even tend to feed as a group."

"Which doesn't mean we can't have a rogue, or that Vinny doesn't know about it. Which is why we need to keep the watch on her, boss."

He was silent for a moment, then said, "Okay, you take over the watch for a couple of hours while I debrief everyone, then I'll send out a replacement so you can get some rest. But I want that report in on my computer before you go home."

"Done deal."

He grunted and hung up. I shoved my phone into my purse and gave Quinn a half smile. "I'm back to work, I'm afraid."

"I heard." He gave me a hug then kissed the top of my head. "I can cancel my night out and come along to keep you company, if you'd like. At least I could keep an eye on things while you grab some sleep."

It was tempting. *So* tempting. But I really didn't want to get Quinn involved any more than he already was, if only because that risked bringing him in close proximity to Kye. And he'd already warned me that would *not* be a good thing.

So I simply smiled and said, "I've only got to last long enough to type the report. By then Jack will have finished his debriefing and he'll send out a replacement." I gave him a long and lingering kiss, then sighed wistfully and added, "Go enjoy yourself. I'll see you tomorrow morning sometime."

"Just be careful out there." He hesitated, and his sexy grin flashed, making my stomach flutter. "And try not to dream about sex again. You really do need to sleep."

"You're just afraid of me having too good a time without you."

His grin faded a little, and I suddenly realized the deeper implications of what I'd said. "Quinn—"

"It's all right," he said gently. "Go to work. I'll see you later."

I went. I found parking only a couple of spaces down from where I'd been earlier, then flipped the rearview mirror up so the headlights of passing cars didn't shine into my eyes and wreck my night vision. After a quick look around to make sure I wasn't going to shock anyone's sensibilities, I changed into the jeans and sweater I'd left in the car earlier. The stilettos I left on. Given where I was and what I might be chasing, they just might be useful.

Typing up my report took all of half an hour. I forwarded it on to Jack, then settled in to wait. Nothing much happened. A dozen or so of Vinny's blond, ghost-like hatchlings drifted in and out of the building, haunting the fence lines of the surrounding buildings and more than likely siphoning the emotions of those within. Nothing I'd classify as interesting happened, however, and before long my eyes started to get heavier and heavier. Opening the window and letting the cooler night air in didn't help any.

I'm not sure what exactly jerked me awake. The night was still. I sat up a little straighter in the seat and rubbed at my eyes, blinking almost owlishly at Vinny's building. The hatchlings had disappeared. While lights twinkled on the upper floor, the rest of the building lay in darkness. No one moved and the night was quiet.

And yet . . .

There was a presence. I couldn't see it, couldn't smell it, but it was there. It tugged at my senses and teased my memories—an itch I couldn't quite scratch.

I frowned and climbed out of the car. The air was crisp and cool, and the breeze drifting in from the direction of Vinny's building was thick with the scent of vampire. It wasn't them I was sensing. It was something else.

Someone else.

I locked the door then shifted shape and took to the sky in my seagull form. Given that I wasn't sure what it was I was sensing, it seemed the safer bet. I might be able to wrap myself in shadows, but that didn't hide my body scent or body heat, and I couldn't risk one or the other being discovered. And most supernaturals tended not to look skyward for shadows.

I drifted around the building, trying to pinpoint the location of the odd sensation. I didn't get much more than the fact that it seemed to be coming from the heart of Vinny's building. I wheeled around and headed for the nearest tree, perching on one of the bigger middle branches where a gull's webbed feet could rest more easily.

I'd barely landed when that odd sensation got stronger, burning across my skin. It felt like the heat of lust, but it was almost as if there were some sort of screen between me and that sensation; I could feel it but wasn't affected.

Of that, I could only be glad. I'd felt that sort of heat once before, and there had been no protecting screen that time . . .

My thoughts froze. I *had* felt that sensation before, and on more than one occasion.

The first time had been in Vinny's den, when she'd tried her emo wiles on me.

And the other times had been in the last couple of nights, in the dreams that had plagued me.

It *wasn't* Kye causing the restless, unbridled lust that disturbed my sleep and drained my strength. It was an emo vampire, somehow feeding on me from a distance. No wonder I felt so goddamn tired—it wasn't lack of sleep but rather the energy I was losing *through* dreaming.

Whether the vampire responsible was this stranger or someone else, I had no idea, but I sure as hell was going to find out. And stop it, before it killed me.

As it had more than likely killed those other women.

The sensation sharpened and, a heartbeat later, a man stepped out of Vinny's building. He was tall and lean, with dark hair and sallow-looking skin. But he moved with a predator's grace, even if his hands were shoved deep into his pockets and his shoulders hunched.

He walked across the pavement and disappeared down a side street. I took wing, following him from a safe distance, not wanting to chance the fact that an emo wouldn't sense me. I had no idea what they were capable of, and while blood vamps usually couldn't sense the heartbeat of a gull this high up, I didn't know if an emo vamp would have similar restrictions when it came to sensing emotions.

He swung into another street, his strides purposeful and long. A vamp who was sure of himself, despite the outward image he was projecting.

He went down another side street and climbed into a blue four-wheel drive. I dipped low enough to memorize the plate number, then continued to follow the car. He didn't flatten his foot, so it was easy enough to keep up.

I wasn't entirely surprised when he parked two streets away from Dante's. The threads twining together our two separate murders seemed to be getting thicker and stronger.

I fluttered down to the pavement, shifting several feet from the ground and landing somewhat awkwardly, running forward before gaining my balance. At least I didn't land on my nose—that had been a common feature in the early months of my learning to fly.

My sweater survived the experience—or at least was still wearable—but my bra was, as usual, shredded. I pulled it off and wished I could find a brand that actually survived the shift into seagull form. Or that Jack would approve my request to start charging the cost of replacements to the Directorate. They were destroyed in the course of my job, after all.

I dumped the silky remains in the nearest bin and followed my quarry. He headed straight for Dante's and went inside, but I stopped in the shadows a street away. I didn't want to confront Dante's owner right now.

And maybe I didn't have to. Not if Kye was there, watching and waiting for his target. I might not want to see the bastard, but I'd damn well use him if it meant an end to these cases.

I turned on my heel and walked away from the building. Kye would be using the latest technology, which meant he wouldn't be close, as the receiving range on spy equipment these days was incredible.

Like most of Melbourne, the streets in this area were set out in neat little squares. I walked around them, gradually widening the search. I was a good five streets away from the club before I felt the familiar tingle of his presence.

I stopped, scenting the night, trying to pinpoint his position. The air held little more than the smell of an oncoming storm, but it didn't matter. My soul knew where he was—all I had to do was let instinct run free.

And that was something I didn't want to risk.

I took a deep breath and blew it out slowly. Fully unleashing the wolf to find him would be dangerous. Her hunger for him was stronger than ever, and once I released control, I feared I might not get it back.

The simple fact was, the two parts of me were at war. And no matter which part won, I would lose.

I gnawed lightly at my bottom lip and walked forward, trying to pinpoint his location without actually unleashing the hunter. His presence was elusive—awareness of him might burn at my skin, but it just wasn't strong enough to grab and pin down.

In the end, I had no choice. It was either go into the club and face Dante, or unleash the wolf and face the man who might well destroy everything I held dear.

It said a lot about my distaste for Dante that the second of those two options seemed the better one.

I took another deep breath then shifted into my wolf form. Instantly the air came alive with a myriad of delicious scents that teased my senses and made my soul want to hunt. And the most delicious one of all wasn't actually a scent but rather the pull of one wild soul to another.

I turned and trotted down a side street. Three houses down and I'd found him.

I shifted back to human form, then pushed open the front gate and walked up the steps. The door opened before I neared and he was standing there, his shirt and jeans undone, revealing the flat muscular planes of his stomach and tantalizing glimpses of pubic hair. I stopped, staring at him, neither of us saying anything. But his eyes were wild and hungry. The hunter in him was free; as free as mine.

As hungry as mine.

I took two steps and was in his arms. His arms went around my waist as his lips crushed mine, his kiss fierce and bruising and passionate. I groaned deep in my throat and tore off his shirt, letting my hands explore the heated expanse of his skin, reveling in the way his flesh leapt and twitched under my touch. He pushed me back against the door frame so hard I grunted in shock and pain. It turned to a gasp of pleasure as his hands thrust under my sweater and flicked my aching nipples.

He chuckled low in his throat then grabbed the edges of the sweater, hauling it over my head and tossing it to the floor. Then his mouth was on my breasts, alternatively kissing and nipping, making me shudder, making me burn. I threw back my head, enjoying the sensations shaking my body, wanting it to last and yet wanting more of him. All of him.

I slid my hands down his sides, then gripped the waist of his jeans and boxers and thrust them down. He kicked free of them, his mouth moving from my breasts to my lips, his hunger even more fierce as his hands fumbled with the button of my jeans then pulled down the zipper. My jeans and panties quickly joined his on the floor. He pressed his body hard against mine, until it felt like the heat and hardness of him was covering me as securely as a blanket.

Then he opened his eyes, and for one brief moment our gazes locked. And deep beneath the hunger in his golden eyes, deep beneath the heat that made them glow like fire, there was both anger and determination. And a need just as intense.

Heaven only knows what he saw in my eyes.

He grabbed my arms and thrust them above my head, holding them secure in one large hand while he lifted my butt with the other. Then he rammed himself into me, and it felt so good I slammed my head back against the wall and howled.

This was no gentle mating. His movements were hard, rough, his body pummeling mine, hitting the right spot again and again, until I couldn't breathe, couldn't think, could only feel. And oh God, it felt *good*. I came, hard, a scream of pleasure tearing itself from my throat and sounding suspiciously like his name.

He came just as hard, his body jerking as his seed shot into me, his face twisting as if in agony.

Then it was over, and the pleasure began to fade, until there was nothing left but sweat, the battle for breath, and the horrid realization that no matter what excuses I'd given myself, I'd come here for this.

I might blame the wolf, but the wolf, like the vampire, wasn't the sum of me.

And if there were two parts of me at war, then it wasn't the wolf and the vampire, but rather heart and soul.

Right now, locked in this man's embrace, I wasn't sure which part of me would win.

Or which part I *wanted* to win.

And that was a scary thought.

"Well," he said, amusement briefly touching the corners of his eyes as he tucked a stray strand of sweaty hair back behind my right ear. "That certainly gave the neighbors something to talk about."

I glanced across the darkened street and saw that we did indeed have watchers. Normally I wouldn't mind, but for some weird reason, this time I did.

Maybe part of me was ashamed of my actions.

I pressed my hands between us and pushed him away. He resisted for a moment, then smiled and stepped back.

"Why are you here?" He turned around as he spoke, stepped over our clothes, and walked naked down the hall.

My gaze drifted to his butt, then I shook my head,

grabbed my clothes, and followed. "Do you still have your bugs in at Dante's?"

All the doors were open, but aside from a bed in one of the rooms, the house was practically empty. There wasn't any form of security equipment that I could see.

"Yes, but it's not set up here. Why?" He pushed open a door and walked in. I followed, my gaze sweeping the small basic kitchen before coming back to Kye, drifting down the muscular V of his back before coming to rest on his well-toned butt. I clenched my fists against the sudden need to touch him.

"Because a suspect I was following went into Dante's, and I'd prefer not to go in after him."

He paused in the middle of making coffee and looked over his shoulder. "Why are you reluctant to go into Dante's? You're many things, Riley, but a coward isn't one of them."

I crossed my arms and leaned a hip against the counter. "I don't like Starke."

He raised an eyebrow. "I would have thought not liking someone was something of a career hazard for guardians."

"And I make it a habit of avoiding the ones I dislike if there are other options available."

He returned to his coffee making. "So that little dance out in the foyer was a way of softening me up?"

"No, that was out-of-control need. I'll do my best not to let it happen again."

He laughed—a sound so cold and harsh that a chill ran down my spine. "We are destined to be one, whether we like it or not."

And he didn't like it. Not one little bit. At least we had *that* in common. "If you're so intent on fighting this, why keep insisting that I come to you?"

He looked over his shoulder, his eyes locking on mine. There was something very chilling in those warm amber depths. "Because to control it, I have to face it. So here I am—and here I will stay—until I have a leash on this. On *us*."

Oh God, oh God . . . I didn't have the strength to keep on fighting this. I couldn't. Not when I hungered so. "The bonds that bind us only grow stronger the more we are together. It would be better if you simply left—"

His hand crashed down on the countertop, the force so great he cracked the stone. "I will *not* retreat from this. I *will* control it."

All I could do was stare at him. This man really *was* crazy.

After a moment, he turned around and offered me a coffee cup. The explosion of anger might have gone, but the embers of it still burned in his eyes.

I clasped the cup and took a sip. The rich scent of hazelnut teased my nostrils, and that only succeeded in increasing the turmoil.

"I only have several minor jobs at the moment, so it gives me time to concentrate on this." His gaze came to mine again and the sensible part of me trembled. Not in fear of the man, but in fear of what I saw there. This wolf might want to control both the situation and me, but he had no intention of actually letting go. "And while I am here, I will have what is mine."

"I will never be yours, Kye."

"If I reach for you now, you would be mine for the taking. We both know it, Riley."

He was right. As much as I might want to deny it, as much as I might fight it, he had my body and he had my soul. But he did not have my heart. *That* I would protect against his assault with my life itself.

I sipped my coffee and said nothing. After several minutes, he smiled. It was a twisted, bitter thing. "What time did your suspect enter Dante's?"

I glanced at my watch. "Twenty-three minutes ago."

His gaze narrowed a little. "Was he a dark-haired man with a hunched demeanor who walked like a predator?"

"Yes." I hesitated. "I thought you said your surveillance equipment wasn't here."

"It isn't. That doesn't mean I can't access it from here. Phones can do amazing things these days."

I guess they could. "What made you notice him?"

"The mere fact he didn't look like the usual type of customer Dante pulled in."

"So you can supply me with a photo of him from your system?"

"I can do more than that. I'll pull up his information." He paused, considering me. "But if you want it, there is a cost."

I snorted softly. "Like I was expecting you to give me something out of the goodness of your heart."

His grin was fierce. "I have no heart. You'd do well to remember that."

"Oh, trust me, I do." I shoved the coffee cup onto the countertop and crossed my arms. "What's your price? Another fuck?"

God, the mere thought had me trembling in anticipation.

Fate needed to be shot.

"Yes and no." His voice was flat, and yet there was an odd hint of amusement teasing his mouth. It made me want to kiss him again, and I hated that. Hated myself for wanting it. "I want you to stay with me."

"What?" I stared at him for a moment. "Why?"

He shrugged. "Maybe because it's the last thing you actually want. Or maybe because I want your vampire to understand just what it's like to know that his mate is in the arms and the bed of another."

He was a bastard. A *bastard*.

Although that wasn't exactly a new revelation.

"I'm not spending the night with you."

"Then you don't get your information and you risk more people dying."

"Maybe I'll just call the Directorate and confiscate your entire system."

"And maybe I'll just call the man following your brother's mate and give him the go-ahead for a little target practice."

Anger and fear surged in equal amounts and I lashed out. Though I moved with vampire speed, he moved almost as fast, and the blow barely even brushed his chin. Even so, there was enough strength behind it to send him sprawling backward.

I stepped forward, wanting to finish it, wanting to punish him for everything he was putting me through, but somehow I got the urge under control and stopped several inches away, my fists clenched and body shaking with fury.

"You ever threaten him like that again—"

He rose and the force of his anger hit me like a ton of bricks. It was all I could do not to step back, to remember this man was *just* a wolf and didn't hold half the threat of some of the other foes I'd faced.

But as I met him glare for glare, he seemed far, far worse.

"I am your *soul* mate," he said flatly. Coldly. "I will do whatever it takes to possess and control what is mine. And if it means destroying everything you hold dear, then that is precisely what I will do."

"But you don't *want* me. You don't want this." My voice rose, until I was almost shouting at him. "So what is the fucking point?"

He smiled again. Once again, it was a cold and harsh thing to behold. "The point, as I have already said, is the fight. It's winning out over base emotion. It's being in control."

I stared at him for several seconds, thinking nothing, feeling nothing, my mind seemingly frozen and his words echoing around in the emptiness of my thoughts.

I was never going to win this fight, because the mere act of fighting was what he wanted, what he enjoyed. No matter what I did, I was going to lose.

If he wanted control, then I'd give it to him.

Or at least, give him the illusion of it.

I stepped back, turned around, and picked up my coffee. "Fine," I said. "You win. I'll spend the night with you."

Surprise flickered through his eyes. "Really? You're giving up, just like that? Somehow, I'm not quite believing that, Riley."

"I don't care what you believe." I rubbed my eyes and suddenly felt a hundred years older. "You want me, you can have me. It's as simple as that."

He raised an eyebrow, the disbelief still very evident, then he held out a hand. "Fine. Come with me now."

I hesitated, then placed my fingers in his. His grip was warm, fierce, and—God help me—a tremor of anticipation ran down my spine. He smiled, obviously sensing the hunger I just couldn't control, then led me from the kitchen, back down the hall, and into his bedroom.

Where we made love, again and again, until our bodies were spent and our wolves sated and all I wanted to do was cry.

But I managed to place the tracker at the base of his neck, just near the hairline as I'd been told, so at least the night was not a total waste.

When we finally slept, it wasn't wrapped in each other's arms, but apart—a physical sign of a distance that would never be bridged, no matter how much fate and our souls might wish it.

*　*　*

*W*hen I woke, I was alone.

I lay in the bed with the sheets twisted around my body, listening to the silence, drawing in the air.

Kye wasn't here.

Hadn't been here for several hours, if the fading aroma of him was anything to go by.

Part of me wanted to hope that by giving in, I'd won the war, but I knew that would be a false hope. Kye hadn't believed I'd meant what I'd said, so he'd be back. And probably when I least expected it.

I untangled the sheets from my legs and sat up. Despite the long hours of intense and often rough sex, I felt refreshed. Maybe because when I finally *had* slept, I hadn't dreamed.

I glanced around the room, noting for the first time it had little in the way of comfort. Besides the bed and a small, somewhat moth-eaten armoire, there was little else in the room. No personal knickknacks, no paintings or mirrors, no clothes lying about. I frowned and walked across to the armoire. It was empty.

A walk through the rest of the house gave the same result. Kye hadn't just left the bed, he'd left the premises—lock, stock, and decent coffee.

I cursed myself for being an idiot and trusting that he'd actually keep his half of the bargain, and stalked into the bathroom to catch a shower. There was no way I was leaving this house reeking of him.

And there, resting on top of a clean towel that was sitting next to the basin, were several sheets of paper. A quick glance revealed not only a printout of my suspect, but what information Kye had found on him.

I wasn't sure whether to be annoyed or amused.

I had my shower and got dressed, then grabbed the papers and headed for the front door.

Only to run straight into my brother's chest.

Chapter 10

"Ow," I said, rubbing my nose as I stepped back. "What the hell are you doing here, Rhoan?"

"I was about to ask you the same fucking question." He'd shoved his hands on his hips and was glaring at me fiercely.

I frowned and wondered what the hell was going on. "I'm getting information about the case. Why?"

"Because you car was found abandoned over near Vinny's, your com-link is turned off, and you weren't answering your phone." He thrust his fingers through his hair, and for the first time I noticed the tension in him. "We thought the worst."

I raised my eyebrows. "Why would you think that? You've always known when I'm in serious trouble in the past."

"Serious trouble, yes, but there've been times when

you've been hurt and in trouble, and I haven't felt a thing." He hesitated and looked sheepish. "I guess I just panicked."

"Whatever game Kye is playing, it doesn't involve hurting me physically." Not yet, at least. "And my com-link isn't turned off. Not completely, anyway. I could hear Jack. He just can't hear me."

Given what I'd been doing last night, that had been a very sensible decision.

"Well, the Directorate is getting nothing from your com-link, just an odd sort of deadness. Hence the panic." His gaze swept me, as if reassuring himself that I really was okay, then rose again. He frowned. "When did you start wearing an earring?"

"I'm not."

He reached out and plucked something off my left ear. It was small and round, with a blue stone at its heart. "*Now* I can feel you."

I barely even heard what he was saying, thanks to the fact that the minute he removed the earring, Jack's voice began to rebound loudly inside my head.

"Jack, slow down, I can't understand a damn word you're saying," I said, then added quickly, before he had a chance to blast me. "It appears I picked up some sort of electronic device that was blocking the com-link and maybe even telepathy."

"There's no device out there capable of that." His voice was gruff and it wasn't all anger. Concern was there as well, and that warmed me.

"Then maybe we'd better check out the device

Rhoan just took off my ear, because I only began hearing you once it was removed."

Had Kye planted it on me? I couldn't remember him actually doing it, but then, he'd played my body like a maestro last night and would have had any number of chances to stick something on my skin without me being aware. After all, I had done exactly that to him. But why would he bother? He surely had to know that me being incommunicado would bring the cavalry running and that we'd find the bug or whatever it actually was sooner rather than later. Especially given how obvious it was.

Maybe he simply didn't realize the com-link was also a tracker. Or maybe he simply enjoyed the thought of creating a little chaos.

"There're several bits of good news to make up for the bad," I added. "I managed to place the tracker on Kye—"

"Excellent," Jack cut in. "Once research homes in on the signal, we'll be able to monitor the bastard's movements. And we'll know whether he's anywhere near if we have another murder."

True. And I really *did* hope he wasn't, because that would only create a bigger mess than there already was.

"I have a name for you to run, too." I glanced down at the papers Kye had left me. "Carlos Martez, born in Spain twenty-nine years ago, immigrated to Australia when he was nine. I have several photos of him I can send through, but no license details."

Although why Kye hadn't retrieved that when he'd

gotten the name is anyone's guess. Maybe he didn't want to make things easy for me.

As if things would ever be easy when it came to him and me.

"And why are we chasing this man?"

"Because I saw him coming out of Vinny's last night, and he's some sort of emo vamp." I hesitated, then decided not to mention the fact that I'd probably gotten several nocturnal visits from him. Jack would only get mad that I hadn't mentioned it before now—although given that, until last night, I hadn't actually suspected my sexy dreams were more than just dreams, I couldn't really be blamed for not saying anything. Besides, until I knew for sure who was doing it and why, it was better not to jump the gun. All I really knew for sure was that it wasn't Vinny; it didn't have her feel. "I actually think he's the one behind the murders of the two women. Interestingly, when I was tracking him last night, he disappeared into Dante's."

"That doesn't mean the two cases are definitely connected."

It didn't mean they weren't, either. "I know. And I have no evidence connecting him to the murders. But I think we need to talk to both him and Vinny."

"I'll get Benson straight onto the trace."

"Have you gotten anywhere with the council? Are any of them willing to talk to us?"

"Given that your attempt to talk to Leon Gordon resulted in him losing his head, the answer to that is a definite no."

"Even Dante?"

"Dante is many things, but a fool isn't one of them. He won't risk talking to you if the others have refused. It would reflect on him badly."

I'd bet a hundred bucks that he *would* talk to me if I asked—but the cost would be sex, and I really didn't want to go down that path. "We need to know what the hell they did to get someone so pissed off at them."

"I realize that, Riley, and it is being dealt with."

Meaning his sister—who happened to be the head of the Directorate—was dealing with it. "Good. Let me know if you get anything."

"No, Riley, I'm going to keep the information all to myself."

I snorted softly. Sarcastic was better than angry. "Thanks, boss."

He grunted and signed off. I blew out a breath and glanced at my brother. "You feel like breakfast? My treat, seeing I caused you so much stress."

He grinned and turned around, offering me his arm. "You know I'll never refuse an offer like that."

"Good, because we need to talk."

"That sounds serious."

"It is." He led me down the steps. His car was on the street and double-parked, blocking the traffic from either direction. There were a couple of cars waiting to get past, and it was probably only the Directorate plates that were keeping them from expressing their displeasure.

Rhoan opened the passenger door for me, then scooted around to the driver's side and climbed in.

"So," he said, starting the car and then driving off. "What's the problem?"

I took a deep breath and blew it out slowly. "Kye."

Rhoan glanced at me, gray eyes considering. "That was his place, wasn't it?"

"Yes."

"And you spent the night with him?"

"Yes."

"For fuck's sake, Riley, I thought you had more sense."

I smiled bitterly. "Tell me, Rhoan, how much success have you had keeping your paws off your soul mate?"

"That's different—"

"No, it's not. Whether I like it or not, that man is a part of me, just like Liander is a part of you. I can't ignore him and I can't get away from him. I have to deal with him—and this whole situation—the best I can."

"And that best is sleeping with him?" He snorted softly. "That's not exactly dealing with the problem. That's giving in to it."

"Yeah, it is. And it was done for a damn good reason, so don't you be looking down your nose at me, brother, or I'll damn well flatten it."

He grinned. "Them's fighting words, babe. Shame to waste them on me rather than him."

"Oh, trust me, I wasted a few of them on him, too." For all the good it did. "What's Liander involved with at the moment?"

He didn't answer immediately, but the tension in the

car suddenly ramped up several degrees. "He threatened Liander?"

"Yes."

"And you believe he'd do it?"

"He's the one who shot you—just to prove the point."

He didn't actually look surprised. But by the same token, the chill in his eyes suggested Kye wouldn't want to meet him on the street anytime soon. Which was the exact reason I hadn't told him earlier. "Bastard."

"Yup."

He blew out a breath and flexed his fingers against the steering wheel. "So we have to get him out of Melbourne. Immediately."

I knew he meant Liander rather than Kye, although I would have loved for him to get Kye out of Melbourne, too. "*You* have to get him out. I have to stay here and not only catch two killers, but deal with said bastard."

He swung into a McDonald's drive-through and ordered breakfast for us both. Once I'd paid and we'd collected our food, we headed for Vinny's. "Liander's not going to be happy."

"Tell him he can't be a daddy if he's dead."

He glanced at me sharply, hope flaring in his eyes. "Does that mean you'll agree to the surrogacy?"

"I can't agree to anything until we make sure everyone survives the current threat. Let's concentrate on that first." I took a bite of my egg and bacon McMuffin.

"According to Kye, he has a tail twenty-four seven, so you'll have to make sure you're not followed."

"They wouldn't want to try." His voice was flat, deadly, and a shiver ran down my spine. He might be my brother, and we might both be little more than leashed killers, but sometimes he scared me. He had a switch that I didn't. He could so easily become everything I was fighting—a cold-blooded, unfeeling killer.

Kye, in another form.

I gulped down some coffee but didn't feel any warmer. Maybe because I knew that, one day, that switch would be mine. It was inevitable if I remained a guardian—and it wasn't as if I had any other option.

"It might be worth warning Quinn, too," Rhoan added. "Although that could be chancy. He tends to get a little annoyed with people who threaten him. And in this case, that wouldn't be good."

Not when he'd already threatened to beat Kye to a pulp. I finished my McMuffin, then started in on the hash browns. "If you don't eat faster, I'm going to finish the lot."

He grabbed one from the container and shoved the whole thing into his mouth. I shook my head in disgust then jumped as my phone rang. I dragged it out of my pocket and saw it was Jack. And he didn't look happy.

My stomach curled. There'd obviously been another murder. I pressed the RECEIVE button and said, "Who's dead this time?"

"I'm hoping no one." His voice was grim. "Sal just hit the EMERGENCY button. You and Rhoan get over to her house ASAP."

"You've tried contacting her via the com-link?"

"Yep. She's not answering." His voice was grim. "Drive fast."

We did.

*S*al lived in a little two-story brown brick terrace near the heart of Brunswick Street's human hot spot. Meaning there were more nightclubs here than there were in any other part of the city. Most supernaturals tended to avoid the area, simply because of the intense human population, but vamps seemed to love it. I guess being close to your food source did have its advantages. Interestingly enough, there weren't any clubs catering to blood whores here. Maybe it was too trendy and not out of the way enough for them.

Rhoan parked several houses down from Sal's, then opened the trunk and tossed me a laser. He pocketed one himself then gripped a rifle. In my brother's estimation, you could never have enough firepower.

"Front and back?"

I shook my head. "These are terrace houses. You'd have to run around the block to get into the back lane." If they had a back lane, that was. Some of these areas didn't. "Let's just hit the front together."

He nodded and walked forward, the rifle held at the ready by his side. A hunter ready to hunt. I turned on the laser and followed. The soft whine of the weapon powering up was a whole lot louder than either of our steps.

The pale yellow picket fence that divided Sal's little front garden from the street came into view. Bright red poppies peaked over the pickets and contrasted sharply to the heavy blue flowers of the hyacinths. Names I knew simply because our mom had loved the cottage garden look when we were kids.

The door—a heavy wooden thing with metal straps running around its length—seemed untouched, as did the front windows. My gaze rose. One of the first-floor windows was open. A lace curtain hung out, fluttering softly in the breeze.

Rhoan opened the front gate and ran lightly to the door. He tested the handle, then shook his head and sidestepped to the window, quickly and carefully peering around the frame.

Again he shook his head, then pointed to the upstairs window. I pressed on the laser's safety, shoved it into my pocket, then shifted shape. In seagull form, I flew up to the window and into the house.

The minute I landed, I shifted to human form but remained kneeling, the thick brown carpet soft on my knees. The house was quiet and smelled ever so faintly of dog and vampire. There was no hint of blood riding the air, no hint of death. And in this room at least, no sign of violence.

I rose, grabbed a blanket from the bed, and dangled one end out the window. Rhoan grabbed the end and swiftly climbed up.

We moved to the door. After a three-two-one count on his fingers, we moved out—him high, me low.

There was no one in the hall. And no one in the two remaining bedrooms or the bathroom.

Which left the lower part of the house. I flicked to infrared and scanned the area immediately below the stairs. There was no sign of blood heat, no sign of life. Relief slithered through me. While it didn't mean there wasn't *un*life, it *did* mean that Kye wasn't here.

Although Jack would surely have mentioned if he was. But I guessed that depended on whether they'd caught the tracking signal yet.

I glanced at Rhoan. "Anything?" I murmured.

He shook his head. "The house is empty as far as I can tell."

Which supported my own findings. I took a step down. The stair creaked softly and I paused, listening. The stillness remained, nothing moved, and yet . . . suddenly I wasn't so sure we were alone.

I padded down more stairs, my laser held at the ready and my muscles jumping with tension. The house remained still and free of any unusual scent or sound.

We reached the bottom step. I pressed my back against the wall, noting the glass littering the hallway. Someone had thrown a mirror—it lay in broken pieces near the front door.

Goose bumps fled up my arms as I stared at the broken shards. Two women had been killed by something that had probably come through their mirrors, I'd been visited in my sleep, and now we had a broken mirror here. Coincidence? More than likely not.

A quick scan of the front two rooms didn't reveal

anything out of the ordinary. We turned and made our way down the hall, our footsteps as silent as the house.

But as we neared the back room, the sensation hit me—an uncomfortable and all-too-familiar wash of heat. The sort of heat that came from lust. The sort of heat I'd felt when I'd followed the man who'd come out of Vinny's building last night.

I stopped abruptly. Rhoan glanced at me, one eyebrow raised in question. I signaled that I could sense someone inside and he shook his head, meaning he couldn't. Which was odd, but it didn't make me doubt what I was sensing. I learned long ago to trust what I felt. It might never have gotten me into less trouble, but at least it did give me a heads-up.

He raised his hand again and began to count down. When the last finger fell, I went in low and fast, slapping down on one knee as I scanned the room with the laser at the ready.

I had one brief glimpse of a man—the man Kye had identified as Carlos Martez—then he was gone, his body exploding into a mass of writhing, boiling black smoke that fled sideways. I followed with the laser, saw the mirror. Fired.

But I was too late.

The smoke that had been a man hit it a fraction of a second before the laser beam, the last of him disappearing into the confines of the mirror just before it shattered. I rose and ran over, but the glass was empty of anything but my reflection.

"What the fuck was that?" Rhoan said.

I glanced at him. He stood near the doorway, his

gaze sweeping the room and his gun still held at the ready. "That," I said heavily, "was probably the vampire responsible for murdering two women. He's possibly also the vampire behind our beheadings."

"Vampires can't just up and disappear into smoke." He scanned the room a final time, then relaxed a little and lowered his weapon. "And they certainly can't disappear into mirrors."

"I don't think we're dealing with an ordinary vampire here."

"But even if he's an emo vamp, the same still applies. They just can't fade into mirrors."

"Unless they were something that could *before* they became a vampire." I pocketed my laser and began picking up the pieces of glass. If he could disappear through a mirror then he could reappear, too, and I wasn't about to chance an ambush.

"So, what was he looking at so intensely?" Rhoan said, walking lightly across the room.

"I don't know." I rose and walked back down the hallway, opening the front door and tossing the mirror's remains out into the garden. Hopefully the bright sunshine would stop him from using the shards as an avenue of return. I did the same to the mirror that had been smashed in the hall, then on the way back to the kitchen, I checked the other rooms. I found a mirror in what looked to be the main bedroom, and dumped it whole and intact outside. It looked old and may well have been an heirloom. And while I enjoyed baiting Sal, I wasn't about to destroy something she held dear.

Rhoan was kneeling where our vamp had been, but glanced up as I entered. "It's a trapdoor."

I raised my eyebrows. "Sal has a panic room?"

"Pretty sensible thing for a vampire to do," he commented. "Especially given the human history of distrust when it comes to vampires."

"It's generally not that bad these days." The door itself wasn't large—it was big enough for a body to slip through but little else. It was also metal, and looked strong enough to withstand a bomb.

"Tell that to the vampires who have lost their heads," Rhoan said, voice wry. "Or to the humans who wanted to belt your lights out."

"That's different." I knelt down beside him and ran my fingers across the cool metal, looking for something that might act as a lock or a switch to get into the thing. "Besides, it's not humans decapitating the vamps. How are we supposed to open this sucker?"

As far as I could see, there was no damn lock. There wasn't even enough of a gap between the door and the metal frame around it to squeeze fingers in and rip it open.

"I don't think anyone is meant to." He raised a fist and pounded heavily on the door. The sound echoed through the stillness, and from what seemed a long way away, a dog yapped.

I grinned. I knew that bark. And if the little terrier I'd rescued was alive down there, then surely Sal was, too.

"Sal," I shouted, leaning forward a little, "it's Riley and Rhoan. The threat is gone. It's safe to come out."

"God," Rhoan said, wincing as he wiggled the earlobe nearest me with one hand. "Give a warning next time you're going to do that."

There was no immediate answer from the room below us, but the excited barking got louder. Two seconds later, there was a hiss of air—similar to that of an air lock opening—then the lid popped upward and slowly opened to reveal a ladder.

"Riley?" Sal almost sounded relieved, which definitely meant the situation had been bad.

"Yeah," I said. "The house is clear. It's safe to come out."

"Good." The sound of steps on metal rungs echoed, then she appeared, looking more than a little disheveled and wearing a white satin nightdress that showed off her curvaceous figure to perfection. The little terrier was tucked safely under her arm, though he was wriggling for all he was worth and giving everyone a silly doggy grin.

She set him down once they were both out, then met my gaze squarely. "Thank you."

I raised an eyebrow. "We were only doing our job. And Jack sure as hell wouldn't have wanted to lose the second-best liaison he's ever had."

A wry smile touched the corners of her mouth. "No, I mean thank you for giving me the dog. He saved my life."

"How?" I glanced down at the mutt in question. He was running excitedly around Rhoan's legs, yipping for all he was worth, stopping only when Rhoan bent down to give him a pat. "I mean, he's a great dog and all, but he's not really a threat, and he certainly wasn't much help to his first master."

Sal smiled and scooped up the little dog as he ran back to her. "I was woken up by his barking. When I went down to investigate, he was frantic. The beat of life was strong on the other side of the front door, and whoever it was wore a very powerful nanowire that I couldn't get past. The intruder scampered the minute I neared the door, but he left a miniature camera sticking through the keyhole. I destroyed it, but it was too late."

I raised my eyebrows. "Too late for what?"

"To stop it." She gave the little dog another scratch. "Fred gave me the heads-up when he started barking at the mirror. That's when I noticed the smoke forming."

She'd called him Fred? A woman with no imagination when it came to decent dog names, obviously. "And you knew what it was?"

"Yes. I've come across mirror wraiths before and have seen what they can do."

"So you smashed the mirror and ran for the safe room?"

"Yes." She smiled, though it held little in the way of amusement. "They can only travel through reflective surfaces, so unpolished steel is a perfect foil for them."

"So why not just destroy the rest of the mirrors in the house?"

"Because I had no idea how long the man at the door had been using the camera or how much of the house he might have seen." She shrugged. "It was safer to hide."

"If these things can come through mirrors," Rhoan said, "why would he be using someone to take images through a keyhole?"

"Because they cannot come through unknown mirrors. They have to physically see them before they can use them."

Which explained the housekeeper's observation that the second man had carried a camera but wasn't using it. It also suggested our two female victims had a tryst with the wraith before he'd started visiting them nightly.

Yet their friends and families had claimed that neither women had lovers. And while you might not tell your family that sort of stuff, most women *did* gossip to friends.

"How come you know about these things and Jack doesn't?"

"Because we come from two very different parts of the world. There are always regional evolutionary differences in species." She shrugged. "The question is, why would the wraith come after me?"

I raised an eyebrow. "Don't suppose you've been having seriously sexual dreams of late, have you?"

She glanced at me. "This is the first time the wraith has attempted to get into my house. So, no, I haven't."

"What about the Melbourne vamp council? Are you on that?" Rhoan asked, moving to the nearest window and looking out. He still held the gun ready, too, though I doubted our felon would risk coming back so quickly. Then I noticed his hand was still near his ear and realized he was in contact with Jack.

"No, I'm not." She frowned. "Although I did a short stint a while ago, when a friend of mine went overseas. And I have to say, most of the councilors are arrogant jerks."

Coming from Sal—who could be as arrogant as the best of them—that was saying a lot. I leaned back against the kitchen counter and crossed my arms. "Those jerks are currently being murdered."

She nodded. "I'd heard, but I really didn't think it would involve me, given that my tenure was so brief."

"How come Jack didn't know?" He mustn't have; otherwise he would have mentioned it. Jack was many things, but he wasn't cavalier with the lives of his people, and he would have at least arranged protection for her.

"Because I only attended a few meetings, and my name never actually went onto the permanent roster."

"And how long ago did you stand in for your friend?"

"Nearly six months ago." She let the little dog down again then moved across to the percolator and began lining up cups. "As I said, it was mostly boring, everyday stuff. You know, someone wanting permission to set up a nest, someone else wanting help with a fledgling—" She paused and frowned as she pressed a button on the percolator. The machine began to spit and hiss, and the rich aroma of coffee filled the air. "There was one request the council refused. A man came to them requesting their help with several fledglings who were having trouble coping with the turn. As it happens, he hadn't actually asked the council's permission to set up a nest, so he was punished. He was severely reprimanded, and the nest was destroyed."

"And how are nests usually destroyed?" The answer was pretty obvious, given the method being used on the councilors, but it was a question that still had to be asked.

"Beheading, then the bodies left to burn in sunlight."

"That would certainly be enough to piss someone off."

"Yeah." She handed me a coffee, then walked over to the window and gave the other to Rhoan. "But it was six months ago. Surely if he was going to seek revenge, he would have done so before now."

"If I've learned one thing in this job, it's that the bad guys never do what you expect," Rhoan said. "And six months isn't a long time when you basically live forever."

"Point taken," she agreed, and took a sip of her own coffee. "He didn't seem particularly angry at the council's decision, though. And he stood by and watched the destruction without saying a word."

"Maybe he was so damn angry he just wasn't able to react." I breathed deeply, savoring the divine smell emanating from my coffee cup, then took a sip. It lived up to the promise of its aroma. I might even be tempted to say the fresh fruitiness and creamy coconut flavor was every bit as good as my old favorite, hazelnut. "What happened to him after that?"

"I don't know. He just disappeared off the radar."

"And the council didn't find that alarming?" Rhoan asked.

Sal's smile was wry. "If the council got alarmed every time a vampire decided to make himself scarce, they would very quickly become nervous wrecks."

"I thought vamps tended to stick to their own territories?"

She arched an eyebrow. "If we did that, then there would be none of us in Australia, would there?"

That was certainly true. Australia didn't have the same history as England, Europe, or even the United States. And when it came to white settlement—and the subsequent inflow of supernaturals—it was certainly one of the last places to be populated.

"So," I said, after taking another drink. "This man who went before the council, what sort of vamp was he?"

She shrugged. "I have to admit, I was bored and wasn't really taking that much notice of proceedings. But his name was Ammon. Ammon Nasser, I think."

It was a start, at least. I pulled out the photo taken from Kye's computer from my pocket and showed it to her. "Is this Nasser?"

She frowned at the printout, then shook her head. "Nasser is tall, with spiky brown hair and odd-colored eyes."

"Odd how?"

She hesitated. "It's almost like the color is unstable. It shifts hue constantly. It's very weird."

It sounded it. "Are mirror wraiths vampires?"

"Generally no, but like any other person born to this

world, they can chose to become one." She took a sip of coffee, her expression considering. "And he uses the mirrors extremely well, so I'd say he was a fairly old wraith when he changed."

"What makes you say that?"

"Because wraiths have certain restrictions when it comes to mirrors, much like vampires with sunshine. The ability really to use mirrors only becomes honed to a true skill as they age."

"How come you know so much about wraiths?" Rhoan asked, voice full of curiosity.

Her smile was bitter. "Because many years ago, one of them killed my family. It took me a very long time to track it down, but I eventually did."

Which was why she'd become a vampire. She didn't say it, but she didn't have to. "So how *do* you kill them?"

"The best way is to catch them in human form. Then you can dispatch them by any means that would kill a normal human. In smoke form, however, they are virtually unstoppable—though I have been told if you can hold them within the surface of one mirror, then smash that mirror in sunshine, you will destroy them."

"That doesn't exactly sound easy."

"No, which is why I chose the more old-fashioned method." Her gaze skated down my body and she smiled when she saw I was wearing wooden-heeled stilettos. "I would suggest stronger stakes. Those would not penetrate the heart of most vamps."

They weren't actually designed to do anything more than cause great discomfort, but Sal knew that. She was just getting back to her normal snarky self. Which was a good thing. "Are you able to give Jack a list of the councilors?" I added. "We really need to give these people protection."

Or, at the very least, warn them to get rid of the damn mirrors in their houses.

She hesitated, then nodded. "As long as Jack promises to keep his source confidential. They'd kick my ass if they found out it was me."

I couldn't help grinning. "I think you'll find there'd be more than a couple volunteers at the Directorate ready, willing, and able to protect that ass of yours."

An eyebrow winged upward. "Why, Riley, is that a compliment?"

"God, gag me with a spoon if I ever did that!"

She laughed—a throaty, warm sound. "Of course. How foolish of me."

"Riley," Jack said into my ear. "Get over to Vinny's and grab whatever information you can about this man you saw leaving her building last night—and by whatever means necessary. You'll have to fly, because I want Rhoan to bring Sal back to base."

Jack was obviously using a party line to talk to us all, because Sal immediately said, "I am quite capable of bringing myself in."

"Yes, I know, but I refuse to lose any more councilors—or part-time councilors—especially when that person is one of my own. So you will do as you're told."

"Boss," I said, "have you managed to get Kye's tracker signal yet?"

"We're only just now picking it up. He's not in the area." Which was no guarantee that he *hadn't* been. "Get moving, Riley."

"As soon as I finish my coffee." Which was a stupid thing to say, really.

"Now, Riley," he said, in that voice that suggested I'd better or there'd be hell to pay.

I blew out a breath, gulped down as much hot liquid as I could, once again burning my insides in the process, then did as ordered and got the hell out of there.

*O*f course, I might have been ordered to drag the information we needed out of Vinny, but that didn't mean I was stupid enough to do it alone. I'd confronted her like that once before, and it was only thanks to the fact that Quinn had been there as backup that Rhoan and I had gotten out relatively unscathed.

Once I'd flown back to my car—which, surprisingly, had been ignored by vandals or looters in what was traditionally a high-crime area—I grabbed my phone, hit the VID button, and dialed Quinn.

"Well, hello there," he said in that softly lilting tone that always made my toes want to curl. "I was wondering when I was going to hear from you."

"Sorry, it's been a horrible night." If you could call great sex with a decidedly unwanted man who also happened to be your soul mate horrible, that is. "Have you got anything important going on right now?"

"Why?"

The way he said it told me it wouldn't have mattered if he did. He'd be there for me, no matter what I needed. God, I really *did* love this man—even if it had taken me forever to realize that fact.

"I have to go question Vinny, and I suspect she's not going to like the subject matter—"

"And you'd like my presence as a motivational tool," he finished for me.

I grinned. "Well, she did become very motivated the last time you accompanied us."

"That's because whatever else she is, she possesses a sensible respect for beings who are far older and far more powerful than she is." He paused, and a deliciously sensual smile touched his lips. "Unlike some werewolves who shall remain nameless."

I laughed. "As you've noted repeatedly, werewolves have no sense."

"A truer point has never been made." He glanced at his watch. "I'll be there in twenty minutes."

"I'll be here waiting."

"Let's hope it always remains that way," he said, and hung up before I could say anything.

Making me feel even more horrible than I already did.

I rubbed the heels of my palms against my eyes and wished it would all become simple. Wished that the problem that was Kye would just disappear and that it could go back to being just me and Quinn.

But that was never going to happen, and I had to learn to deal—no matter how much pain that caused both to me and to those I loved.

Of course, Quinn would never understand the way I'd dealt with things last night. He was an old-fashioned sort when it came to sex, and giving in to what was basically blackmail would be something he'd never understand.

Or condone.

Not that he'd ever learn of it. Not if I could help it. I might love the man, but I also knew what he was capable of, and the one thing that worried me was him taking out Kye in a fit of anger. Or—worse—a fit of jealousy.

He might know about the soul mate bond of were-wolves, but I doubted he understood the true depth of it. Doubted he believed it could really lead to the death of the surviving partner, even though he'd witnessed the devastation Rhoan had gone through when Liander had almost died.

I leaned back against the headrest and turned on the music. But it didn't stop the thoughts from going around and around in my head, like cats chasing their tails. Nor did it help ease the worry that, sooner or later, this was all going to blow up in my face.

Fifteen minutes later, Jack buzzed me. I picked up the phone from the seat and hit the RECEIVE button. "If you're wondering why I haven't moved, I'm waiting for Quinn. I've got a feeling I'm going to need his help if we want Vinny to talk."

"Good idea," he said, "but that's not what I'm calling about."

The edge in his voice had my heart just about leaping into my throat. "Nothing has happened to Rhoan or Sal, has it?"

"No, they're safely on their way into the Directorate. But we did a full trace on Carlos Martez and have discovered that he died some five and a half years ago in a traffic accident."

"Well, he looks pretty good for a dead man."

"Obviously, we are dealing with someone who has usurped his identity."

Had Kye known that the real Carlos was dead when he'd given me his name? And if he had, why not tell me? Or was it simply another of his games? Another way of maintaining some form of control over me? "Was Carlos listed as human or vampire?"

"Vamp."

"Then how could he die in a car accident?"

"Easily. He ran into the back of a truck, which subsequently lost its load and decapitated him."

"And it was definitely an accident?"

"Yes. There was a witness." He paused. "Interestingly enough, that witness is a young woman currently residing in Vinny's nest."

"How convenient."

"Yes." His voice was heavy with sarcasm. "We've also done a preliminary search for Ammon Nasser. We have no records of him entering the country, but that's not unusual, given we only list those who come here legally. I've applied to the greater council for details, but it may take some time."

"You know, they're not exactly falling over themselves to help us, and that's damn strange, considering it's their people being chopped up."

"We're dealing with a very old, very formal organization here, Riley. And there are set processes in place for good reason, whether they chafe you or not."

I grinned. "Hey, they're the ones with their necks on the line, not me, so it's no skin off my nose."

He snorted softly. "Make sure the com-link is on so we can hear the conversation when you're in Vinny's."

"It'll be my first priority." Which was a blatant lie, because my first priority would be kissing the hell out of Quinn.

Which is precisely what I did when he arrived eight minutes later.

"You're late," I murmured, when we finally came up for air.

He smiled and lightly traced his finger around my well-kissed lips. "Unfortunately, the traffic was worse than usual. A four-car accident, according to the news."

I kissed his fingertip and barely resisted the temptation to draw the digit into my mouth and suck on it. That would only lead to activities we really didn't have time for.

"Shall we head inside?" he said, even as the scent of desire began emanating from him. I guess after all the time we'd been spending together he'd know exactly where my thoughts had been heading.

"Yeah." I swung around and led the way. He walked beside me, not touching me physically but close enough that the scent of him, the heat of him, swirled around me—a blanket of warm protection that I just wanted to roll up in. But that was a distant likelihood for the next several hours, at least. "Our dear Vinny has been keeping secrets from us. We're about to lean on her to discover them."

"I always did appreciate a good 'lean,' " he said, amusement in his voice. "But she's grown stronger since our last visit, and since she thinks she knows exactly what I'm capable of, she will be less tractable."

"Even *I* don't know exactly what you're capable of," I said wryly, "so she's a fool if she thinks she knows all there is to know."

And Vinny was many things, but a fool wasn't one of them.

My phone beeped as a message came in, and I dug it out of my pocket and glanced down. My heart skipped several beats when I saw it was from Kye.

Lunch is canceled, it said. *Have meeting with a client, Will contact you later.*

Hope surged. Maybe last night—and my decision to stop fighting and give him what he wanted—was already beginning to pay off. With the challenge gone, maybe—just maybe—he'd pack up and move on.

It was a slim hope, but one I had to cling to nonetheless.

"Anything important?" Quinn asked, his voice nonchalant.

I glanced at him, noting the sudden remoteness in his expression.

He knew.

"Just a canceled lunch meeting." I shoved my phone away. "Nothing important."

"Uh-huh," he said, voice still noncommittal.

I wanted to reach out and catch his hand in mine, but that would only confirm his fears. And even though those fears were very real, I didn't want to cause him any more pain than I already had.

We walked though the doors of Vinny's high-rise and began to climb the stairs. A rumble of excitement began to touch the air, growing stronger the higher we climbed. I pressed the com-link, making sure it was on.

"Vinny knows we're here," Quinn said, the amusement back in his voice. "She is excited about it."

I glanced back at him. "Is that why the air feels so charged?"

"Yep. Our mistress of emotions is planning to challenge our authority."

"Then she's a damn fool."

He smiled, but this time there was nothing warm about it. "All youngsters challenge authority at some point in their lives. But most choose their targets more wisely."

We reached the top floor. A different girl guarded the door, but like the previous one, she was dressed casually but had a suspicious bulge on her right hip. And this girl looked arrogant. Confident.

If the fledglings were taking their lead from their master, then Quinn was right. Vinny *had* grown overly confident. So why the sudden change? There'd been little evidence of this attitude when I'd talked to her yesterday.

Did the man who'd visited her last night have anything to do with it? If so, it was more important than ever that we find him. And that she help us.

"We're here to see Vinny," I said, stopping little more than a foot away from the guard.

"*You* may go in, but the old one stays here—"

"His name is Quinn and he accompanies me or I will bust Vinny's ass and drag her down to the Directorate." I raised my voice a little. "So call off your dog, Vinny."

The guard's gaze went blank for a moment, then she said, her voice several octaves lower than it had been moments ago, "She does not wish problems with the Directorate, but she does not wish the old one inside her sanctuary."

"The old one can rip your precious little world apart whether he is inside or outside, Vincenta." Though Quinn's voice was still decidedly mild, there was a hint of steel underneath that was warning enough to anyone with any intelligence. "But perhaps a demonstration is in order?"

The wash of power that suddenly burned across my senses was unlike anything I'd ever felt before. It was dark, dangerous, and somehow unholy, and it sent chills racing across my flesh. My gaze jumped to Quinn, and for a moment he didn't really seem whole or real, but rather a creature of shadow and imagination.

And somewhere deep inside of me, a memory twitched. I'd seen him do that once before, but that time he'd done it to save my life.

From within the room, there was a weird ripping, popping sound, then the screaming began. High, terrible screaming.

God, I said telepathically, *what the hell did you just do?*

I showed them just what an old one is capable of. I do not believe Vincenta will cause you any more problems.

Did you have to kill one of them to do it? But even as I said that, I knew it was a stupid question. If Vinny was beginning to test the Directorate's authority and control, then yeah, something drastic had to be done. And whether I liked to admit it or not, the Directorate maintained authority in this city—and others—by the knowledge that they would do whatever it took to hunt down those who went against the rules.

Vinny was an emo vampire, and her methods of rebellion were far subtler—and possibly more dangerous—than those of regular blood vampires. We couldn't afford to have her flexing her muscles when the city was already in turmoil.

I killed the one armed with silver who was standing in the shadows of the wall curtains. It wasn't one of her main concubines.

I'm sure Vinny will appreciate that consideration.

The sarcasm in my mental voice had his lips briefly twitching, but there was little amusement in his tone as he glanced at the somewhat paler guard and said, "Open the door, or I will do it for you."

The guard stepped back and opened the door. Quinn held out his hand and added, "Give me the gun and the extra bullets."

The note of command was in his voice and the girl obeyed without question. Those bullets were silver, as well. I felt the burn of them as Quinn pocketed both them and the weapon.

I stepped inside the warm room, my gaze sweeping the velvet lushness before stopping at what could only be described as an explosion of flesh, blood, and gore. There were no bones, no body parts, just an oozing, awful mess.

He'd vaporized her.

God.

Just . . .

God.

How on earth could you do that to another living being? I flicked my gaze across to Vinny and her cozy little setup down the far end of the room. If I was shocked, then Vinny and her entourage were positively scared shitless.

And with good reason.

Damn it, Quinn, just how long have you been concealing this little ability from me?

I was born with it. It is a gift—he paused, then added darkly—*or a curse of my Aedh heritage. I do not use it much, because it has severe consequences.*

Yeah. I was looking at the dripping remains of them. *And yet . . . I've seen you do something like this before?*

He hesitated. *Yes. A while ago, when you first started dating Kellen. One of the chameleons from Starke's underground labs came after you.*

Chameleons are a rare breed of nonhumans who can

take on any background and literally become a part of it. They are also ferocious flesh-eaters and extremely hard to kill.

How come I've only just remembered it? Or is that a stupid question?

Our relationship was still very tenuous, he said gently, *I did not wish to scare you away.*

I told you to keep out of my head.

And I have. As I said, this was a while ago. Before you civilized me.

I snorted softly. As if there were *ever* a hope of civilizing this particular vampire. He might have an urbane and polished front, but underneath he was still very much a powder keg—and just as dangerous if handled the wrong way.

And yet I felt safer with him than I ever would with Kye.

I kept striding forward. Vinny was attended by her usual passel of toga-clad teenagers, but this time the clothing of those nearest the curtain bore the splattered remains of what had once been human. Or nonhuman. Their faces were positively green, and I guessed it was only Vinny's influence that was keeping them in the room. There was no caressing of their master's skin, no languid eyes or secretive little smiles. It had all been annihilated by the show of Quinn's power.

Vinny had definitely paled, and her normally seductive lips were little more than thin slashes, but the abject terror I'd glimpsed earlier was gone. She met my gaze squarely and there was now a hint of steel in the brown of her eyes.

She might still be scared shitless, but she wasn't about to let on to her fledglings *or* us.

And for that, I had to admire her.

I stopped several feet in front of her, with Quinn standing just behind me, his breath stirring the little hairs on my neck.

"I told you once before never to mess with the Directorate, Vinny. Now you know the consequences."

She glared balefully at me for several seconds, then pointed with her chin at the man behind me. "He's not Directorate."

"He's an advisor, so that makes him one of us." I hesitated, then added, "One fledgling dead is better than the whole nest. And trust me, that is currently an option if the Melbourne council is informed of your recent activities."

"I have no idea what you mean."

She was lying. I could taste it, even if I couldn't see it in her expression. And while there was little to be seen in *her* face, the toga-clad teenagers behind her rustled nervously. Pale fingers reached out and began to caress Vinny's arms and shoulders, and a gentle hum of energy tinged the air.

I wondered if they were reassuring themselves or Vinny but didn't really care enough to ask. Not when there were more important questions.

"I'm talking about your association with the man calling himself Carlos Martez."

"I have no idea who—"

"Vinny, he was seen leaving your building last night,

and we all know no one can get in here without your permission."

"He was merely here paying his respects. There is nothing sinister in that, guardian."

She changed tack as swiftly as a tiger snake, and was probably just as deadly. Or would have been, if Quinn wasn't standing behind me.

"Except for the fact that Martez has just tried to kill a Directorate employee."

"He wouldn't do that. You're mistaken."

"I was there, Vinny. I saw him."

Amusement flared briefly in her eyes. "If you were there, you should have stopped him."

"It's hard to stop someone when they can escape through mirrors."

"If you've come to me for information about how to destroy such a person, I'm afraid you're out of luck. I have no idea."

Quinn didn't move, but his power whipped out again. This time it was the barb of telepathy. Somewhere behind us a door slammed, the sound echoing across the silence.

"Do tell your people not to try and sneak up behind us," Quinn said mildly. "I'd hate to kill any more of your concubines."

Vinny's fingers clenched. With a visible effort, she flexed them again. "I've already said I can't help, so I don't understand why you are still here."

"Vinny dearest, we haven't even started." I stepped forward, grabbed the front of her gown, and yanked her out of her chair and away from the caressing, calming influence of the teenagers. She yelped and briefly struggled, her pale arms flying. I ducked the blows and shook her a little more. "Carlos Martez died over five years ago. Tell me who has assumed his identity."

"I don't—"

I shook her again, hard enough to rattle her teeth. "One of your fledglings was a witness, so you *knew* Martez was dead. Who did you deal that information to?"

"I can't," she said, fury mixing with fear in her eyes. "He'll kill me."

"And the Directorate will kill you if you don't," I commented. "So choose which side of the bed you want to lie on, Vinny, because these games of yours are getting a little tiresome."

Something flickered through her eyes. The snake was twisting yet again. "He is my creator. I had no choice in doing what he said."

Is that true? I asked, without turning to look at Quinn. Without my full attention, the serpent I held just might strike, even with Quinn at my back.

To a degree, yes. The power of the creator over the fledgling lessens with time, but Vinny is not old enough to be totally free of his influence.

"Give me a name, Vinny."

She hesitated, then said, "Ammon Nasser."

The man the council had all but destroyed. He obviously had to be similar in looks to Martez to be able to maintain the fraud for so long. "And why did he come here?"

"Because this is my territory. It is considered polite to state one's aims when entering the territory of another."

Also true, up to a point, Quinn said. *Vampires tend to tolerate other vamps within their hunting grounds if they are not causing problems.*

I knew you guys were territorial, but I didn't think it actually meant having defined territories.

Why do you think there is such a wide spread of vampires? Unlike werewolves, we cannot easily live in each other's shadow.

Which had to make life in a nest interesting. Obviously, though, emo vamps had no such problems. To Vinny, I said, "Would you even have a say in him setting up another nest, given you're one of his creations?" Surprise flitted through her eyes, and I smiled grimly. "Yes, we know all about it. The council is not so staid and set in their ways that they wouldn't feed the Directorate information when someone is killing them off."

Yeah, they totally wouldn't, Quinn said, his amusement running through my mind—a river of warmth that made me want to smile.

"I did warn him of that danger," Vinny said, her sincerity almost believable. Almost. "I tried to talk him out of his plans, but to no avail."

"Then why did he wait six months to begin his revenge?"

She snorted softly. "Why do you think? If he'd begun straightaway, the culprit would have been obvious. He is many things, but a fool isn't one of them."

"So what was he doing in the six months since the council wiped out his nest?"

She shrugged, pulling against my grip. "I didn't ask and didn't care to ask. He keeps out of my way—mostly, anyway—and I keep out of his."

"But you know where he's currently residing?"

"No. As I said, Nasser isn't a fool." Her brief smile was amused. "Apparently, he doesn't trust me."

Obviously, Nasser was well aware that he'd raised a snake. "Is he a mirror wraith as well as an emo vamp?"

She smiled. It set my nerves on edge. "Yes, he is. I'm surprised you discovered it, because not even the council would have known that."

"Why not?" I asked, more out of curiosity than any real need to know.

"Because he came into this country illegally, and therefore would not be listed on the council's books."

Wouldn't have mattered if he was, Quinn commented. *The council wouldn't have shared the information with you.*

The council are rather large pains in the butt. To Vinny, I said, "So why did Nasser come here last night?"

"Because he supplements his feeding by feeding off of us."

I raised my eyebrows. "And you let him?"

"I have no choice." She almost spat the words. "He is an old and hungry soul who cannot be satisfied with feeding off a woman or two. He needs the energy supplied by a nest."

Maybe that's why Vinny's nest has grown substantially

in the last few months, Quinn commented. *She's been supporting her creator's needs as well as her own.*

She's using him as an excuse. She wants her own empire, and would be growing as fast as she could anyway. To Vinny, I added, "So he *has* fed apart from the nest?"

"Yes." Something flickered in her eyes. Amusement, perhaps. Or cunning.

"And is he capable of killing?"

The cunning in her brown eyes got sharper, and I suddenly realized that she wanted her creator out of the way. She'd give us what we wanted, all right—not only to save *her* skin but to get rid of his.

"If you're asking me if his feeding killed Renatta Bailey and Janette Crowley, then the answer is yes. He boasted about it."

"And why would he do that when he knows you're as trustworthy as a snake?"

Her smile was bitter, hard. "Because it was a reminder that he could and would do the same to this nest if I stepped out of line."

I frowned. "How could one man kill an entire nest? Even if that man is your creator?"

It might be possible to kill Vinny, but there'd still be an entire nest to cope with, and even Quinn with his Aedh powers wouldn't have an easy time of that.

"It is *because* he's my creator that he can do it. I cannot deny his demand that we feed him, and he could, if he wished, drain us so completely that we die."

Hence her sudden desire to use us to get rid of her master.

"And you have no idea where he is staying?"

"No. I would give him to you if I could, but I really do not know."

She telling the truth? I asked Quinn.

Unfortunately, yes.

I grunted and released my grip on Vinny. The movement was so sudden she staggered backward and fell into the chaise longue. The toga-clad teenagers instantly began to caress her skin, and the soft humming I'd heard earlier resumed.

"I appreciate your help, Vinny."

It was sarcastically said, and the old arrogance flared in her eyes. "And I'd appreciate it if you leave and never come back."

"I'm afraid that is never going to happen. It's the price you pay for empire-building."

She didn't say anything to that. I turned and walked for the door—and felt safe only because Quinn was at my back. Had I been alone, I probably would have had a dozen silver bullets in it long before I ever got there.

The outside guard swung the door open as we neared, but before I could exit, Vinny said, "Riley?"

I paused and glanced at her. "What?"

"There is something else about Nasser you might want to know. Something that is vital if you're to have any hope of tracking him down."

I met her gaze and saw the cunning in it. "We're not paying you for the information, Vinny."

"Oh, consider this a freebie."

I snorted softly. "Hardly, when us getting rid of your creator means we'd actually be doing you a great favor."

"There is that, as well." She smiled benignly. I didn't believe it for a second. "Mirror wraiths have two interesting sets of skills. In vapor form, they can use reflective surfaces to travel through, therefore releasing them from the usual restraints of blood vampires."

Which explained how he managed to attack Sal during the day. "And the second?"

"The second will make your hunt more interesting." She paused—just to be annoying, I'm sure. "You see, they are flesh-shifters. They can mold their skins to resemble any person they touch."

Chapter 11

"Well, that sure puts a wrench in the works," I grumbled, once we were clear of Vinny's building. "He could be anyone and we'd never know it."

"I think you would," Quinn said. "You've crossed paths with him several times now, so even if he assumes another form, you'd probably pick up his scent."

Maybe, and maybe not. There were ways and means of covering a base scent, and if he was an old vampire—or wraith—then he could probably also tone down his energy "vibe" or whatever the hell it was. "At least it explains how he managed to use Martez's identity for so long without anyone picking it up."

"The obvious place to look is Dante's. That's where the murders happened."

"And that's where Martez went when I was following him last night." I raised my face to the morning sunshine, letting it warm my skin. "He could even be Dante himself."

But could an emo vamp who was also a mirror wraith constantly exude the sort of sexual glamor that Dante did? Vinny could seduce just about anyone, but it was a power she could switch on or off and one that drained her after a while—unless she was feeding while using it. Dante was simply "on" all the time.

"That is very possible."

For the first time, there was a note of weariness in Quinn's voice, and I glanced up at him. His normally tanned skin seemed redder than usual, suggesting the sunlight was beginning to burn him even though midday—the dangerous part of the day for him—was a ways off yet. I lightly touched his arm. Despite his color, his skin was cool, which was unusual, considering that generally happened only when he wasn't feeding enough. "Are you okay?"

He nodded. "As I said before, using the Aedh skills has its consequences."

"Meaning it drains you?"

"Depending on how much I use, it can drain me to the point of unconsciousness. Luckily, that was not the case here."

Meaning he hadn't used full power and yet had still been able to pulverize that person . . .

The thought had another tremor running through me. It was scary to think that one man could contain so much power . . .

Jesus, *Risa*.

"Yes," Quinn said, before I could ask the question.

"Risa will have the skill, which is why I so readily agreed to train her. If she doesn't know how to control it, she could be a threat to everyone around her."

"Maybe that's why Dia is so desperate to get your help. Maybe she saw something in her dreams." And hopefully, the death she'd seen for herself wasn't at the hands of her beautiful little girl. "Do you need to feed or something?"

He hesitated, then shook his head. "I do, but Jack will have my head if I drag you away from this investigation right now."

"You're older than Jack, and more dangerous besides. I don't think you're in any danger from him—metaphorically or otherwise."

"Jack is not someone you should brush aside so easily," Quinn said wryly. "Especially when he's probably listening."

"Hey, he knows I love and respect him. He just can't do what you just did." And thank God for that, I added silently. One and a half atom-splitting beings in my little world was more than enough.

"I do not think I need to know the details of what Quinn just did," Jack said into my ear, confirming that he had indeed been listening. "But I agree with him that we need to start with Dante's and its owner. Do you think Kye still has the place monitored?"

"I have no idea."

"Then find out and get back to me. If he hasn't, then we'll need to put cameras and bugs in place."

"We could just go in and talk to Starke." Then the

undercurrent in his words hit me, and I added, "You have him marked as a suspect, don't you?"

"Starke *is* the likely starting point, now that we're dealing with a flesh-shifter. For all we know, the real Dante Starke is a rotting headless corpse in a cellar somewhere."

"Someone would have smelled him by now if that was the case." I hesitated, then added, "Would an emo vamp have the same sort of sexual glamor that Starke has? Because the Starke I've been meeting is dynamite."

"If he is old enough, yes. And if he has refined his methods, you wouldn't even know he was feeding. All you would feel was lust."

Well, I'd certainly felt that around Starke. And if he was our wraith, then he'd also paid me a visit. Which presented another problem. "There's one sticky point in all this—neither Renatta Bailey nor Janette Crowley apparently had a lover, and yet Sal claims wraiths can only travel through mirrors they've physically seen. How did he drain them nightly if he's never been to their houses?" He'd certainly never been near *mine*.

"I don't know enough about wraiths to answer that question," Jack said heavily.

Quinn and I reached my car and stopped. "Where do you want me to go once I find out whether the bugs are still online or not?"

"Come into the office."

"Will do." I clicked the com-link off and caught Quinn's hands in mine. "Are you going to be okay to drive, or do you want me to drop you off somewhere?"

"And leave the Porsche sitting around here for the vandals? Bite your tongue, woman."

I grinned. "It's not like you can't afford another one. Or a hundred."

"I didn't get rich by being wasteful."

"No, you got rich through becoming a thief."

"Which I did for only for a very brief period in my life. Most of my money has been honestly gained."

"Hey, I've seen the prices your airline charges for tickets. There's nothing honest about that."

He smiled, then leaned forward and kissed me. His lips were light on mine, his kiss gentle and yet potent.

"Be careful when dealing with the spirit wraith," he said, his lips still so close that his breath warmed mine. "Have you still got that knife I gave you?"

"It's in the car's weapons stash."

"Then carry it. It works on more than just demons—and on more than those who inhabit flesh."

Then I'd be carrying it. Anything that gave me a slight advantage was a damn good thing right now. I ran my fingertips down his chin. "I do love you. You know that, don't you?"

He raised an eyebrow. "And what has bought about this sudden declaration?"

"I sometimes think I don't say it enough."

He smiled. "Well, it *is* nice to hear it said out loud every now and again, even if I do know it for a fact."

It didn't stop him from fearing Kye, though, or what he might do to us. He might not have said it, but that darkness was there in his eyes. And there was nothing

I could say to ease those fears, because they were mine, as well.

I gave him another quick kiss. "I'll see you sometime tonight."

"Make sure that you do." He hesitated, his gaze sweeping my face, as if memorizing it. "Shoot to kill, Riley. Don't hesitate."

"Why do people keep telling me that?" I muttered, even as goose bumps ran across my flesh. It was almost as if everyone around me were having premonitions of impending doom. "I'm a guardian. I'll do what I'm paid to do. I think I've more than proven that."

"I know. It doesn't stop me from worrying, though."

At least he didn't try to stop me, or ask me to give up being a guardian. That made him a far better man than Kellen ever was.

"Go get yourself some sustenance." I hesitated, then grinned and added, "Just don't go enjoying the experience too much."

He laughed, touched my chin lightly—almost reverently—then walked over to his car. I waved him good-bye, then dug out my phone again.

"Well, this is an unexpected pleasure," Kye said, his golden eyes glowing on the vid screen.

"For you, maybe," I said tartly. "For me, it's all business."

He laughed. The sound was so different from the one I'd heard only moments before and yet, in its own way, just as powerful. "That's what I like about you, Riley. You cut straight through the crap."

And yet there was still tons of it in my life. And I was currently talking to the primary source.

"Have you still got your bugs and cameras in Dante's?"

He hesitated. "No, I pulled them this morning. Why?"

I ignored the question and said, "I hope that doesn't mean you've completed your mission, because if it does, I'm going to have to arrest your ass."

"What it means is the client's wife has moved on to greener pastures." He paused, and his voice lowered several octaves as he added, "Although I'd really like to see you try and arrest me. That could get interesting."

The way he emphasized "interesting" sent a shudder racing down my spine, and it wasn't entirely the ice of fear.

"And I'd hate to make things interesting for you," I said tartly. "So maybe I'll send someone else." Someone he *couldn't* seduce.

"I refuse to be caught by anyone else but you." He paused. "I don't suppose you feel like handcuffing and interrogating me now, do you?"

"No," I said briskly. Though the usual stupid part of me wished I did. "I have far more important things to do with my time. And I thought you had a meeting with another client?"

"It's just finished." His smile flashed. "Don't suppose you want to know who it was?"

"No." *Yes.*

"Shame, because it's someone you've had a long association with."

I knew who he meant in an instant, and my stomach curled. Why the hell would he be meeting my pack leader? "Not Blake?"

"The very man."

"You could have done me a favor and shot him."

"And why would I do that? Unless, of course, you pay me to do so." Again his grin flashed. He was obviously feeling mighty fine this morning. Whether it had anything to do with our marathon last night or the meeting with Blake was anyone's guess. "And from you," he added, "I'll accept a currency other than cash."

I just bet. "He's tried to hurt me once before. We both know he wants to do so again."

"True. And believe me, if he does anything that threatens your life, then I *will* kill him, and free of charge." He paused. "You are mine to kill, Riley, no one else's."

"Kill me and you kill yourself," I snapped back. "And you don't seem the suicidal type to me."

Crazy, yes. Suicidal, no.

He laughed. There was nothing warm or comforting about it. "You really have no idea what I'm capable of, Riley."

That was certainly true. "Was Blake behind the bug you placed on me last night?"

"Maybe. And it wasn't a bug but a deadener." He paused again. "Why do you need to use the cameras and bugs at the club? Is Dante a suspect?"

I countered his questions with one of my own. "Why didn't you put the bug somewhere more subtle?"

He smiled. "Maybe I wanted you to know what

Blake was up to. Or maybe it was designed as an earring so I had no choice. Your turn to give an answer."

"At this point in time, everyone is a suspect."

"Even me?" Amusement laced his tone. "Riley, I'm hurt."

I snorted softly. "We know there are two people involved in these killings, so there's no reason why you can't be one of them."

"That's true," he said cheerfully. "So, are you coming to arrest me? Perhaps we can get hot and heavy with the questioning."

"Sorry, you'll have control your deviant fantasies a little longer. I've got a club to bug."

"You never did explain why Dante and his club are suspect."

"No, I didn't. Shame," I added cheerfully, then hung up, climbed into my car, and drove to the Directorate.

Jack glanced up as I walked into the otherwise empty squad room. "Any luck on the bugs?"

"Which bugs are we talking about? The one found on me or the ones Kye placed? Have the labs said anything about my bug?"

"Only that it's black market and not something we've even heard whispers about." His expression was grim. "Which makes me wonder why he left it on you."

"He said it was a warning. And that he couldn't conceal it better because it was designed as an earring." I wasn't entirely sure I believed *either* reason.

Jack grunted. "And the surveillance equipment he placed at the club?"

"He says his target has moved on and that he's removed them."

Jack raised his eyebrows. "Is that a sarcastic note I hear in your voice?"

"Me? Sarcastic? Never." I walked over to the coffee machine and poured myself a cup of the horrid stuff. Beans had been packed, and this was better than nothing. But only just, I thought, wincing as I took a sip. "I just think it's a little convenient. Either he's made the kill and is covering his ass so we won't arrest him when and if we find the body, or something else is going on."

"You don't think he's involved in these murders, do you?"

"Honestly? I have no idea. The fact that he's been so helpful suggests not—and we have absolutely no evidence pointing to the fact that he is—but he's a twisted sort of soul, and he may be getting an inordinate amount of pleasure seeing just how close we get."

"The other man your ghost talked about wasn't a vampire, so it's possible that he could be a werewolf."

"But it's also possible he's a shifter of any other make and model." I took a sip and wondered why I was defending the man. It wasn't as if I actually wanted to help him out. But I didn't want to see a possibly innocent man accused, either—even if he was as rotten as Kye. "So, what's next?"

He grimaced. "Kade talked to the woman whose car was stolen, but she didn't give us anything new. He's downstairs now collecting the appropriate bugging gear for the club. We've arranged for an electrical outage to happen"—he glanced at his watch—"at twelve forty-five. We'll divert their call to ensure our people are the ones phoned and tell them we have vans in the area. Lunch seems to be a busy time for them, so they won't be looking too closely at what the electricians are doing when they've got a room full of people to cope with."

I frowned. "Dante will more than likely be there at that time, and he doesn't miss much."

"I know. Which is why you're going to be there at twelve-thirty to interview the man."

Oh, *great*. "Boss—"

"Don't 'boss' me, Riley. You *will* go talk to him." Meaning the one thing I'd been trying to avoid was the one thing I was now being ordered to do. He continued, "We need those bugs in there—and this case solved—as soon as possible."

My frown deepened at the tension in his voice. "So why do I suspect there's more than the usual urgency behind that order?"

"Because the Melbourne council—what remains of them—is meeting tonight, as usual—against our advice, I might add—and that just makes them a very juicy target."

"Why on earth would they do that? I thought they were all hightailing it out of the state until the crisis was over."

His expression was grim. "They were ordered not to by the greater council, who plans to use them as bait."

I blinked. "Talk about a bloodthirsty method of getting your man!"

"And if they get the *wrong* man, things could get

very nasty for all of us." He pointed his pen at me. "So you will wear something pretty to Dante's and distract the hell out of Starke."

I glanced at my watch. It was after eleven, so I really didn't have time to go home and clean up. "I'll need some fresh clothes if I'm going to distract Starke. And you need to let me know the minute Kade and his people have finished so I can get the hell out of there."

"We will. Now go. And don't expect the Directorate to cough up huge amounts of money for the outfit. Think budget sexy."

"I'll try." I gulped down the last of the horrendous coffee, then headed up the stairs and down the street to the Direct Factory Outlet Center to find something suitable to wear.

It was just after twelve-thirty by the time I arrived at Dante's. I climbed out of the car then adjusted my skirt, smoothing the tight material over my hips. I'd been tempted just to wear jeans and a T-shirt, but Jack had ordered a complete distraction.

The tight black skirt with the teasing split that went high up my right thigh and the dark-green, button-up top that was almost—but not quite—see-through were certainly that. And there were just enough buttons undone to reveal a slight hint of breast. A tease, not a full-on show.

Now I just had to survive the full force of his "distraction" and try to avoid getting laid.

Of course, the outfit made the knife and its protective sheath sitting at the base of my spine somewhat obvious, but I wasn't going to go into that place without some sort of weapon at hand. In fact, I had several, because my purse held my laser as well as my keys—and in the right hands, those little bits of metal could be quite dangerous indeed.

Especially when they had the power of a dhampire behind them.

I glanced at my watch, saw that it was time, and strolled toward Dante's. The guard at the door was new—to my knowledge, at least—and he eyed me intently, his face giving little away.

"I need to talk to Dante Starke," I said, taking my badge from my purse and showing it to him. "Is he in at the moment?"

His gaze swept the badge then he nodded. "One moment, and I'll see if he's available."

His gaze went blank, meaning that, like the guard who'd worked here before him, he was a newer vampire. Maybe Starke couldn't afford more seasoned personnel.

"He said he'll meet you in his office shortly." He opened the door and I walked inside the gloom of the club. Once again, the smell assaulted my senses, making me pause. The riot of hunger and lust, all entwined with the scent of humanity, vampire, booze, and blood, had my stomach turning. Yet once again, a tiny part of my soul was turned on by it.

I walked toward the bar. The same man was there, still chewing gum and looking superior.

"Hey, you're looking pretty special today," he said, his gaze sweeping my body and lingering on the length of thigh. "The boss is a lucky man."

"This outfit is not for your boss's benefit but rather for the man I have a hot date with after this interview. So if you could hurry your boss along, it would be most appreciated."

"If I had known such a delicious treat waited for me," Dante said, his voice sliding up from behind me and wrapping around me as seductively as a caress, "I would most certainly have been here to receive you."

I turned around. He was standing four feet away and I hadn't even heard him approach. His golden hair was tousled and his tight-fitting shirt was untucked and not fully buttoned, revealing teasing glimpses of tight golden curls. He was wearing black pants that were neatly creased and seemed to emphasize the sheer size of him, and his feet were bare.

He'd just come from his bed, I thought, and tried to shake the image from my mind.

"As I just said, the treat is not for you." I might be under orders to distract the man, but any sudden change of attitude was going to raise suspicions—especially if he *was* our man. "I just have a few quick questions, then I'll be gone again."

"I'm shattered," he said, his expression crestfallen but golden eyes twinkling. "Boris, a bottle of our finest."

"You know I can't drink it." I crossed my arms, forcing my breasts a little closer together and making it totally obvious that I wasn't wearing a bra.

"Of course you can't," he agreed, his gaze barely flickering to my chest, yet the heat of him seeming to leap substantially—flaring white hot then just as quickly disappearing, as if he were controlling it tightly. "With two glasses, please."

Boris grinned and wandered off to wherever they stashed the good stuff. Starke waved a hand toward the office. "After you, sweet thing."

I snorted softly and led the way, trying but not entirely succeeding in keeping the distance between us.

"That knife is an interesting addition to your outfit," Starke commented, his voice low and gently seductive. "And it does put an interesting twist on what you consider a hot date."

"That knife is for you." I wrapped my hand around the handle of the office door and pushed it open. "And if you get too touchy-feely, I *will* use it."

He laughed. The sound rumbled pleasantly across my senses. "I shall consider myself warned."

But not frightened off, obviously.

The office was no less sparsely furnished than before, although one additional item had been added more recently. As well as the two plush velvet armchairs, there was now also a huge chaise longue.

Its message was obvious.

I thrust the images of golden skin and hard bodies delightfully entwined away irritably and forced my feet firmly in the direction of the chairs. I sat down, crossing my legs and ensuring the skirt's split revealed plenty. Including, if he looked hard enough, the fact I was wearing lacy black panties. I glanced at my watch and saw it was now twelve forty. The power should be failing at any minute.

"I just have a few questions to ask," I said briskly,

entwining my fingers and resting them on my lap. His gaze followed the movement and lingered on the skin being revealed. "It shouldn't take that long."

"Please, take all the time you want." He pulled the other chair closer and sat down, the action grace itself. "I am quite enjoying the view."

I made a slight attempt to adjust the skirt. "I would prefer it if you didn't."

"And I'd prefer it if you were naked and putty in my arms, but we can't all get what we want, now can we?"

"Thankfully, in this case, no."

He smiled and touched a toe to my calf. Delight shimmered up my leg, heating me in ways I couldn't even begin to describe.

I shifted so that his touch fell away. His amusement grew stronger, twitching his lips.

"Do you know a man called Kye Murphy?"

He frowned, pretending to consider the question as his deep-lidded gaze slithered up to my breasts then down to my legs again. "Should I?"

"We know he's been to this club."

He arched a pale eyebrow. "And how would you know that? I do hope you haven't bugged the place. That would be most inconsiderate, considering I've gone out of my way to help you."

"It's the Directorate's business to be inconsiderate— especially when we're chasing a killer." I paused, and allowed a small smile to touch my lips. "However, we haven't bugged you. I saw him when I was viewing the security camera tapes."

"Ah, of course." He laced his fingers and dropped

them on his lap—drawing my gaze to the bulge that was his crotch. I have to say, it seemed even more impressive now than it had before. But then, if this guy *was* a flesh-shifting wraith who could alter his body any way he wished, he wouldn't exactly be gifting himself with small bits, would he?

The lights chose that moment to go out, plunging us into darkness. I breathed a silent sigh of relief. At least things were going to plan.

So far, at least.

A few seconds later, the lights flickered and came on again, but this time their glow was much dimmer. A backup generator was powering the emergency lighting, obviously.

There was a knock at the door, and when Starke said "Enter," Boris opened the door, a tray of Bollinger and two glasses in hand. "The power has just crapped out, boss," he said, placing the tray on the little table beside Starke's chair.

"Then deal with it," Starke said, "and ensure I'm not disturbed for as long as Ms. Jenson is here."

"Which won't be long at all," I assured them both.

The barkeeper smirked. Starke merely looked amused. Once Boris had left and the door was once again closed, he said, "So why is this Murphy fellow of interest to you?"

"Because he's a hired hit man, and we don't believe his reasons for being in town."

Starke's toe was somehow caressing my leg again, and desire began to unfurl inside of me. But I didn't shift my leg, if only because it was already hard up against the arm of the chair.

"So you suspect that he's behind these beheadings?" Starke poured two glasses of Bollinger and handed one to me, his fingers lingering briefly against mine.

I pulled my hand away and placed the glass on the floor. He tut-tutted. "Come now, Ms. Jenson, you know the rules. I cannot answer questions if you're going to waste the nectar of life."

"I thought blood was the nectar of life for you vampires?"

"Only to those who do not have the good taste or the fortune to afford life's true necessities."

"Which blood is to a vampire."

"Only to some. For me, the only thing sweeter than Bollinger is the taste of a woman dripping with desire."

His gaze met mine, and caused all sorts of havoc to my breathing. I reached down, picked up the glass, and tried to get my breathing under control. *Slowly in, slowly out.* It was simple, really.

Only my mind fastened on the words and suddenly began imagining other things going slowly in and slowly out. And *that* caused still more chaos.

I took a sip of the deliciously cool liquid, but it didn't do a lot to stamp out the sparks threatening to become a bonfire.

God, if this man *wasn't* the wraith, then he was something just as dangerous. Hell, the use of werewolf auras was restricted by law, and this damn well should be, too.

I cleared my throat and said, "So, Kye Murphy."

He shrugged. It was an elegant movement. "He could have come here. I don't know everyone who visits my establishment. But perhaps a description would help?"

"He's several inches taller than me, with dark red hair, golden eyes, and a strong build."

"And a werewolf, like you?"

"Yes." I took another sip of champagne.

"Then I doubt it." His sudden smile was wicked. "We don't really cater to their addiction."

"We like sex, but it's not an addiction." It might be a necessity during the full moon, but that was different. I glanced surreptitiously at my watch. Little more than ten minutes had passed. Time had obviously decided to slow to a crawl. I hoped Kade and his crew weren't intending to do the same.

"So, you're admitting you like sex, and yet you refuse to have it with me. I find that most disappointing."

"I'm working. And did I mention my hot date?"

He smiled. It was lazy, insolent, and oh so sexy. "I simply thought I could get you primed and ready."

I was primed and ready to go right *now,* and if I didn't do something to distract this man—or whatever the hell he actually was—I was going to be exactly where he wanted me to be. In his arms and naked.

But there was only one thing more I could think to question him about, and if he *was* our flesh-shifter, it would warn him we were onto him.

And yet, better he be warned than me having sex with him. That was my only other option right now.

I exchanged my drink for my purse and pulled out

the picture Kye had given me. "I don't suppose you know this man, then?"

He reached for the printout, his fingers briefly caressing my wrist before sliding down to grasp the piece of paper. A tremor ran through me and I took a large slug of champagne. If Kade didn't hurry his ass, I was never going to get through this.

Either I was getting depressingly staid in my old age, or he just felt too dangerous for my wolf to handle.

Or maybe I'd finally realized that the real joy in sex was not just the motion and the pleasure but the emotions that clicked in when you became involved with that one special person.

Of course, I had two special people to contend with, but that was just fate being a bitch.

"I think I have seen him around a couple of times," Starke mused, looking at the printout.

"And can you tell me anything about him?"

"Perhaps." Amusement twitched his lips. "But I can't possibly say anything without getting something in return."

"I am not going to get naked and sweaty with you." I took another drink, and realized I'd somehow finished the glass. "I already have a plan to do that with someone else."

A full-blown grin erupted. It was stunning. "All I ask is for you to undo two buttons."

"Two buttons?"

"Yes." He picked up the champagne and refilled my glass, his knees pressing briefly and sensually against mine. "Just two little buttons."

I pretended to consider the request, then swiftly undid the buttons. The flimsy shirt fell farther open, revealing the dark pink edges of areola.

"Lovely," he all but purred. "Simply lovely."

"The information, Starke," I said dryly.

"Of course." He filled his own glass then added, "He's not a regular here, but I have seen him on a few occasions."

I raised an eyebrow. "Why would you notice him when you didn't notice someone like Murphy?"

"Because this man didn't come here to feed or be fed on. He had several drinks at the bar and walked out again. *That* we notice."

"When was the last time he was here?" I took another sip of Bollinger and a nice little buzz began to fill my head. Champagne—and most other alcohol—didn't really affect wolves to the extent that it did humans, thanks to our higher metabolic rate, but it did provide a happy little high before said metabolism kicked in.

Starke said, "I believe it was last night. He stayed an hour, then left again."

I studied him, unable to tell whether he was speaking the truth or playing a dangerous game. Either one was a possibility, given the amusement in his eyes.

"Riley," Jack said into my ear, his voice fading in and out, as if there were some sort of interference. "We need you back at the office immediate—"

The rest of his sentence was cut off, but it didn't matter because I got the gist of it. Relief slithered through me. Never before had I been so happy about being called back to the Directorate.

I finished my drink in several unladylike gulps, then grabbed my bag and rose. "I'm afraid I've just been called back to the office, so the rest of my questions will have to wait."

"What, so no hot date, either?" He pushed gracefully to his feet, moving altogether too close. "It seems a shame to waste such a hot outfit."

"I've learned to live with disappointment." I gave him an insolent grin. "You should, too."

"Oh, I try not to." He caught my hand and raised it to his lips, kissing it gently. "And I don't believe you should, either."

And with that, he hit me.

Not physically, not mentally, but with the full force of his aura or mojo or whatever the hell it was.

My reaction was instinctual. I threw up my own aura, trying to use it as a shield as I had in the past. But I might as well have been using a tissue to block out the force of a gale.

And that gale was instant, burning *need*.

It was deep and violent and it ached. Literally ached.

He smiled and his grip on my hand tightened, forcing me backward. Not to the chaise longue but to the desk. I fought it, I really did, but the need was all-encompassing.

My body shook with futile anger and the ever-increasing tide of lust, but at least my thoughts—while a little scrambled—were my own. I might not be strong enough to fight him—and who would have thought a werewolf would ever be saying *that*?—but at least I wasn't a complete automaton.

Not that *that* made the situation any better.

My butt hit the desk and his grip on my hand forced me to slide up on top of it. His free hand traced the line of my cheek, his fingers so heated against my skin it felt like a burn.

"So lovely," he murmured, his gaze following the journey of his fingers. Down my neck, past my shoulder blade, and onto the soft swell of breast. One fingertip gently grazed a nipple and I couldn't fight arching my back—an age-old invitation for more. Part of me might be screaming in frustration and fury, but that part was a flea fighting against the might of a storm right now.

He chuckled softly and his touch moved down. The remaining buttons came undone and the shirt was completely open.

His fingers continued their downward journey and my skin twitched and burned, pleasure and pain mingling into one. He ran his hands down my thighs, then grabbed the end of the skirt, ripping upward, so that the split tore all the way to my crotch.

"Much better," he said, rubbing his thumbs down the inside of my thighs before gently pushing them apart. God, I was wet, so wet with the need for him that when he stepped in between my legs, I moaned. And hated the fact that I did.

"I have desired to do this in the flesh," he murmured, thereby confirming he *had* visited me in my dreams and therefore *was* our wraith. His fingers slid back up my thighs. "Have long wished to know what it is really like to be inside you, heated flesh in heated flesh."

I didn't say anything. Couldn't say anything, caught between expectation and ecstasy. His touch brushed lightly over the lace of my panties, then lifted my butt with one hand and pulled them down my legs. He tossed them aside then reached up and did the same to the shirt, so that I was all but naked.

Then his caress thrust deep inside of me, making me shiver and moan.

"So wet," he said, almost in awe. "I ache with anticipation."

He wasn't the only one. The brain might not want this, but the body was a slave to his mental juju and there was nothing I could do to stop it.

He stepped back and began to strip. His body was as glorious as I'd imagined, all sculpted golden flesh topped by a thick, engorged cock that seemed to grow even larger before my eyes.

And I both ached for and was repelled by it. Or maybe I was just repelled by the sheer fact that this was all being forced on me.

Then he stepped back between my legs, his hands grabbing my butt and holding me steady as that gloriously engorged piece of flesh slid deep inside of me.

A deep sound of pleasure rumbled from his throat, then he began to move, slowly at first but gradually getting faster, harder, until our coupling was a wild mesh of fury, lust, and unbridled pleasure. Heated flesh slapped against heated flesh, bringing me to fulfillment, again and again, even though he himself never reached that peak.

The more it went on and on, the more I was being drained.

I had no doubt he'd suck me dry so completely he'd kill me if I didn't find a way to stop him. Because even if he didn't think we suspected *him,* he knew we were close to one of his identities, thanks to my line of questioning earlier.

Then I remembered the knife at my back.

It was still there, still pressing into my spine. Either Starke had forgotten about it, or he didn't believe it was a real threat.

Bad mistake.

But his aura was still surrounding me and I wasn't entirely sure I could summon the strength to fight it long enough even to move my hand . . .

Then, like sunshine breaking through a storm, the strength was there. It wasn't mine, but I grabbed it nonetheless, thrusting a hand backward, wrapping my fingers around the hilt, drawing it free.

Starke didn't notice the movement. He was too busy sucking me dry.

I shifted slightly. Then, as the realization that I was no longer under the influence of his aura hit him, I plunged the knife into his back.

Blue fire exploded from the blade and spread out like little bolts of lightning across his skin. Starke screamed and arched backward, his skin bubbling and boiling and shifting—becoming something less golden and a whole lot less real.

Then the office door crashed back on its hinges and Kye stood there, a wild mix of lust and anger in his eyes, and a large silver gun in his hands.

He fired before I could move, and Starke's head exploded into a rain of flesh and bone and God knows what else.

As Starke's body fell to the floor, Kye's gaze met mine. His breathing was harsh—as harsh as mine still was—and he smelled of sex and lust and hunger.

He'd been the source of that rush of strength, I realized. The link between us had grown strong enough that I'd been able to call on his reserves to bolster my own.

It had also been strong enough that he'd known exactly what was being done to me, and who was doing it.

Strong enough for him to feel every sensation and desire right along with me.

"Kye, now is not—" I said.

"There is no better time," he cut in ruthlessly. "No one takes what is mine. *No one.*"

I'll never be yours, I wanted to say, but the words died in my throat as the force of his need hit.

That need was as much about control as it was desire.

He kicked the door shut and strode over to me. Then his fingers were tangling themselves in my hair and his lips crushed mine, kissing me savagely as my hands found their way to the waist of his jeans, undoing the button and zipper before thrusting them down his hips.

Then he was in me, claiming me, and it felt glorious.

Because this was *real* and solid, a meeting of flesh *and* soul—even if the man now claiming me was as unwanted as Starke had been.

He fucked me more fully and more savagely than Starke had, and it felt so damn right tears stung my eyes. I came seconds before him, my body shuddering and twisting as his body spasmed and the hot flush of his seed flooded into me.

Then there was nothing but utter exhaustion.

He rested his forehead against mine, his fingers still locked in my hair and his harsh breathing searing my lips. Slowly, surely, my breath and my thoughts steadied, and I found the strength to ask, "Why aren't Starke's men battering down the door after that gunshot?"

He finally released his grip on my hair, sliding his hands down to my hips instead, holding me firmly against him. The wolf wasn't finished with me yet, apparently. But then, I'd learned last night he had an amazing recovery rate and a *huge* sexual appetite. And while I might not want him in my life, he was still my soul mate, and I couldn't deny just how good it felt to be locked against him like this.

"Because I told them the Directorate was on the way, and if they valued their lives, they'd get the hell out of here."

I raised an eyebrow. "And they believed you?"

"Why wouldn't they?" He began to rock gently, his body continuing to harden inside of mine. Part of me wanted to slap him away, and part of me wanted to use every inch of him to erase every second of my time with

Starke. "You were already here and, for all they knew, it could have been the first part of a plan."

It made sense, and yet . . .

I didn't know what it was, but something niggled. Intuition didn't believe him, and I couldn't ignore it.

"But that makes no sense." I paused, my breath catching in my throat, as his cock—once again hard—slid so very deep inside, sending a wave of pleasure rolling across my body. I licked my lips and somehow said, "As far as they're concerned, you could be just another crackpot trying to cause mischief."

"They thought I was an angry husband." His words were distracted. "How do you think I initially got upstairs to place my bugs?"

And if he'd left those bugs in place, it would have made our job a whole lot easier. "Why would Starke let you up there and yet meet me downstairs?"

"He didn't. I bribed the barman and several security guards to give me five minutes."

My mind was having a hard time concentrating against the delicious assault on my body. And yet I couldn't quite let the questions go. That would be giving in totally to the needs of my body, and I'd done enough of that for one day.

"You shouldn't have killed Starke. We needed to question him about his partner—"

The words died as his lips crushed mine, ending all attempts on my part to continue the conversation.

I conceded defeat and closed my eyes, enjoying his caresses and kisses, until the slow burn of desire exploded and we came once again.

He kissed me a final time, soft and lingering, then said, "He needed to die for what he was doing."

"Kye, he was only fucking me. In the larger scheme of things, that really didn't matter."

Anger spurted, spinning around me, a firestorm that would not be tamed. "He wasn't just fucking you," he said, his golden eyes flashing. "He was taking what was mine, and he was *draining* you."

"I was dealing with it—"

"Yeah," he exploded. "I felt how you were dealing with it. Believe me, I *wasn't* impressed."

"He didn't end up with a knife in his back through magic," I retorted, and thrust a hand against his chest, trying to push him away from me.

He tightened his grip on my thighs and didn't budge. "I warned him," he growled. "I told him not to—"

He stopped.

Oh my God, I thought.

I had been soundly fucked not only by one murdering son of a bitch today, but two.

"Come alone," he said, and before the meaning of his words had even really registered, his fist smashed into my jaw.

I was unconscious before my head hit the desk.

Chapter 12

I was awoken by the sensation of ice pressing against my jaw. It wasn't helping the ache in my face much, but at least it meant there was someone present who cared enough to try.

The sunshiny scent that teased my nostrils told me it was Kade, but the musky scents that were entwined within his also said that he wasn't alone. As did the murmur of conversation.

Kye wasn't here. His scent still was, but the heated, tingly awareness that always hit when he was close was absent.

He'd obviously run.

Part of me hoped he ran far and fast, because then I wouldn't have to deal with him.

But the other part—the part so angry about being so

completely fooled *and* used—wanted the chance to confront him.

To get her own back.

To ask *why*.

The surface under my hips was soft, not the hard wood of the desk, and the slide of material against my skin told me I was no longer almost naked.

I opened my eyes. Kade was kneeling down in front of me, holding the ice pack to my decidedly tender jaw. Behind him, Cole and Dusty were examining Starke's remains.

"The cavalry arrives," I commented, wincing as the mere act of speaking had pain flickering along my jaw. Not that it would actually *stop* me. I flicked my tongue across the left side—one loose tooth and several others feeling as bruised as my jaw. "But it arrives too late, as usual."

"Well, you will get yourself into situations where the cavalry has no option but to arrive late," Cole commented. "Next time, give us a little warning and we'll be on time."

"I'll try and remember that," I said wryly, and pushed upright. Aside from the sore jaw, I was actually feeling pretty good. But then, good sex and multiple orgasms tended to do that to you. "How did you know that I needed help?"

It wasn't as if I'd actually *called* for it.

"We didn't." Kade removed the ice pack and sat back on his heels. "When the com-link went dead again—this time midsentence—Jack feared the worst and sent us scurrying."

Meaning Kye had not only been wearing a deadener similar to what he'd placed on me, but that it had a fairly decent range. The com-link connection had been severed long before he'd kicked his way into the room.

And *that* was a scary thought, because it had huge ramifications for the Directorate. It could become deadly when it came to on-street personnel. "Who hit you?" Kade added.

"Kye." I hesitated, a mix of anger and hurt and confusion rolling through me. Part of me—the wolf part, no doubt—still couldn't accept the fact that my soul mate was one of our killers. Where the hell did that leave me? What options did I have? If he didn't have a kill order on him already, he soon would. Because I couldn't—and wouldn't—conceal the truth. And yet if they killed him, they'd very likely kill me. "He wasn't here when you arrived?"

"No." He eyed me closely, his expression concerned. As an empath, he'd be feeling every bit of the twisted, tortured emotions currently running riot through me. "Why would he be here?"

"Because he's one-half of our beheading team, and he came here to warn his client that the Directorate knew several of his identities." Of course, Kye himself had given us one of those identities, and I had to wonder why.

"Oh, fuck," Cole said. Obviously, Kade had been sharing the news about just who my soul mate was. "What the hell are you going to do?"

I glanced over Kade's broad shoulders at him. His expression was one of horror. He might not be a werewolf, but he was familiar with the werewolf culture and understood exactly what it meant. "I don't know."

Kade's expression was decidedly confused. "Why is this a bad thing? He's a cold-blooded killer—you've said that yourself multiple times. So we take him out and he's gone from your life forever. Which is what you wanted, isn't it?"

"He's her *soul* mate, Kade," Cole said, as if that explained it all. And it did—for those in the know.

But Kade obviously didn't understand the full impact of the bond. "The soul mate bond is unbreakable," I explained. "If one-half dies, the other generally follows."

His frown deepened. "Ben didn't."

Ben was a big, black wolf I'd met while investigating a case a few months ago. We'd become firm friends since then, and though he'd made continuous efforts to seduce me, it could never have amounted to anything more than sexual gratification. Ben's soul mate had died long before I'd met him, and he, in his own words, existed. Nothing more, nothing less.

"That's rare. I don't want to take the chance." Not given the way fate liked playing her games with my life.

"So," Kade said. "We can't kill him. What about just capturing the bastard, beating him up, then throwing him in a nice dark cell somewhere to rot?"

"I don't know if Jack will go for that." Or rather, I wasn't sure that the council—higher *or* lower—would let him go for that option. "But it's certainly a solution that appeals to the animal side of *me*."

Kade raised an eyebrow. "Animal? Or betrayed lover?"

"They're one and the same," I muttered. "And before we can talk about beating him up and tossing away the key, we need to find him."

"The signal from the tracker is erratic. Given the bug placed on you, we suspect he's got others in his possession and that they're interfering with the signal," Jack said into my ear. "But we're in the process of trying to boost it. I've ordered a lockdown on all the airports, so he won't get out that way."

"There are plenty of private airfields, and he has the money to use them."

"Private planes still have to register their flight details, or they're forced down. And once the problems with the tracker have been sorted out, it won't matter."

I didn't think it would matter anyway, because Kye wouldn't do the obvious. His mind just didn't work that way.

"Do you want us to come back to the office or wait here?"

"Not here," Cole muttered, voice disparaging but amusement evident in his brief glance. "We do not need the crime scene disturbed any more than necessary."

"Come back," Jack agreed. "If we get a location in the meantime, we'll let you both know."

"Okay." I pushed to my feet. Kade rose with me, his fingers under my elbow. Not really supporting but ready to steady me if I actually needed it. "Looks like you got your wish, Cole."

"Sometimes fate does take pity on me," he murmured.

I couldn't help wishing that fate would take pity on me occasionally. "Hey, I want my silver knife back when you finish with it, too."

Cole raised an eyebrow. "What silver knife?"

"The one I left sticking in Starke's back when I stabbed him."

"There was no such knife when we arrived."

"Then the bastard's taken it."

"I gather we're talking about Kye?" Kade said.

I nodded. "It was a gift from Quinn, and had some unusual properties. I don't want to lose it."

"Then we'll retrieve it before we pummel the shit out of him," Kade said cheerfully. "Don't you wish all problems were that easily fixed?"

I certainly did. I hooked my arm through his and let him escort me outside. I didn't feel like driving, so I climbed into the passenger seat of Kade's car.

"Thanks for dressing me," I said, once we were on the road.

He gave me an odd sort of look. "I didn't. You were fully dressed when we arrived."

I closed my eyes. *Kye* had been the one who'd cleaned me up and covered my nakedness. And somehow, that just made the whole situation even worse.

Damn it, *why* did he have to do this? Why did he have to take this job and risk losing both our lives?

But I knew the answer even as I asked the question.

It was all about control. Controlling me, and controlling the situation.

Yet I very much suspected it was also about the risk. The high of knowing that everything was at stake and that one wrong move could end everything.

Literally.

I knew that high, but I wasn't addicted to it. Kye, I suspected, was.

What a fucking mess this was all turning out to be. And I bet fate was having a jolly old time watching all her plans unfold.

We didn't make it into the Directorate. Jack called on my phone when we were still ten minutes away. I hit the button and put it on speaker.

"You got a location?"

"We do. His signal is coming from an old biscuit factory out near Broadmeadows. Benson's sending the address through to Kade's onboard now."

The computer beeped as he said it. I hit the switch and shifted the address over to the nav-com. Kade glanced down then nodded, doing a fast U-turn and hitting the gas.

"We're on our way. Can you get hold of a floor plan of the place?"

"We're searching now. And I've called Iktar back from his vacation, but he's not going to get there before three-thirty."

I glanced at my watch. That was nearly an hour away, meaning Iktar was at the spirit lizard's reservation up in the mountains near Taradale.

One way or another, the action would probably be over by then. Which left Kade and me alone against a professional hit man.

The odds should have been in our favor. We were as well trained—or *better* trained—than he. And yet uncertainty gnawed at me.

Or maybe it was just the memory of his last words. *Come alone.*

He had to know that I wasn't that stupid. The link between us had grown a lot stronger over the past few days, and I wasn't about to trust my ability to bring him to justice.

"And Rhoan?" I asked Jack. Part of me wanted my brother there, and yet it was also a risk I didn't want to take. Kye knew that stopping Rhoan would stop me, and if it meant the difference between him escaping or not, then he'd shoot to kill and to hell with the consequences.

"Rhoan's apparently in the process of escorting Liander out of town. He'll get back here as soon as he can." Jack paused. "Be careful going in, you two."

"We always are," Kade murmured, amusement twisting his lips.

Jack made a disparaging sound. "You might be, but your partner has a definite tendency toward carelessness."

"I resent that," I said mildly, then frowned and added, "Boss, if Kye still has those deadeners on him, you may lose contact with one or both of us when we get within range."

"We know. I've ordered our cleanup teams to be on standby, and they'll be ready to go if we lose contact for more than five minutes."

"Teams? It's not going to be *that* big a mess."

"Maybe not, but the teams are trained to defend themselves and can legally render armed help if the situation calls for it."

Which meant he was sending us help the only way he legally could, but he was also giving us the chance to do our jobs first while trying to avoid endangering the lives of men and women who weren't trained killers. "Oh. Thanks."

"Just be careful," he said, and hung up. I rubbed a hand across my eyes and wondered if I was ever going to wake up from this nightmare.

A killer was on the loose and the lives of non-guardian personnel were being put on the line because of me.

Because I hadn't been able to really believe that Kye was as cold and as ruthless as he portrayed himself. Because I'd been unable to see past my own twisted feelings for the man.

"Riley," Kade said softly, "don't be too harsh on yourself. None of us seriously suspected that Kye could be involved. It's as much our fault as yours that he's on the loose."

"But I was with him a lot over the past few days. I *knew* he was playing some sort of game, but I—"

He placed a hand on my bare knee, squeezing it gently. "Enough. You did what you could. No one could ask for anything more."

"Jack could."

"Jack hasn't. The only person angry at you is you, and you don't deserve the beating you're giving yourself. Besides, you *did* take out one of our killers."

"That was more Kye than me."

It might have been the truth, but Kye hadn't really come there to save me. He'd gone there to preserve the *ideal* of control. He was a man who kept a tight leash on every little aspect of his life, and he'd needed to prove to me—and to himself—that nothing and no one could get past him.

That's why we'd made love. He might have wanted me, but it was also another means of proving that I *would* comply with his wishes, no matter what the situation.

Which was probably why he wasn't running now. That would be messy. Kye didn't do messy, or leave unfinished business behind.

It could only mean he planned a more personal ending to this. Maybe that's why he'd warned me to come alone. The man who needed to be in command of every little aspect of his life planned to end all this *his* way.

And his way meant guns and death.

"Riley," Kade said softly, squeezing my knee again. "*Enough*. I mean it."

"You're such a sweet man, but—"

He snorted softly. "You wouldn't be thinking that if you knew just how good your skin feels under my fingers, or what is currently going on in my thoughts."

I grinned. "Once a stallion, always a stallion."

"Too true, my dear." He sighed wistfully and withdrew his hand.

The computer beeped again. I hit another button and a floor plan popped up on the screen. I studied it for a moment, then said, "It looks like we have two main entrances and a fire exit. There're two floor levels and several outbuildings."

"He'll be in the main building. There are more options there for running and hiding."

Neither of which I could really imagine Kye doing. "He's run there for a reason."

"Of course he has." Kade turned off the ring road at Pascoe Vale Road and slowed down for the lights, checking the traffic to the right before pulling out and slapping his foot on the accelerator again. "Professionals always have their escape routes planned beforehand, and I'd be very surprised if Kye didn't have every expectation of walking away from this."

And I'd be very surprised if he *did*. Kye was a realist, if nothing else.

All too soon we were pulling up several buildings away from the one I suspected held Kye. Kade climbed out and opened the trunk. He had a veritable arsenal inside.

"Good grief," I said, sweeping my gaze over the rifles, lasers, guns, and stakes stashed in neat little secured rows. "Does Jack know you've raided the weapon store like this?"

"Nope," he said cheerfully. "And a man can never have enough firepower."

I snorted softly and reached for a laser. He slapped my hand away. "Take a gun. Lasers don't fire up instantly, and you can't afford to give a man like Kye even a half-second advantage."

He had a point. I reached for a Browning simply

because it was a lighter weight than some of the others and fit my hand better, yet still packed a hell of a punch.

"So what's the plan? We sneak in front and back and pin him down in the middle?" Kade said, stashing several different pistols and knives about his body before picking up a rifle, then slamming the trunk shut.

"You take the back. I'm walking right in through the front door."

He frowned. "I really don't think—"

"Kade, we're soul mates. He's going to know I'm here the minute I walk into that building." If he wasn't already aware that I was here, that was. "So it's pointless to try any subterfuge. But doing the obvious might just give you the chance to get close enough to bring him down."

"I like the last half of that plan, but the first is decidedly unpalatable." He ran a finger down my cheek, his touch warm and not at all sexual. "He's the sort of man who'd want to go down in a blaze of glory, and it may be that he plans to take you with him."

"Trust me, I'm more than aware of that possibility. But I've been tested by Gautier, the best guardian the Directorate ever had, and I'm the only person to ever score a hit on him. Trust the skills behind that, if nothing else."

But yet, even that didn't make me the killer Kye was, and *that* put the advantage squarely in his court.

I stood up on tippy-toes and gave Kade a kiss. "Please be careful. I don't want to have to explain your death to Sable."

"Ditto." His bright smile flashed but just as quickly

faded. "We both know that this job is a walking death sentence. Sooner or later, it's going to happen, Riley, no matter what precautions we take."

"Well, you're not dying on my fucking shift," I said, and slapped his arm. "So please be careful."

"Oh, I have many more mares in the stable yet to service, so don't worry your pretty little head." He flashed me an insolent grin. "I'll see you in the middle, my sweet."

I watched him walk away, took a deep, calming breath that didn't do one iota to ease the churning in my stomach or the trembling in my limbs, then walked toward the front gate.

It was unlocked, as were the front glass doors that led into what looked to be an old office area. I paused and blinked, briefly flicking my sight to infrared. There was no sign of body heat in the offices lining the walls of the office area, and nothing in the immediate area behind the double swing doors. But there were huge blobs of darkness preventing me from seeing deeper into the factory.

Frowning, I walked forward, pushing the swinging doors open and letting them slap closed behind me. The noise echoed, filling the shadowed silence.

I walked on, the click of my heels against the concrete grating against my nerves. One way or another, I wanted this done and over with.

The blobs of darkness that had foiled my infrared turned out to be vast metal machines and long tracks of conveyors. They looked to be still in a usable condition, despite the cobwebs and the dirt that draped them.

Maybe the factory hadn't been closed all that long, despite all the smashed windows high up near the roof line.

I punched open another set of swinging doors but paused in the doorway, my gaze sweeping the room and my senses on high alert. This room was also double height, and as before, silent machines lined the concrete floor. But it also had storage rooms or offices lining the walls of the upper story and a walkway that ran around the entire perimeter.

No familiar, joyous warmth rose to warn me of Kye's presence, but I suspected he was near, regardless. It was the perfect place for a showdown.

"Kade?" I said softly. "I'm in the second machine room. I suspect he's here."

"I just got into the back loading bay," Kade said. "The bastard's set up some trip wires, so I'm going to have to move forward cautiously. Play for time if you can, Riley."

"Will do." I hesitated, then added, "Just remember that this link will go dead once I'm near him."

"At least that'll let me know the game is on."

I stepped forward and let the doors swing closed. They clipped each other on the way through, and the sharp slap of sound had my nerves jumping.

I scanned the room with infrared as I walked forward, but there were still huge swathes of darkness, on both this level and the upper one. Kye could be hiding anywhere.

I was about halfway across the room when I sensed him. It was a rush of warmth that flashed across my skin then settled somewhere deep inside. I stopped and turned around, sweeping my gaze across the walkway above the swing doors I'd come in through. I couldn't see him, either through normal vision or infrared, and I couldn't smell him, but he was up there nevertheless.

"Stop hiding and come out, Kye."

For a heartbeat, nothing happened. Then he appeared in a doorway, a teasing smile on his lips and a gun held loosely in his right hand.

Much like me—in both respects.

"You're here sooner than I thought you'd be," he said, stopping a foot away from the walkway railing. His pose was relaxed, his golden eyes warm, and yet he reminded me of a predator about to strike.

"It's always a bad move to underestimate the Directorate." My fingers were starting to sweat against the metal of the Browning and there was a sick, churning sensation beginning to build in my stomach.

I wanted this over with, and yet I didn't, because that would mean actually having to act against the man who was my other half.

"I don't ever underestimate anyone, Riley, least of all the Directorate." He studied me for a moment, and his smile grew. My stomach twisted at the beauty of it. "You've bugged me, haven't you?"

"I'm hardly likely to confirm or deny that."

"Meaning you have. You're good, because I never even suspected."

Neither had I when he'd tagged me with that deadener, so I guess that made us even.

"Why did you do it, Kye? Why take the job from

Starke—or whatever the hell his real name was—when you knew it was only going to bring you up against me?"

His smile was lazy and insolent, and so damn sexy my breath caught in my throat. "You said it yourself a million times—I go where the money is, and Nasser offered a lot to take his photos and guard his back while he killed. Besides, I would not have had this opportunity to enjoy time with my oh-so-loving soul mate if I had walked away."

I ignored the sarcasm in his words and said, "So why didn't you run when you had the chance? What is it you want? Because you've left me with no option but to bring you in."

"You know what I want."

"I haven't got a fucking *clue* what you want. I never have." But I did, and it scared the hell out of me.

"Odd, because you actually hit the nail on the head several days ago."

"I've said a lot of things over the past few days." And some of them I'd even meant. "And you've said even more—none of which I've believed. So what is it now, Kye?"

"It's the same thing I've always wanted." His gaze darkened. "I want you. *You.* Heart, body, and soul. Not for one night, not for pretend, but for real."

"And the answer is the same one I've continually given you. You have my soul, you can have my body, but you will never have my heart. *Never.*"

"I don't accept that."

Because his need to control his environment

wouldn't accept anything less than the whole. "That's your problem, not mine."

Anger flared in his eyes. Anger and determination. My stomach twisted and I flexed my free hand, trying to calm the tension. But that was an impossible task.

Because the confrontation I'd feared was coming.

"Kye," I added softly, "put down your weapon and come down off the walkway."

"You know I can't do that."

"There's a kill order out on your head if you don't come in with me."

"And if I come in with you, I'll still be killed."

"No. Jack knows you're my soul mate, and he won't risk losing me to kill you."

"If you truly think that, then you are the biggest fool on this green earth." He shook his head, as if in disbelief. Sunlight caught strands of his dark red hair, turning them a rich, molten gold. Deep inside, part of me raged—against fate, against what was going to happen, at the ashes that my long-held dreams were rapidly becoming. "He's a vampire, Riley. He may run the Directorate in a fair and even way, but his true allegiance will always be with the council—one of whom is his sister. And *they* want me dead."

"You're wrong."

"I'm very rarely wrong, Riley." His brief smile was so sad and gentle it made my soul ache. "I guess that leaves us with only one option."

Something inside me clenched, and for a moment I had trouble breathing, let alone thinking. "That's not an option," I somehow managed. "That's suicide."

"It's only suicide if I lose."

Don't do this, I wanted to plead. *Don't destroy us.*

But there really wasn't an "us" to destroy. Just two people fate should never have thrown together.

"How should we play it, Riley?" he continued softly. There was an odd light in his eyes—a joyous light. A maniacal light. "As an old-fashioned stand and shoot, or shall we play cat-and-mouse in this big old mouse-trap?"

Trap being the operative word, given what Kade had told me. "There isn't an option number three?"

"No," he said, then raised the gun, the movement so fast it was almost a blur.

I dove to my right, throwing myself behind a machine, landing on all fours and crushing the fingers on the hand that held the gun. I swore, but the words were lost to the sound of his gunshot. It *ping*ed off the top of the metal above my head, sending sparks flying into the shadows.

"You're as fast as any vampire I've come across," he said, his voice coming from my right. I raised the gun but didn't fire, simply because he was on the move.

"That's because I *am* part vampire." I was answering more to let Kade know—if he was close enough to hear our voices—I was okay rather than out of any real desire to speak to the man who was trying to kill me. "And that's also the reason you can never have what you want, Kye."

I shifted position, keeping the machine at my back as I scanned the walkway above me. A shadow flicked between one office and another, and I pressed the trigger. The shot reverberated and my heart froze, waiting for that moment of soul-death that would indicate I'd aimed accurately.

It didn't come, and I breathed a silent sigh of relief.

God help me, I didn't want to do this. Didn't want to kill my soul mate no matter how intent he was on killing me. No matter what Dia had said, no matter what Kye himself had said, I just didn't want to do it.

"If what you have with the vampire was truly strong, you would not have kept coming back to me," he said. His voice was coming from the shadows just to the left of the doorway. I raised the gun, my mouth so dry it hurt, and fired.

I waited, for what seemed an eternity, as the bullet sped across the distance between us and blasted its way through the wall.

And heaved another sigh of relief when there was no indication that I'd hit anything, let alone flesh.

I ran across to the next machine, hunkering under its protecting weight. Though I could feel his presence in the room, I had no real grip on his actual position. It was as if the deadener he was wearing was somehow blocking my more basic senses as well as the psychic and electronic ones.

I flicked to infrared, quickly scanning the upper floor. There were no telltale blurs of red, but that could just mean he was hiding behind the thick patches of darkness that my infrared couldn't see past.

"What I have with my vampire satisfies one half of my soul, but I am a being with two very different souls,

Kye." Even if I'd spent most of my life denying that the vampire half of me had needs every bit as strong as the wolf. "I might not be able to deny the pull of the soul mate bond, but that doesn't mean it's all I want in my life."

Even if I'd spent most of my life wanting that very thing.

I slipped through the small gap between the floor and the machine and came out the other side, moving quietly across to another machine.

I still had no sense of him. The air was rich with the scent of machine oil, dust, and metal but remained steadfastly free of the man who prowled above me. Unless he spoke, I had no idea where he was, and that was scary. I relied so heavily on my senses in situations like this that being without them left me feeling almost helpless.

And I *hated* that sensation. It reminded me too much of my years growing up and being thrown from pillar to post by Blake, the man who now led the Jenson pack.

I shook the memories of him from my head, even as I wondered why he was in my thoughts so often of late, and scanned the rooms above me again.

Nothing.

It was *so* frustrating. I knew he was there somewhere, but I just couldn't—

The thought froze as a prickle of warning ran down my spine. I rose and spun in one swift movement, the gun held at arm's length and my finger on the trigger, close, so close to pulling it.

Kye stood near my original machine, his gun raised, his golden eyes so cold they froze my soul.

I couldn't pull the trigger. I just couldn't.

I didn't want to destroy the dream.

"I think what we have here is commonly called a standoff," he said, voice calm, expression so cool.

And yet I could feel the heat of him, taste the desire in him. Heard the answering response from deep inside of me.

"Put the gun down and give it up, Kye." *Please put the gun down.* "We both get to live that way."

He smiled. Again, it was a sad and wistful thing that tore at my heart. The heart that supposedly *didn't* belong to Kye. "Run away with me."

I blinked. "What?"

"Run away with me," he repeated softly. "We make a good team, you and I. We could make a fortune together."

"I'm not a killer, Kye. I can't do what you do for a living."

"You already do."

"No. I chase people like you, people who destroy others for the fun of it. Money might change hands in your case, but we both know that is not the motivating factor."

"Then we die—as simple as that." He gave me a smile. "Pull the trigger, Riley. I dare you."

I stared at him for the longest of moments. I was holding the gun so tightly my hand ached, but no matter what I did, I couldn't force my finger to retract against the trigger.

I just couldn't kill the dream, no matter how much of a nightmare it had turned into.

I lowered the gun. "If you're going to kill me, just pull the damn trigger and get it over with." My voice was weary, yet filled with anger and sorrow.

He smiled. "I never said I wanted to kill you. All I wanted to do was control this situation."

"Some things will *never* be controlled, Kye, no matter how hard you try." Especially when it came to something as nebulous as love.

"I've never yet hit such a situation. You, on the other hand, have wasted a number of good opportunities. Take, for instance, your much-despised pack leader. When you put the fear of God into Blake rather than taking him out like you should have, you placed the control back into his court." His gaze narrowed a little. "That will come back and bite you in the ass, you know. He has a serious yen for revenge, and already his plans have begun to unfold."

"Right now, I don't fucking care. If you don't want to kill me, and you won't be arrested, then what the hell do you want?" I paused, then added heatedly, "And don't fucking say *me,* because I've answered that."

"What I wanted—" He paused, and his nostrils flared.

I sucked in a deep breath, tasting the air. Kade was near. His rich, summery scent was coming in from behind me.

"Riley," Kye said, his voice flat and yet filled with an odd sense of disappointment. "I told you to come alone."

"And you really thought I would?" I hoped Kade was listening, hoped he was aware that he'd been sensed. "I'm not that stupid, Kye. Nor is the Directorate."

"This was between you and me," he said, and something in his manner hardened. It sent goose bumps skittering across my flesh and had the hairs on the back of my neck rising. "It didn't have to be this way. It didn't have to end this way."

My gun was up and focused on his head even before he'd finished speaking. "Last warning, Kye. Drop the fucking gun and put your hands up in the air."

He smiled. There was nothing sad, wistful, or beautiful about it now. "I told you once before, bad things happen when you hesitate, Riley."

It was a warning I'd heard from too many people, and suddenly I felt sick.

His weapon fired. I threw myself sideways but knew I was never going to be fast enough. Even as my body sliced through the air, I waited for the moment of metal on flesh, waited for that moment of death.

But it wasn't my death he wanted.

The bullet ripped past my ear and found its home.

I hit the concrete, rolled to my feet, and spun, a scream of denial tearing past my throat. I saw Kade standing on the walkway behind us, saw the hole in his chest, the dark blood just beginning to ooze from the wound. Saw the mess of blood and flesh on the wall behind him. Knew he was a dead man standing.

His gaze met mine briefly, and he smiled—a warm, wistful sort of smile that spoke of the things we'd done and the things we would now never do, and then the life left his eyes and he fell, his body plummeting over the metal railing.

I didn't see him hit the concrete. I don't even remember turning or firing the gun.

All I saw was the surprise on Kye's face a heartbeat before the bullet exploded into his brain.

Then pain, unlike anything I'd ever felt in my life— pain that was heart and soul and body—hit. I dropped the gun and doubled over, gasping for breath, gasping for life.

I couldn't find either, and I hit the concrete hard. Darkness swept in, and then there was nothing.

Nothing except the need to let go.

Chapter 13

$\mathscr{I}$n the darkness, I existed.

The urge to let go, just to walk away from all the hurt, the pain, and the futile fury over what fate had done might have been strong, but there was one thing that was stronger.

The other half of my soul, the one that had struggled to retain sanity under the weight of the werewolf's needs and desires, hungered to survive, and she would not let me give up.

But I didn't have the strength to wake, either.

Waking would mean facing the pain and a world without my wolf soul mate.

Waking would mean facing up to the fact that my inability to kill Kye when I had the chance had led to the death of a good man. A man I'd cared about, a man who had deserved far more than the screwed-up partner he'd been landed with.

I'd been warned so many times, and I just didn't have the strength to face that sort of guilt.

So I existed in the darkness, neither living nor dead, hearing nothing, feeling nothing, doing nothing.

As time drifted on, voices occasionally broke through the nothingness. Voices I cared about, people I loved. Quinn was strongest of them all, and yet neither his lilting voice nor his desperate pleas for me to come back could shatter the shadows that were locked around me.

I continued to exist, to survive, but that was not a state that could be maintained forever. Eventually, the darkness began to grow thicker, deeper, and through it I could feel the presence of another. Not someone I knew, but a stranger. A stranger who waited for the moment of finality.

My guide to wherever it was my shattered soul was destined to move on to.

Part of me screamed for him to back off, that I wasn't ready, that there was still too much that I had to do and had to achieve, but the words swirled into the abyss and the shadows got stronger, and I knew my body was shutting down. That the silly, insistent part of me that was struggling to survive was losing the greater battle.

The stranger moved closer.

Held out a hand.

Then another voice entered the shadows. A tiny,

happy voice that tugged at my heartstrings and made my soul ache.

The shadows around me stirred, becoming fainter, until a sliver of sunshine in the form of a silver-haired, violet-eyed little girl appeared before me.

Riley, she said, her mind voice holding an edge of censure that made her seem far older than her years. *You cannot leave with Death.*

I sighed. The sound whispered through the shadows, stirring them. The man that was Death neither retreated nor moved forward, but simply continued to hold out his hand.

It was tempting.

So tempting.

My gaze went back to the sunshine sliver that was Risa.

Death is the easier choice, little monkey.

Death doesn't love you. I do. You can't go. Tears filled her eyes and her little face crumpled.

My own shattered heart felt like it was splintering into even tinier pieces. *Risa—*

No. She stamped her foot, her expression filled with stubbornness. She was a child who had no understanding of what she was asking—who just wanted what she wanted, and she wanted it *now. You can't leave me, Riley. I won't let you.*

It's not that easy, monkey—

It is. We love you. And suddenly she was gone, the darkness was gone, and I was seeing a hospital room. Not through my eyes but through hers, because I was there on the bed, surrounded by the machines that were not only keeping me alive but tracking my progress into death. Rhoan, Liander, and Quinn were there, all looking gaunt and gray and worried. Dia was there, pale and unhappy. Even Jack and Sal were there, sitting in the background, waiting patiently for a decision.

People I cared about, people who cared for me, even if we weren't exactly always friends.

People I didn't want to walk away from forever, even if it meant facing up to all the grief and the pain and the loss.

The image swirled away and the shadows returned. The sunshine beam that was Risa held out her hand.

Please, Riley, she pleaded. *Walk back with me.*

I hesitated. Turned to look at the shadow that was Death. Studied his outstretched hand.

Please, Riley, that little sunshiny voice said.

I turned and placed my hand in hers. Her little fingers clenched around mine, and suddenly the darkness was gone. In its place were scents of antiseptic and humanity, wolf and vampire, death and unhappiness. Deep, deep unhappiness.

But the most overwhelming scent of all was the scent of soap and powder and everything that was good in this world.

Risa.

I opened my eyes. Dia's little girl was sitting on the bed right in front of me and her smile shone out, warming my shattered soul in a way few other things could right now.

"Riley's decided to live," she said happily, and flung

herself into my arms, her chubby limbs giving me a hug that just about threatened to cut off my air supply.

And I didn't care one little bit—just wrapped my arms around her and held on tight.

The minute I moved, Rhoan gasped and flung himself out of his chair. But it was nothing, absolutely nothing, compared to the storm of love and relief and pure unadulterated love that Quinn flooded into my mind. I grabbed it, hugged it to me, filling the dark, empty places deep inside. Used it as a shield, a barrier to hold back all that pain and hurt and the need for forgiveness—at least temporarily.

I met his gaze and smiled. A simple smile, and yet it said so much that tears rose in his eyes.

Then my gaze went to my brother and in those familiar, haunted depths, I saw the shadow of death. He'd known just how close I'd come.

I smiled and reached out a hand, clasping his. "I had to come back," I said, my voice croaky and stiff with disuse. "Because I hadn't given you and Liander my answer."

"Answer?" he said, confusion flitting briefly across his face.

"Yes," I said, and glanced at Liander. "Let's do it. Let's start a pack of our own."